PENGUIN BO

The Other Guest

Heidi Perks is the *Sunday Times* bestselling author of *Now You See Her,* which was a Richard and Judy Book Club pick, *Come Back for Me, Three Perfect Liars* and *The Whispers. The Other Guest* is her fifth novel. Heidi is a voracious reader of crime and thrillers and is fascinated by the darker side of our closest relationships. Heidi lives in Bournemouth with her husband and two children.

Also by Heidi Perks

Now You See Her
Come Back For Me
Three Perfect Liars
The Whispers

The Other Guest

HEIDI PERKS

PENGUIN BOOKS

PENGUIN BOOKS

UK | USA | Canada | Ireland | Australia
India | New Zealand | South Africa

Penguin Books is part of the Penguin Random House group of companies
whose addresses can be found at global.penguinrandomhouse.com

First published by Century in 2023
Published in Penguin Books 2023
001

Typeset in 10.68/16 pt Palatino LT Std
by Integra Software Services Pvt. Ltd, Pondicherry

Printed and bound in Great Britain by Clays Ltd, Elcograf S.p.A.

The authorised representative in the EEA is Penguin Random House Ireland, Morrison Chambers, 32 Nassau Street, Dublin D02 YH68

A CIP catalogue record for this book is available from
the British Library

ISBN: 978–1–529–15874–8

www.greenpenguin.co.uk

PART ONE

LAILA

Day Six – Thursday

I have been watching the other guests. Not obsessively, as my husband, James, accused me of last night – just people-watching around the pool since we arrived on Saturday. Six days into our holiday and I have seen the way the couples and families interact. You can't help it in a resort like White Sands, you're around the same people every day.

It's an intimate hotel, or 'luxury boutique' as it refers to itself on its website. Though there are at least fifty or sixty rooms that are filled with predominantly British guests, the faces quickly become familiar. White Sands is a resort built on the northernmost point of the small island of Ixos and a long way from any villages. You can't just walk out and amble past Greek tavernas and restaurants with waiters keen to usher you inside, like I'm used to doing.

I thought I would miss that. The fact that we would have to hire a car or go by taxi if we wanted to escape the hotel seemed like it might make the place feel claustrophobic, but then I had never stepped foot inside anywhere like White Sands before. I didn't realise somewhere could so effortlessly sweep you up into its plush velvet sofas and perfectly aligned wicker sunbeds and make you feel that if you never left again you would be happy.

Besides, as James pointed out, there wasn't really anywhere else to go on the island. Ixos is relatively unknown to tourists and undeveloped, save for our resort, and its only village is a half-hour drive along winding roads.

So instead I have given myself over to everything White Sands has to offer, heart and soul. My early reluctance about the holiday soon dissolved as I acquiesced that maybe James was right. That this was exactly what we needed. In spite of the cost.

Every morning I've woken up to go out walking before James or any of the other guests are up and about. There is something magical about stepping into the warm Greek morning air and wandering past the sunbeds, plumped with cream mattresses and rolled towels ready for guests. To see the sun rise and the water in the pool catch its first beams, dancing in ripples, before any guests have emerged to disturb the calm. To hear only the sounds of birds and the occasional words spoken by staff in a language I don't understand.

I left our room this morning in much the same way, slipping on my complimentary flip-flops, opening the door and shutting it quietly behind me, breathing in like I had never taken a breath before. Today the bedroom had felt stifling, James splayed on his back, his mouth hanging open; clearly he wasn't going to wake any time soon. It was the first morning of our holiday that I had wanted to get out to get away from him.

I was surprised I wasn't feeling worse, given the amount we had both drunk the night before. Yesterday was the White Sands gala night, a high point of the week, and it had been talked about since we'd first arrived. Table service, instead of the usual buffet, and all laid out on the hotel's private beach with live music and dancing on the sand. It was a real party atmosphere and was supposed to be such a different evening to the one it turned into. Now everything had unravelled. James and I weren't speaking.

We had never before gone to bed on a fight. Not even after James told me he'd booked this holiday and our conversation ventured into unsafe ground, and he ended up breaking my heart with an admission I can still barely think about. Even then we'd found a way through. But not last night.

My mind was still on the events of the previous evening as I walked along the path that wove past the other rooms, each one individual and set apart from its neighbours. This isn't a hotel with two-storey buildings; its luxury is evident in the space we have all been given, each room detached and with its own private garden.

I cut across the grass and veered away from the steps that led down to the private beach. All I could think of were James's unkind words, my unanswered questions, and the mystery over what had happened to him yesterday when he went on the fishing trip alone. He had come back seemingly spoiling for a fight.

It was so unlike my husband, who I have known for ten years. James has always been laid-back and easy-going, eager to please me. I was surprised he wanted to go fishing in the first place; he's never shown any interest in it before, but at the same time James is more active than I am. He has never been one to laze on sunbeds by the pool like I can for hours at a time. His Kindle is thrown into his suitcase at the last minute but rarely opened, unlike my carefully chosen pile of paperbacks, selected for a week in the sun.

I suppose it was because I was busy filtering through last night's memories that at first I wasn't aware of the commotion around the pool at 6 a.m., or the voices shouting at each other in Greek. I was too intent on piecing together fragments of last night and trying to fill in the many blanks to question why one of the waiters, Jonas, was racing across the path ahead of me, not stopping to wave and cheerily greet me like he usually does.

I couldn't even say with certainty the exact moment I realised something was gravely wrong. Whether it was when I saw the crowd of staff gathered around the pool, or the seconds immediately after when I noticed the body, clothes billowing out, arms and legs in a star shape and face down in the water as they tried to pull it out.

Three hours later I am beside the same pool, only with my back to it now, and seated at a table near the bar where a detective pushes a glass of water in front of me. I hadn't lingered here earlier, after it became clear that something was so terribly wrong. I didn't go over to see who it was, although from where I stood I had a very good idea. Instead I turned and threw up into the bushes and then ran back to the room, my hands and legs shaking as I sat on the edge of the bed, not knowing whether to wake James or not.

I did, of course, because a dead body in the hotel swimming pool is not something you keep from your husband, even when you are both still simmering in the aftermath of a fight.

I knew that the detectives would likely want to question every one of the guests at White Sands, but this particular conversation hasn't come about because of such a routine. This one was sprung upon me, and I have only myself to blame for leaving our room again when James specifically told me not to.

'Was it an accident?' I ask the detective as I hold the glass between my hands and lift it to my lips to take a sip of water. This is what James presumes. He told me so enough times earlier, though it was possibly an attempt to calm me down.

Out of the corner of my eye I see my husband pacing back and forth like a caged animal. He came out looking for me after I left our room again and found me only five minutes ago, but by then I was already sitting with the detective, who in turn ushered him away.

James doesn't want to be at White Sands any longer, not after a death. He has suggested we look for another hotel over in Crete, but that is a two-hour boat ride away.

The detective bites his bottom lip as he mulls over what to say to me and in the end simply answers, 'We do not know what has happened.' His words are clipped but his English is very good. He has introduced himself as Police Lieutenant Kallis, and told me that he is in charge of the investigation.

'Surely it must be?' I plead; the thought that it could be anything else is too terrifying to contemplate.

Kallis doesn't respond and I feel the need to clear up the fact that I stumbled across the discovery of the body earlier. To tell him the truth, because James had pretended we didn't already know at 7 a.m., when a room-service waiter delivered a breakfast I didn't even want.

'You cannot go to the pool today,' the waiter had said as he'd set down the tray of pastries and berries that James had ordered.

'Oh?' James said. 'Why is that?'

The young boy shook his head gravely. 'There has been a – a drowning?' He said it as if it were a question, though I think he was just checking he had the right word.

Now I want to be open and so I say to the detective, 'I saw what had happened this morning.'

He raises his eyebrows.

'Every morning I wake early and I go for a walk, and so I already saw the … the pool,' I finish.

'What time?' he asks.

'Six a.m.,' I tell him. I had woken an hour earlier, but it was six when I eventually left the room. 'But there were other people there,' I add quickly. 'I don't mean I was the first to come across the body.' The staff were already heaving it out of the water.

I squeeze my eyes shut before opening them sharply as if that will somehow rid me of the image that I have not been able to get out of my head.

Kallis makes a note in his pad and asks, 'Mrs Burrow, you have seen the deceased before?' He shows me a picture and I nod. 'When was the last time?'

'Yesterday,' I say. 'Some time yesterday – I'm not exactly sure when.'

'You were at the gala night? Down on the beach?'

'Yes,' I say. 'I was.'

'Did you see them then?'

'Maybe. I …' I think back, the night continuing to flash in distorted pictures. 'Yes, I did.' Of course I did. At the beginning of the evening I saw most of the guests I'd come to recognise, seated at their various tables looking happy, laughing. Later in the night I saw the way some of them gaped over at James and me. I had tried to keep my voice down, but I don't know how much anyone else heard. 'Only from a distance,' I add.

'What time did you leave dinner last night?'

'I think it was about ten p.m., maybe ten thirty – I'm not sure.' Most people had still been sitting at their tables, listening to the music, some of them dancing.

'Mrs Burrow,' he says now, 'is there anything else you want to tell me?'

I wonder if he knows there is. That there are words on the tip of my tongue. By the way he is regarding me so suspiciously it feels like he knows I have something to tell him. My mind ticks back and forth like a metronome, not knowing if I should. Or if I can, more like.

If I'd confided in James, my husband would tell me to say nothing, keep out of it. After all, I don't know anything with certainty. I can almost hear his words ringing in my ears. But I didn't confide in him. I didn't tell James anything about what happened yesterday, because I didn't get the chance before our argument started.

Slowly, I shake my head. If I say anything I will have to admit *how* I know. I will have to tell Kallis what I have observed over the last five days when all the while I should maybe have been paying more attention to my marriage. Right now, perhaps the best thing would be not to say anything and focus on me and James. Somehow we have to put ourselves back together, and speaking up might be the worst thing I could do. But then what if there is a killer among us? What if my silence means they will get away with what they have done?

Chapter One

Day One – Saturday

Despite my love of water and the fact I live by the sea, I have never been good with boats. James knows this because we have laughed enough times about my stories of when my dad used to take me out in one and I would often hurl up over the side. Though I rarely get travel sick these days, I still feel queasy. I pointed this out to James when he told me it was a two-hour transfer between Crete and the small island of Ixos. He'd only mentioned it a few days ago, apologising and telling me he would buy me a sickness band to wear around my wrist. Someone at his gym had told him they worked, and maybe it did help, but it didn't stop me stepping onto the small harbour in Ixos Old Town feeling like I was going to throw up.

It was 6 p.m., which meant it was 4 p.m. back at home. The heat of the Greek sun burned through the few puffs of cloud that had found their way into the sky as the egg sandwich I'd had on the plane from Gatwick to Crete lurked nauseatingly high in my throat.

James rubbed my back and pulled my bag off my shoulder, transferring it to his own. 'I'm sorry,' he said again. 'I really didn't think—'

'It's fine, I'll be fine,' I said. 'I just need some air.' I took exaggerated breaths as I slipped off my cardigan and tied it around my waist. On the opposite side of the road sat a twelve-seater coach that was waiting to take us to the resort. Out of its windows, faces peered blankly. I wasn't sure if they were looking at us or just staring aimlessly as they waited, tired from a long journey and eager to get to the hotel.

'There's no hurry,' he said. 'The bus can wait.'

'But the others will be getting annoyed.' I already felt like the poor cousin compared with the guests that had boarded the coach, not a piece of matching luggage in sight for James and me. Everything about White Sands was far out of my comfort zone.

'So what?'

I shrugged. 'I'll be fine,' I muttered again. 'Come on, we'd better go.' I took my bag off James so he could pull our cases over the road and hand them to the driver who stood by the side of the coach with its luggage door open. James put his hand in the small of my back as we wound round the front of it and up the steps to where we found two seats halfway back. I twiddled the knobs above my head until a blast of air conditioning hit my face. James was frowning, looking at me cautiously.

'Stop worrying,' I said quietly. 'I won't actually be sick.'

I sat with my bag on my lap, clutching it to me, my fingers weaving through the brightly coloured tassel that hung from its strap and that I had made two years ago in some art-and-craft class I joined for eight weeks. I was always starting these things and then stopping them. I gave up the classes because my heart wasn't in it, though I had enjoyed them at the time. For an hour a week I had actually forgotten about everything else.

'How long is the journey?' I asked James.

'Well it's not far,' he said as he pulled out his phone and expanded a map that was already on the screen. 'I don't know, ten, fifteen minutes?'

'It'll be longer than fifteen minutes,' I said, narrowing my eyes to focus. 'It's the other side of the island.'

'Yeah, but it's not a big island.' He closed the screen and put the phone back in his pocket.

I tried not to sigh as I leant my head against the seat. I had worried over this holiday enough, questioning James about the money and about why he'd chosen a resort like White Sands. It wasn't, after all, our usual type of holiday, but then we hadn't had one in so long that maybe we didn't have a type any more.

'We need this, Laila,' he had told me. 'We need some time together, just to reset.'

It was more than that and we both knew it, but I'd told myself that maybe he was right. And that maybe the holiday was going to be some kind of turning point, because God knew we both deserved it after the last few years.

On the coach James took hold of my hand and squeezed it, holding it up to his lips as he kissed the back of it and smiled at me. 'I love you,' he whispered.

'I love you too,' I told him.

'We haven't been away in years.'

'I know.'

'I'm excited.'

'I am too,' I said, although this wasn't strictly true. I had plenty of reservations and yet I was trying to brush them to one side. To make the most of it.

'Do you remember our first holiday together?' he asked.

'Of course I do,' I laughed. 'How could I ever forget it?'

'I don't know, I'm not sure how much you remember these things.'

'James?' I questioned. 'Why do you say that?'

'We don't talk about those days so much.'

'No, I know but . . .' I trailed off. He was right. It was as if a line had been drawn across our path, separating the then from the now, although I couldn't pinpoint exactly where the divide was. Whether it was as far back as five years ago, a halfway point in our relationship, or more likely at some time since.

'I still want us to travel together, Laila,' James said, visibly getting excited. 'Do all the things we talked about when we got together. Do you remember how we used to lie in bed for hours on Sunday mornings with the papers and coffee and just plan stuff?'

I nod. 'We had dreams.' Dreams that didn't seem unrealistic at the time.

'I wanted you to see the world. I wanted to show you some of the things I'd seen.'

'Is that what this is?' I asked. James had travelled the Greek islands with an ex-girlfriend years before we had got together. It was one of those things I had never grilled him about, though somehow I sensed its importance. I'd picked up on the way he avoided talking about Stephanie. How he clammed up and brushed over their months of travelling. He wasn't the same about Addie, the girlfriend before. James didn't care about admitting what a screw-up she'd been, but Stephanie remained an enigma.

And now we were here, in Ixos, and suddenly Stephanie was looming uninvited into the forefront of my mind, and so of course I imagined the same was true for James. I had only ever seen one photo of her, found by accident, tucked into the back of a book, and at the time I hadn't been able to put her picture down, poring over her features, her long wavy sun-bleached hair that hung like a mermaid's around her thin, tanned face. Her large blue eyes and the way her head tilted to one side as she laughed at the camera. In many ways Stephanie and I couldn't have been more different. Her hair blond to my dark brown. Her waiflike frame to my curves that James professed to love.

'Of course not,' he said now. 'This is just a holiday. For us.'

Us. It was a word I rolled over my tongue, one I had questioned when I spoke to my best friend, Claire, a few weeks back when I told her what James had done. Was there still an 'us'?

Claire had told me categorically there was. 'How could you and James not be together?' she had said. 'You two are …' She'd momentarily grappled for the right words. 'Christ, you're the couple we all want to be, Laila.'

I had nodded, tears rolling down my cheeks as I tried to trust she was right. I didn't want to lose my husband and yet if there was an *us* then something would have to give. And that's when she said it, reaching over and stroking my hand: 'Possibly it means you need to try to accept that you and James might not have children, and that it isn't the end of the world.'

The coach rumbled into action and I clicked my seat belt into place and pulled my hand away to reach into my bag for a bottle of water. I was 'reframing my future', taking steps to concentrate on James and me. This holiday was about us reconnecting again, and all those other words that were bandied about in the articles I read. As I'd said to Claire, I didn't want to lose my husband – but I was aware that I *had* been losing him. White Sands was a perfect chance for us to get back on track.

James turned to look out the window and so I glanced around at the people on the coach who I would be bumping into every day, sitting next to at dinner and looking at as we sat around the lagoon-shaped infinity pool that occupied pride of place in the resort's grounds.

To my right were a couple who intrigued me and who had been on the same flight as us, sitting two rows in front of us on the plane. They were newly married and on their honeymoon, which I knew because he had announced it loudly to one of the aircrew, making a show of himself.

'My new wife and I,' he had chuckled like an overgrown schoolboy, winking at the British Airways stewardess as he nodded to the front of the plane, 'were just wondering if there were any spare seats up there?' I grimaced at the way he made a show of saying 'up there'.

'I'm afraid not, sir,' she replied with a smile, and I'd smiled myself then, glad he hadn't managed to score a free upgrade. She had, however, told him she would see what she could do for them since they were celebrating, and had returned with two glasses of champagne.

I guessed there must be about ten years between them. She looked to be half my age, about twenty, while he was clearly tipping thirty with the very first signs of grey hair around his ears and lines around his eyes.

She sat in her seat by the coach window ramrod straight and staring out to her left, her long fake fingernails making an irritating tapping sound on the leather handbag that rested in her lap, until her husband stopped it by swatting at her. He was hunched over his mobile, scrolling through Facebook. For honeymooners, their body language was all wrong. Neither of them seemed remotely happy.

I shuffled in my seat to peek at the family of four behind us. Directly behind James and me were two boys in their teens, and in the seats behind the newlyweds sat the boys' parents. I had seen them all on the boat and wondered what two teenagers would find to do with their time somewhere so remote. It had to have been the parents' choice to come here; their sons would surely have preferred a livelier resort.

Maybe this wasn't the only holiday they'd be having this year. Possibly they had a Mark Warner trip booked for the end of the summer. I assumed that for the majority of White Sands guests, money was no object. The telltale signs of wealth were evident in the way the parents dressed and carried themselves. Over the weeks since James told me about the holiday I had wrestled with the thought of how I would fit in at a resort so luxurious in my maxi dresses from H&M and Next. 'I don't know why you don't have more confidence in the way you look,' Claire said when I told her as much. 'Honestly, Laila, you're stunning.' She had pinched a roll of the baby fat from her stomach and widened her eyes at me, and I smiled in return but didn't respond.

Now the mother had caught me looking and so I quickly turned back to the front of the coach, trying to make out I hadn't been watching the way her husband's fingers curled around hers.

I already knew that the boys behind me were called Isaac and Theo, because their mum had addressed them by name during the boat journey. I liked the sound of both their names and tried them out, mouthing them soundlessly the way I had done with so many names over the last five years. It was hard to stop myself mentally adding them to my constantly growing list of baby names, because by now it had become habit.

Isaac was the older of the two – I put him at seventeen, though I'm not good at ageing teenage boys – while his brother looked to be about fifteen. I found myself doing another thing I needed to stop: guessing how old she would have been when she'd had her children.

She had wavy, highlighted blond hair that fell just below her shoulders, and nails that were painted bright pink and were so shiny they must have been gelled. Her face was bare of make-up and I put her in her mid-forties, which meant she couldn't have been more than thirty when she'd had Isaac, possibly even late twenties. Nine years younger than I was at the very least.

Stop torturing yourself, Laila, I reprimanded myself. *What does any of that matter now?* But regardless of how often I repeated the mantra, I wasn't so sure I believed it.

*

The bus had started now, making its ascent over the hills then dipping down again as the road hugged the coastline. I looked past the newlyweds and out through the window at a lone fisherman on the rocks, the patches of beaches and whitewashed houses with their blue dome roofs and doors. Occasionally there was a restaurant perched on the edge of the road, remote and mostly empty, its tables covered with checked tablecloths as if the owners were confident of customers arriving shortly.

This was an island that was sparsely inhabited and had managed to hold off the tourists for as long as possible. I wondered how much say the locals had against a resort like White Sands. Whether they were grateful for the money it brought to the island, or if they'd been bullied into agreement. I was inclined to believe it was the latter, and it made me sad for them.

'Don't you think it's a shame they've built a hotel on this island?' I murmured to James, resting my head on his shoulder.

He was staring out of his own window, his attention elsewhere, and so he didn't hear me.

'James.' I nudged him. 'Don't you think it's a shame they've allowed such a huge resort to be built out here? It's beautiful as it is.' My voice was low, I didn't want anyone else on the bus to hear me.

He turned sharply, as if surprised I was talking to him. A frown creased his forehead as he said, 'Yeah. Yeah, I do.'

He looked like he wanted to say more, but he didn't, and I had a sudden urge to ask him again if he had visited Ixos when he toured Greece. He had brushed off my question previously, leaving me wondering if I really wanted to know. What if James were to admit he had been to this island with Stephanie? Some things you are better off not knowing.

Besides, half an hour in and we turned a sharp corner and suddenly the hotel loomed ahead of us. 'This must be it,' said James. Whether or not he had been to Ixos before he'd definitely not been to White Sands; the resort had been built less than ten years ago, after we had met.

The hotel stuck out against the green rocky landscape like a piece of modern architecture, all white straight lines and glass that reflected the sun, which was dipping behind us, and yet it didn't look out of place. The coach slowed as it swung into the driveway and two men emerged through the hotel's revolving doors with trays of champagne-filled flutes.

James leant towards me and kissed my forehead. 'This is going to be awesome,' he whispered.

'Yes,' I agreed. Such a small word, but it caught in my throat as I said it.

James had surprised me with the booking six weeks ago. He had pushed his laptop in front of me, pointing at the images of the resort, a smile spreading across his face as I stared at them stonily and asked him outright, 'How much did it cost?'

I felt him shift awkwardly beside me. Undoubtedly it wasn't the response he was hoping for, but while I didn't really want to know the answer I needed to ask.

'It doesn't matter.'

'Yes, it matters,' I said, and looked up at him.

He shook his head once, his eyes narrowing. I could see he was embarrassed.

'James?'

'Five thousand.'

'Five thousand pounds?' I choked. 'For ten days in Greece?'

My eyes stung with the amount. We had never spent anything like that before and I couldn't comprehend why we would, especially now. The last thing I wanted was to start crying, but I knew it wouldn't take much before I did.

'Don't say it like that. It's not just *ten days in Greece*,' he said.

'If you wanted us to get away we could have gone to Corfu or Kos or anywhere where there's a choice of hotels, not somewhere like *Ixos*,' I said. 'A five-star luxury resort – I mean, I don't get it, James.'

When he didn't answer, I asked him again: 'James? You've spent all our—' But I stopped short, unable to finish the sentence. My husband had spent all our IVF money.

My hands were trembling against the table as I tried to fathom what this meant.

'No, I haven't spent it,' James was telling me. 'I've had a bonus.'

My heart lifted, but only a little. 'What kind of bonus?' The last time James had received one, it had been a pitiful sum over eighteen months ago that angered us both, although James did nothing about it. At the time I wondered how much his younger brother, Carl, had received, because there was little doubt their father had given him more, but I never brought it up.

'The holiday is paid for,' he said, leaning down and pressing a kiss onto the top of my head. 'So will you stop worrying about it. Please.'

'But still,' I'd gone on, 'you know it could have been better spent. What happens when the next round doesn't work?' We had been through the process enough times by now that I was certain it might be the case. 'We could have left your bonus money in case we needed to try again. James?' I had implored him.

It had been a month since I had taken yet another pregnancy test only to see one thin red line appear. James had found me in the bathroom. Not crumpled into a ball on the floor tiles by the toilet as I had been on the five occasions before. This time I was staring at my ageing reflection in the mirror, one hand loosely covering the test as it lay on the sink beside me.

The 39-year-old woman in the mirror didn't look like the girl I still imagined myself to be. It wasn't that I had grey hairs yet – like my mother, I'd been lucky in that respect, especially for someone so dark. I only had thin lines around my eyes, my forehead wasn't as smooth as it would be if I gave in to Botox but neither did it crinkle badly when I frowned. It was the hollowness of my eyes that got me. Sometimes they just looked dead. Like all the life had been sucked from within me and I was nothing more than a shell.

At the time James had peeled my fingers back so he could see for himself that we weren't having a baby. His hand stayed on mine, but with his other he picked up the test and tossed it in the bin.

We didn't speak of it. There seemed little point. We had dissected my failed pregnancies enough over the last five years, each time picking ourselves up and brushing ourselves off, ready to start again. Six rounds of IVF had produced nothing and yet as I heard the clink of the test hit the bottom of the bin, I was already preparing myself to go through it again, my mind racing through when my body would be ready and how quickly we could find the required money.

But a month later James was telling me he'd spent £5,000 on a holiday and I was struggling to make sense of it when he said quietly, 'I can't do this any more, Laila.'

I knew what he meant immediately. I could tell by the way he was looking at me: cold, fearful. But I asked anyway: 'Do what?'

'I can't go through another round. It's been five years of living like this and I can't do it any more.'

'No,' I'd replied, shaking my head vehemently. 'Don't say that.'

'We always said we would stop at five. We've had six lots of IVF now and it hasn't happened for us …' He had let the implication hang: if it hadn't worked after six attempts then surely it never would.

Had we once said we would stop at five? I no longer remembered, but maybe we had when we first started out. When our hopes hadn't been crushed time and time again. When five attempts seemed like an impossibly huge number of treatments and we'd both assumed it would surely have happened by then.

'We can't,' I'd whispered, afraid to say too much, to say the wrong thing in case he found some way of convincing me that this could be the right decision.

'It breaks me every time we get the results,' he said. 'I can't bear watching you go through it.'

'But I want to go through it,' I protested. 'It's my decision, and I'm happy.'

James shook his head. 'It's our decision,' he said slowly. 'And you're not happy, Laila.'

Maybe happy was not the right word, but that wasn't the point. He had spent thousands on a holiday – so what did that mean? That in his mind it was definitely over?

'How could you?' I'd cried as I ran out of the room. There was no way I could let James do this to us.

It was too big a discussion to be resolved in one night. We'd picked at it in the days following, both coming at it from our opposing sides, neither of us knowing how we could resolve something so monumental.

I had intended my question to Claire to settle things in my head, wanting her to confirm that I couldn't possibly give up. Instead she answered truthfully: 'Laila, I'm worried about you and I have been for some time. After everything you've gone through, you're not the same person. For what it's worth, I think James is right. I think you should at least take a break from IVF.'

No. That hadn't been the answer I was expecting, and so I sought out my parents, whose hopes had been resting on news of a grandchild. I knew I didn't imagine the flicker of relief that passed over Mum's face when I told her what James had said, and what Claire had advised me. She had taken me into her arms and clasped me against her chest and said, 'Laila, I think this may be for the best.' It broke me knowing that, to so readily put her hopes aside, she must have really believed this.

Something shifted in me after that. Could we really give up our dreams so easily? Then again, weren't dreams only worth having when there was the slightest chance of them becoming reality? As the days blurred into weeks I couldn't help admitting that something had been lifted. A weight. A darkness – call it what you will. It was still early days, but I was beginning to think that I could imagine a life for *us*. One without children in it. And if that were the case, then this holiday was exactly what James and I needed.

Day Six – Thursday

There is something George Clooney-esque about the detective, Lieutenant Kallis, that makes me even more uneasy. As if answering questions about a dead body isn't enough, the fact his deep brown eyes pierce into me under thick bushy eyebrows and the way his stubble is shaved to what feels like perfection, sets me further off-kilter.

There is a flurry of activity around me, although I have my back to the pool and I can only see what is happening in a blurred reflection of movement in the thin slice of mirror behind the bar. The body has been removed. The water is draining. Sunloungers have been pushed back to the edges, parasols folded and laid out on the ground so there is room for the police to work.

They are trawling the area, carefully stepping over the manicured lawns and shedding bags and jackets across the pathways, peering over the top of the emptying pool and combing through the bushes beyond. It is hard to reconcile the area with the image of what it was like before: guests sunbathing on the loungers, the ripple of the water as someone slices through it, waiters carrying trays of cocktails.

Though Kallis won't say much, the police seem to be treating the death as suspicious. The handful of police who turned up early has grown to a swarm.

I don't know what this means for us or what the rest of our holiday will entail. It feels wrong to even consider this when someone is dead, but I guess most of the guests will be doing the same. Do we stay? Do we leave?

James is firmly in the latter camp. 'What do you think it's going to be like, Laila?' he said earlier. 'There are police everywhere, they're draining the pool. One of the guests is dead!' He shouted the word, *dead,* like I might not have understood it.

Of course I did. I saw the body with my own eyes, and I cannot rid myself of the image however much I try.

I wish we weren't sitting so close to where it had been floating earlier. I should have done what James suggested this morning and stayed in our room after I'd got back and told him the news. I shouldn't have said I needed to get out for another walk, just so that I could slip away. If I hadn't done that, Kallis would never have found me.

I have answered his question of whether there is anything else I want to tell him with a shake of my head.

'In that case, Mrs Burrow,' he responds, 'can you tell me what you were doing fifteen minutes ago, loitering outside the deceased's room?'

Chapter Two

Day One – Saturday

James stepped off the coach outside White Sands and we both stood for a moment, staring at the building in front of us with its huge glass windows flanked by white stone pillars and palm trees.

'I have wanted to do something like this for you for so long,' he said as I joined him. 'I wanted to treat you, Laila.' He glanced at me, almost shyly. Sometimes I felt like neither of us was sure what the other wanted any more, not like we used to be, though we were making every effort to change that. 'I just . . .' His words faded before he said, 'I just want to give you everything you deserve and—' He stopped abruptly. It was the wrong choice of words.

I found out only recently he blamed himself for us not getting pregnant. But it was not James's fault we couldn't conceive. In the last few weeks I'd found out a lot of things that James had bottled up, having started to prise them out of him. It's not hard to see that he'd pushed down his own feelings for five years to focus on mine. Maybe if we had talked sooner, maybe if we'd been more honest … There were plenty of maybes tossed around, but now it was time to start focusing on the two of us.

'It's beautiful,' I said. 'Thank you.'

James smiled and picked up two flutes of champagne, passing one to me as he clinked our glasses together. We walked through the revolving doors and into the white and airy reception lounge with its high ceiling and glass walls that led out to the back. While James checked us in, I strolled over to look out at the perfectly manicured squares of lawn bordered with low stone walls and small bushes with their bright pink and orange flowers. To my right and down some steps I could see the tips of the white parasols that surrounded the pool. I stepped aside as a woman walked in wearing a sarong and flip-flops, and knew I must have the bewildered look of a new arrival, my eyes heavy with tiredness from the journey, my cotton trousers crumpled.

'I have a map,' James said, suddenly at my side. 'They can take us to our room by buggy, but I said we'd walk. Then we can get to know the place on the way. Dinner's served from six thirty to nine thirty and we should pass the restaurant so we can have a nose.'

He led us through the glass doors and down the path and the steps to the right where the restaurant lay ahead as promised, its doors wide open. Tables spilled out onto the veranda beyond. A smattering of guests were taking seats for an early dinner. 'Oh my God, look at the pool,' I said, grabbing James's arm as I pointed to where the lagoon-shaped swimming pool lay.

At quarter to seven in the evening it was empty of guests; already the sun was low behind the reception area. Staff were gathering towels that had been left on loungers and folding up parasols. 'It makes you want to jump right in,' I said.

James grinned as he kept on walking, weaving us around the pool until we could see the private beach nestled into a sandy cove a few steps down from the hotel's grounds. Here more loungers and parasols sat in uniformed lines, two by two with little wicker tables between them. There were still a few guests here, making the most of the evening sun warming the beach and skimming the turquoise water.

Our room sat within a staggered row of others, all of them facing the sea and with private gardens separated by lines of hedges. I felt like a kid as I skipped across the deck and through the bifold doors, running my hand along the white sofa with its pale blue throw. 'We've got chocolates!' I declared, grabbing one from the tray on the coffee table. I was so tired from an early start I could have thrown myself into the queen-sized bed had I not been desperate to make the most of our first evening.

'Is that what you're most excited about?' James laughed.

'No. All of it,' I said as I checked it out. The dressing table with its large oval mirror and fresh flowers that stood in a tall glass. The bed plumped with throws and cushions that were perfectly positioned in rows; the complimentary slippers, dressing gowns and flip-flops, all branded with the White Sands logo, waiting on the end of the bed.

There was a wall dividing the bedroom from the bathroom, and the side of the latter was tiled in tiny green mosaic tiles that sparkled as they caught the light. There were two basins with toiletries in between, glass bottles filled with oils in tempting shades of orange. The shower was a huge walk-in affair that was bigger than our downstairs toilet at home.

I could get used to this, I thought. *Quite quickly.*

Forty-five minutes later and I'd already had two mojitos, on top of the champagne we'd been given on arrival. I could taste the generous measures of alcohol and felt light-headed as I unpacked and folded our clothes into drawers. It was too easy to order from the gold-embossed menu that sat on the desk in the corner of the room. Whatever I wanted I could have, and it was already paid for. I felt like a child on Christmas morning as I soaked up the luxury.

James had barely been in the villa five minutes before he set off to check out the grounds. As soon as he was out of sight, I'd called room service and ordered the cocktails, drinking them both in one go.

They gave me a looseness in my shoulders that I hadn't experienced in a while, and I wanted to savour it – though something stopped me from telling James what I had done. Instead, I rinsed the glasses and put our toothbrushes into one of them, keeping my drinks a secret from my husband. It was something else about our marriage that I would have to address at some point, but not now.

'You OK?' he asked, making me jump when he returned. I nodded as I arranged the rest of my toiletries neatly beside one sink and placed James's washbag by the other. I had placed my jewellery bag inside one of the drawers, taking out the watch my grandmother had given me before she died, and clasping it around my wrist, wondering if I'd done the right thing in bringing something so irreplaceable on holiday. Then I took a photo of the room on my iPhone and sent it to my mum and dad, telling them we had arrived and the hotel was lovely. My phone pinged with a message from them and as James started telling me about everything the hotel had to offer, I read the reply from Mum: *Oh darling, it looks wonderful. You're both going to have a lovely rest. We miss you xx*

I wondered how my mum was truly faring. She had been almost as desperate for grandchildren as I had been to conceive. As an only child, their hopes rested solely on me, yet she had assured me that my happiness was paramount and she knew that numerous rounds of IVF were doing anything but making me happy.

I had seen the way her own body crumpled every time I told her another round had failed, how she visibly stopped herself from offering me pity because she understood it made everything harder. I hated giving them bad news, and now I wondered if Mum was just relieved she wouldn't have to hear it any more.

Yes, there were plenty of reasons to believe this was the right decision. Not least that I was beginning to 'see' my husband again. For the last five years everyone's attention had been on me. Did anyone even think to ask James how he was feeling? I wasn't sure that he'd talked to anyone apart from my parents and our closest friends. He'd certainly never unburdened himself onto me.

I remembered the first time I hadn't been pregnant after an IVF cycle. The two of us had sat on the bathroom floor, curled into each other.

'I thought it would work,' I whispered through my tears.

'I did too,' he admitted.

'I don't know if I can do this again,' I said. It was a knee-jerk emotional response; deep down, I knew I would keep doing it forever if I had to.

'You can do anything you put your mind to, Laila,' he had said.

'What if it doesn't happen next time?'

'Then we decide what you want to do after that.'

It was always about me. James giving himself over to me like he had always done, and me accepting it, because he adored me and I adored him and that was just what we did.

Only, I never asked him how he felt. The night after he told me he couldn't do it any more, I'd begged him not to give up. 'Just one more go,' I'd pleaded.

But James had looked at me with eyes that had lost all their life, and speaking as if it was with his last breath, he said, 'I'm not going to change my mind, Laila.' So flat, so adamant. So unlike my husband. He had reached a point where he couldn't go any further.

Now, on our first night of holiday, he looked at the dress I was wearing and his eyes sparkled. 'You look beautiful.' He smiled.

I had chosen a bright orange maxi dress that looked good against my olive skin, and had piled my hair up into a loose bun. Around my ankle I had a gold chain that I hadn't worn since the last time we were abroad.

'I'd better put on a shirt and then we can go and eat?' he said.

I nodded and finished laying out my things – perfume on one side of the basin, my make-up on one of the shelves by the side of it. James pulled out a blue shirt and buttoned it up save for the last two. If I could have let myself, we would be back there again, in those early days of our relationship that were all about love and sex and not needing anything but each other. This was what James wanted. 'I need you again, Laila,' he'd told me a few weeks back. 'Somewhere along the line I feel I've lost my wife, and I want you back.'

Now I took his outstretched hand and returned his smile. We couldn't go back to how it used to be because there was too much hurt and loss that we were carrying, but somehow we would find a way forward.

At the restaurant we were asked if we wanted to sit inside or out and we both said out – along with every other guest, it appeared, as we were shown to a table for two that sat alongside the glass wall of the restaurant. 'Do you think it's OK to leave my bag?' I said to James as we both got up to peruse the buffet.

James grinned. 'I don't think any of these guests are likely to steal it, do you?'

'No, I suppose not,' I agreed as I flicked my gaze around at the other diners, mostly couples, their attention focused on their meals or the wine that was being poured for them.

My biggest dilemma was deciding what to eat. I resisted the urge to fill my plate from the buffet, instead picking out a warm square of flatbread and adding spoonfuls of tzatziki, olive paste and fish-roe mousse far brighter than anything I'd seen at home. I ladled out a heap of Greek salad then wandered back to the table, passing dish upon dish, from moussaka to beef stew to buttered vegetables and everything in between.

'I'm going to leave here the size of a house,' I said as I joined James back at the table, where he was studying the wine list. We were more accustomed to hastily thrown together meals, often eaten in front of the TV, or I'd eat alone while waiting for James to come back from the gym. I couldn't recall the last time we had been out for dinner, just the two of us. It didn't happen the way Claire and my other friends thought it must, given that we were a couple without the burden of childcare. When you were reaching your forties and the stress of work overlay a heavy tiredness, you realised you just couldn't be arsed.

On the first night of our holiday I searched my husband's face, looking for the familiarity we once had. How could I draw the lines of his face or the shape of his eyes and angular chin from memory and yet at the same time feel like I was with a stranger? We were conversing over our dinner but it felt oddly like small talk, and it unnerved me that we could be like that.

I remembered a night, after our second failed attempt, when James and I were in bed and I suddenly said, 'We're incompatible, aren't we?' It was a term that had been bandied about by fertility specialists in an attempt to explain why we hadn't managed to conceive. 'What if we aren't meant to have children together?' I asked him.

It was a dark thought that possessed me. The idea that James and I were not meant to be together. How could that be possible when I had known from the night we met that he was the man I was supposed to marry? He'd approached me at a house party neither of us wanted to be at, and we had sat outside on a wooden bench and talked into the early hours of the morning. From then on not a day had passed that I had been able to imagine myself without him.

James had taken my hands in his as he shifted around in the bed until he was in front of me and I could see right through his bright blue eyes and into his soul. His eyes were one of the first things I'd noticed about him – so deep they looked like pools of water. I always thought you could tell so much about someone by their eyes.

'Laila, we were made for each other,' he had said, his hands clasping tighter, as if he were afraid he might lose me. 'Don't you ever forget that. I would never be without you.'

I wanted to ask James if he still felt that way now. As we sipped our wine and pushed our food around our plate, and sat there with five years of stress and failures behind us, did James still think we were made for each other? Did I?

But I didn't ask. Instead I drank the wine, which went down particularly well, topping up the alcohol I had already secretly consumed earlier, and I gave in to the bliss of being on holiday. I scanned the poolside, picking out the guests I had seen on the transfer coach. The newlyweds were seated close by. She had her hair scraped back off her face in a band, he was bending to one side as he leant against the window of the restaurant. They were both on their mobiles, neither of them talking to each other, until he finally looked up and asked her something and she scowled in return. She looked like a child as she turned away from him and stared at the buffet, shrugging. I found myself leaning across the table as if hoping to catch some of their limited conversation, intrigued as to why neither of them looked like they wanted to be here and certainly not in each other's company.

She was pale, her skin translucent, almost white. She looked ill, I thought, and yet he showed no concern; he'd been too caught up in his phone to notice anything amiss. Now he tossed the phone on the table and set off to the buffet on his own. Her plateful of food remained untouched in front of her.

Not far away from them were the family I had seen on the plane, the mother looking effortlessly glam in her white jeans and pale pink chiffon top. Her husband pulled out her chair for her as she sat down, her oldest son, Isaac, holding her attention as he spoke to her from across the table, making her laugh so that she barely noticed the gesture from her husband, who was now sliding into a chair next to her. I thought he looked forlorn as he settled in his seat, his wife still captivated by their son. Their private conversation seemed to go on for so long that in the end the younger one, Theo, got up and helped himself to food. Their dad followed and when the two of them returned, their plates full, Isaac and his mum looked up in surprise, only then registering that they'd been gone from the table.

I found myself frowning in concentration as I studied them. I have loved working out the intricacies of family dynamics and people's relationships ever since I studied psychology for A level. I'd intended to take it further, but allowed myself to be persuaded by a careers adviser to take a more vocational course in business because at the time I didn't know what I would do with a psychology degree.

Eighteen years of working in offices and I now know that I would have become a counsellor. Even now I would swap my spreadsheets and marketing budgets for my own practice were it not for the fact I've got caught in a trap of waiting for maternity pay.

It dawned on me as I sat in the restaurant that first night that this no longer applied. If I wanted, I could give up my job and pursue an alternative career. My heart fluttered at the prospect. There was still one dream I could follow, and I was certain I would make a much better therapist than I did a marketeer.

I was so engrossed in the thought that I jumped when I noticed a waiter at our table. Introducing himself as Jonas, he asked if everything was OK with our meal. 'Oh yes, it's lovely,' I told him. 'Thank you.'

'I noticed you do water sports on the beach,' James said, engaging him in a conversation that I zoned out of.

I tuned back in when Jonas said, 'May I tell you about our gala evening? Every Wednesday we set up the restaurant on the beach. It's a very beautiful occasion – everyone dresses up and there's live music and dancing. You will come?' he asked.

'Of course we will,' I told him. 'We wouldn't miss it, would we, James?'

'No, I suppose not,' he replied, although he seemed unsure. Possibly it was the dressing up he didn't like the sound of, or most likely the dancing. But after half a bottle of wine on top of the drinks I'd already downed, the gala night sounded perfect.

Day Six – Thursday

I wasn't 'watching' their room. I wasn't spying or anything like that, though I can see how it might have looked that way to Lieutenant Kallis when he found me hanging around outside, peering in and wondering whether I should knock on their door.

From the corner of my eye I see James pacing along the outer edge of the restaurant. He knows he cannot come over and ask what is happening because he has already been told by Lieutenant Kallis to wait. James doesn't know why I am being questioned; he doesn't know why I slipped out of the room for a second time. Right after we had discussed how awful it was going to be, that we wouldn't be able to go anywhere near the pool now that it was being emptied and police were crawling over it. He'd been shocked when I suddenly announced that I needed air, and he'd tried to stop me leaving.

'Where do you think you're going? You can't go snooping.'

'Snooping?' I'd said. 'Do you really think that's what I'm doing?'

James's eyes have been hard since last night, filled with something more than anger, but I can't fathom what because I've never seen my husband like this. He looks through me, like he can't even bear to look at me and yet I don't believe it's because of what was said at the gala dinner. The more I think about the way he spoke to me when he came back from fishing, his voice so urgent but his focus somewhere else entirely, makes me believe there is more going on that I don't know about.

If that's the case, last night's fight was masking something else. All I know is that when James returned from yesterday's fishing trip he was a different person to the one who'd left that morning.

I am aware my attention keeps flitting between the detective's questions about the body found in the pool and the odd actions of my husband. I need to focus on the present, but I can't stop thinking that everything I had hoped for from this holiday, one final chance to get our marriage back on course, has been irretrievably damaged.

Perhaps I just need to stop worrying about my marriage and tell the detective what I know. After all, a death is surely more important than the breakdown of my relationship. Maybe I should begin by telling him how it all started last Sunday when I realised my watch had been stolen.

Chapter Three

Day Two – Sunday

Even at 10.15 a.m. when we got to the pool the sunloungers weren't reserved with towels or bags. I had been fretting during our leisurely breakfast that we wouldn't get a spot by the pool, I was so used to towels being clipped onto beds to stake a claim. I'd wanted James to hurry up and not linger over his coffee as he was doing.

'Does it matter?' he'd said. 'We'll just do something else if they're all gone.'

I screwed up my face at him. Of course it mattered. Getting a sunbed was of utmost importance. 'What else would we do?'

James shrugged. 'I don't know, there's plenty. Take out some kayaks or jet skis, hire a boat ...' He had stopped by reception last night after dinner to find out what the resort had to offer. 'We won't get bored,' he told me, like that might ever be a problem.

But I didn't want to throw myself into activities. I wanted to relax by the pool and read my book. I wanted to feel the sun on my eyelids and not have to think about what I was cooking for tea that night, and have an Aperol spritz with my lunch if I wanted it.

So I was pleasantly surprised and relieved when we made it to the pool to find there were plenty of loungers to go round. Better yet, when we pointed out the ones we wanted a man carried our towels to them and laid them out while we lingered, waiting for him to finish.

'It's not good for the environment, is it?' I said to James. 'This many towels. Look, there's a woman over there with three.'

He turned in her direction but didn't comment as he sat down beside me and reached in my bag for the sun cream. 'Do you want me to put some on your back?' he asked.

I shook my head. 'I'm lying on it for now.'

'Can you do mine then?' He passed me the cream and shuffled to the edge of the bed while I sat behind him and ran my hands over his back. By the end of the day he would have patches of red whatever I did. And by the end of the holiday his hair would be even blonder and his skin would have a light tan, but he'd also have large rings around his eyes because he never took his sunglasses off.

As soon as I finished, he jumped up. 'I'm going in the pool,' he announced, and wandered round to the far edge of the lagoon, diving in without so much as a splash and slicing effortlessly through the water. I was left wondering why he'd insisted on lathering up with cream when it would all wash off.

He seemed restless that first morning. How long would he be able to sit still before cajoling me into one of his activities? He was like this at home, always wanting to do something and never able to be in one place for long. 'In case his thoughts catch up with him,' my mum had once joked. At the time I'd thought my husband was an open book, sharing all his thoughts with me. Now I was beginning to wonder if there were things he wasn't telling me.

He was swimming freestyle lengths, muscles rippling as his arms sliced through the water. Those hours in the gym were paying off, but then he had always seemed so strong. I remembered the first time he had wrapped those arms around me. I'd felt so small against him, so protected. I knew from the start James would always look after me.

As he continued to swim laps I became distracted by the family with the teenage boys arriving at the other side of the pool and I lost interest in my husband as I pulled my sunglasses over my eyes and sank into the lounger.

Today the mum was wearing a long green-and-gold sarong that was tied on one shoulder. On the other hung a large wicker bag. She was chatting to Isaac as his younger brother, Theo, trailed behind and their dad behind him, talking into his phone.

There was something similar about the two boys, I'd noticed the day before, around their eyes that made it obvious they were brothers. Other than that, they were physically very different. Where Isaac was lean and lighter haired and at least a head taller than his mum, Theo was much shorter and squatter.

Theo bounced a ball as he walked, his head down, like he had no interest in being here. Despite the heat he was wearing a long-sleeved sports top, burgundy with a white stripe and an emblem on the top left. Like it belonged to a private school team.

He reminded me of my ex, Sam, though Theo was a much younger version; Sam had worn his hockey top like a badge of honour, making sure everyone knew he was good enough to play for a team, though there was no pride to be had from the fact he spent nights in the hockey club bar racing his pints and tipping the empty glass on top of his head. Agreeing to ridiculous dares that saw him come home with a chipped front tooth or two broken fingers that had been tied together with a splint.

Both Theo and Isaac managed to carry off that look that teenage boys have when they come from money; Theo with his dark tousled hair, sunglasses perched on top of his curls, and Isaac in contrast with his hair cut so sharply and clothes that hung like they were made to fit.

'You're staring.' James pulled himself out of the pool in front of me. I ignored him as I watched the mum pointing to some sunbeds. A man with a stack of towels in his arms followed her over and started carefully laying them out as he had done for us. Beside the beds all four of them hovered with none of the embarrassment I had felt when the man did the same for me.

'Who's caught your interest this time?'

'No one,' I replied.

James started rubbing himself down with a towel. He was standing in my sun and so close to me that drips of water sprayed onto my legs as he shook himself off like a dog.

'I was just watching that family,' I admitted. 'They look like they've stepped out of a catalogue.'

James squinted as he glanced over. 'Really?' He didn't seem to share my opinion.

'What do you suppose he does for a job?'

'How would I know?' he laughed. Then, 'You're serious, aren't you?'

'Deadly,' I replied. 'I think he works in finance. He has that look about him, he always looks kind of serious.'

James rolled his eyes. 'How do you think you can know what someone does by looking at them across a pool?'

'He's been on his mobile since he got here, so he can't leave the office behind. Whatever he does it's important. His hair's cut smartly, he has the look of someone who sits on a board and he's definitely the type to wear suits to work. Plus' – I paused – 'he earns a lot of money to bring the whole family out here. Don't you think?'

'You're in the wrong job, you should have been a detective.'

'No . . .' I hesitated. But I was in the wrong job, James was right. My interest in other people was more than just people-watching, and maybe I should tell him I was thinking about a career change, that I wanted to look into a counselling course. But something was stopping me, and I had a feeling I wasn't ready to do anything about it. If I did, I would be kissing goodbye to the prospect of maternity pay, and I just couldn't go there quite yet. 'Anyway, you haven't told me what he does,' I said.

'I don't know. He's a teacher.'

'No, he's not a teacher! And you're not playing the game properly.'

'Do you want a drink?' James asked.

I glanced up at him. It was 10.45, too early for a drink, yet James was telling me he was getting a beer. I squinted at him, watching him sit down and beckon to a waiter. I did want a drink. I wanted an Aperol spritz but there was a knot low in my stomach that was telling me I should make a point and order a large bottle of water.

I had commented on James's drinking lately though not too pointedly. It wasn't that he came home rolling drunk or poured himself whiskies at four in the afternoon. There was nothing I could specifically say was worrying about his behaviour, other than the fact James had never been a drinker.

When we'd first met and were only touching thirty, something like sobriety was noticeable enough for both me and my friends to question him about.

'I don't like the taste of it,' James had told me once. 'And I'm happy driving.' It was a refreshing change to meet a boyfriend who wasn't downing pints as his mates counted along with him, or accepting tequila challenges like my ex, Sam, was always doing.

Yet over the last year James's taste for it had seemingly changed. 'You're drinking more,' I had pointed out when he asked me if I could drive home from a party, and James had shrugged and told me I could hardly say it was unfair. He was right, I couldn't, and so I didn't. Still it didn't answer my question: why was he?

I had never known James to *want* a beer, especially so early in the day, and I couldn't help myself when I said, 'That's unlike you.'

'I'm on holiday,' he said, as if this were an obvious reason. Like it didn't matter whether he actually wanted it or not.

'I know but ...' I drifted off and found myself making my point that James likely didn't even notice by not ordering an Aperol, and somehow it only served to create an awkwardness between us, although it was possibly one that was solely in my head.

I picked up my novel and attempted to focus but now the young newlyweds had arrived and the man was talking so loudly that even James glanced over at them.

He was striding towards the sunbeds next to us as she ambled behind, twiddling with the end of her blond hair that was hung loosely in a plait over her shoulder. She seemed almost apprehensive in the way she followed her husband, which intrigued me.

'Bit arrogant,' James murmured.

I shrugged. Was he arrogant, or did she just fall into his shadow? There definitely appeared to be an imbalance of power between them, which could have been their age gap, but it felt more than that.

The young wife stood by a lounger, looking over the pool as the man with the towels rushed over. She didn't acknowledge him, she didn't even seem to notice him preparing her sunbed for her as she gazed into the distance. As soon as he left, she stripped off a short white dress to reveal an equally dazzling white bikini. She hovered for a moment before settling down in a way that suggested she was expecting people to notice her.

I gave up with my book pretty quickly. There was too much to look at to bother trying to read. In contrast, by lunchtime James had walked around the resort twice and been in the pool three times.

He was bored. It was barely one o'clock when he suggested we had lunch. I followed him to the poolside bar, where I finally ordered myself the Aperol I'd been craving for the last two hours.

'You're fed up, aren't you?' I said.

James shrugged. 'A bit.'

'I've not seen you this bad before.'

'The last time we went on a beach holiday was five years ago,' he pointed out.

He was right. Since we had started IVF treatments we had ploughed all our money into them leaving little to pay for holidays. We'd managed a few short city breaks, but we hadn't spent so long away in years. 'What do you want to do then?' I asked him.

James pulled his pint glass to his mouth and took a gulp. 'I was thinking of booking something, a fishing trip maybe,' he murmured, his gaze on the bar ahead of him.

'I hate fishing, you know that,' I said.

'Yeah, I know you do but . . .' He shrugged. 'Would you mind?'

'If you went on your own?' I asked, surprised.

He nodded. 'There's a guy who can take me on Wednesday.'

'Oh.' I didn't know what else to say and James looked away, sipping from his pint, ignoring the froth that had gathered on his top lip. Would it be wrong to say I didn't want him going? To stop him from doing what he actually wanted to do on his holiday when I was happy lazing by the pool? But then this was supposed to be about us spending time together. 'Since when have you liked fishing?' I asked.

James sighed. 'I don't have to go.'

'No, it's fine,' I said. 'It's one day. It doesn't matter. Just be back in time for the gala evening.'

'Of course.' He smiled.

I inhaled my Aperol as James and I sank into a silence. Eventually he beckoned the waiter over for another drink, when I asked, 'Shall we go for lunch?'

James nodded and stood up. 'You are happy here, aren't you, Laila?' he asked.

'Of course I am,' I said, though I was agitated in that moment. I was disappointed he wanted to spend a day fishing without me, and bothered by the pints he was drinking, and then in turn I was annoyed with myself for feeling irritated by these petty things when I should be enjoying my holiday.

James seemed happy enough with my response, but then I had become adept at telling people what they wanted to hear. Words had become meaningless when I'd uttered them enough times to colleagues at work and even friends. 'Yes, lovely weekend,' or 'everything's fine, thank you'.

In the early days of trying for a baby I often found myself making excuses as to why I wasn't pregnant yet when for some reason people expected me to be. 'Do you want kids, Laila?' Keeley, from HR, who was in her late forties, once asked me as I was pouring myself a coffee in the breakout area. 'You've been married a while now, haven't you?' It was clear that in her eyes this meant I should be reproducing by now.

Only the week before had I found out my latest attempt at IVF hadn't worked, so in that moment it was as if the world around me stopped; I could almost see the stream of coffee pausing in mid-air.

In my head I said, *Actually, Keeley, it turns out it's not proving that easy for us. My womb lining has to be pumped with drugs just to make it thick enough, and my husband has sperm that like to swim in every direction but forward. And to be totally honest it's none of your business anyway.*

What I actually said was, 'Yes, maybe one day. Can I get you a coffee?'

It wasn't a lie, more an omission. But I wasn't just covering up for myself, I was pathetically doing it for Keeley because I didn't want the conversation to get awkward.

Later it happened with my friends too. I'd confided everything to Melissa and Claire, then one after the other they fell pregnant and I could see the apprehension in their eyes as they told me their news.

I was always happy for them, but I couldn't deny the deep hole gnawing inside me, the constant refrain of 'Why isn't this happening for me?' running through my mind.

As their babies arrived and I was asked to be a godmother, and my friends' lives became wrapped up in their own families, I stopped burdening them with what we were going through. Instead I began to confide in strangers online who were in the same position as me. The faces on my screen who I would likely never meet and who James once commented were 'helping you close yourself off from the real world, Laila'.

I had to admit I'd had a welcome morning of respite from these thoughts. In the last three hours I hadn't once drifted into the dark whispers of babies and lack of them; instead I'd wrapped myself up in the lives of the other guests, particularly the mum whose name I overheard was Em, and the young married girl whose name, Rosie, had been yelled across the pool. And it had been refreshingly pleasant.

As James and I strolled to the restaurant I steered the conversation away from my own irritations and on to safe ground in the form of these strangers. 'There's something odd about the couple who are here on their honeymoon,' I observed.

'In what way?' James asked.

'She doesn't look happy. They barely speak to each other – or at least she doesn't speak to him. He seems all right, I suppose.' My comment was based solely on the fact he had smiled at me as he walked past my lounger and commented that it was a lovely hotel, which I realised seemed fickle of me. 'I wonder if he knows his new wife doesn't want to be with him.'

'I don't like him,' James said. 'He reminds me of Carl. Up his own arse.'

'Your brother?' I hadn't seen it myself, but then I didn't really have much to go on. James had always kept his dad and his brother at arm's length. His mother died when he was twenty, but despite them being the only family members he had left, they'd never been there for him in the way you'd expect. His dad coerced him into working in the family business though it wasn't what James wanted, then always promoted Carl ahead of him. I often asked James why he stuck at the job, why he didn't get out when he clearly wasn't happy, and he always answered with a resigned, 'What else would I do now?'

'Anyone else got the Laila treatment?' he joked as we reached the restaurant. It was light relief to talk about other people, and that was all it had been at the start. Having a harmless laugh with my husband as I told him about Em and her family, and how Em was the polar opposite of Rosie.

What I didn't divulge was that I hadn't been able to take my eyes off the way Em was with her teenage son, Isaac, laughing and joking like they were the best of friends.

In the past, James had accused me of idolising certain women, demanding, 'Why do you think she's better than you?' I didn't want to risk him accusing me of doing the same with Em.

It wasn't that I thought they were better, just that what they *had* was better, and I'd never understood why James didn't realise this. On the first day of our holiday I found myself experiencing the familiar pang of wanting what Em had: a family. Only I was desperately trying to suppress it.

That afternoon we were back on our sunbeds when I reached for my wrist and realised my watch wasn't on it. In a sudden moment of panic I rummaged through my bag, and the books and T-shirts that were strewn over the table between us.

'I've lost my watch,' I said, furiously searching.

'The one your grandma gave you?'

'Yes.'

'You brought that to the pool with you?' James asked.

'Yes.'

'Why would you have done that?'

'James! Don't do that, I've lost it. It's gone, you don't need to tell me I shouldn't have brought it, just help me look.'

He sighed, shaking his head infuriatingly. I didn't need to be reminded I should have left it in the room but I hadn't. I'd worn it this morning, I remembered taking it off and putting it down. 'Shit,' I muttered, looking about the pool. 'Someone must have taken it.'

'Why do you say that?'

'Because I think I left it here.' I patted the table as tears pricked at my eyes. I was furious with myself for being so stupid.

'Then you need to go and tell reception,' he said. 'If you really think that happened.'

'It must have,' I said. 'Oh God, James, what if I've lost it for good?'

'Don't panic,' he told me. 'We can just go and sort it now. I'll come with you.'

'No. Stay here,' I said, 'look after the rest of our things.'

James frowned as I got up. 'I just don't see anyone stealing it,' he murmured as I grabbed my bag and walked off to reception.

Rosie's husband was at the desk in front of me, asking for a replacement key card and being told to wait one moment while it was sorted. He turned to smile as I approached the desk. Lowering my voice, I told the second receptionist: 'I believe my watch has been stolen from the pool.'

'Oh?' she said, 'I am sorry to hear it is missing, let me take some details.'

I described the gift my grandmother had given me, the last thing I'd received before she died. All the time I could feel Rosie's husband staring at me.

'You didn't lose it somewhere?' he asked.

I shook my head. 'I put it on the table.'

'So someone nicked it?'

'I'm – well, yes, I'm guessing so.'

I was turning back to the receptionist when I caught sight of Theo, Em's youngest son, hovering by a tall potted tree and watching with interest, what looked like a smirk hanging off the corner of his mouth.

I couldn't make out if he was just amused by the whole exchange or if there was more to him standing there, watching me. Either way, there was something about his expression that felt sinister. Like he might have known exactly what had happened to my watch.

Day Six – Thursday

Kallis was still waiting for my reply. What was I doing outside Em's room this morning? When the family were grieving, why on earth would I be hovering so close by?

I'd found her room earlier in the week. It isn't on one of the main paths. In fact it is tucked away over the other side of the resort, at the end of a path that leads nowhere else, set aside from any other rooms with its own private pool.

It made me wonder at first why they spent so much time around the communal lagoon pool with the rest of us when they had their own. A swim-up villa, as it's described online, where you can step from the decking right into the water. But then the following day, when I was back at reception, asking if there was any news of my watch, I had overheard Em complaining.

'We aren't facing the sun,' she'd said to the same woman I'd spoken to previously. 'I wanted a villa that at least got some sun in the afternoon. It's gone by midday.'

'There isn't anything I can do. This is where all the swim-up rooms are, I am afraid,' the receptionist answered.

'So you mean there aren't any we can move to?'

'They're all fully booked, but I can move you to a sea-view villa instead, if you'd prefer?'

'Without a pool?' Em asked.

'These ones don't have pools, that's correct.'

I wished I had been able to see Em's expression at that moment. Was she aghast at the idea of not having a swim-up room, or was she prepared to consider it? In the end she said, 'No. Don't worry. We'll stay where we are.' Her words were clipped as she turned on her heel and strode out of reception, barely looking at me.

There is no excuse for me being outside her room. I can't pretend I was walking past it when the path goes no further. The truth of it is I was there because I wanted to speak to Em. Because even though I, along with the detectives, am still waiting to find out what has happened and why a body has ended up in the pool, there are things I want to tell her. Things I think she needs to know that I am pretty sure have something to do with her son's death.

Now another police officer has hurried over to speak to Lieutenant Kallis in hushed Greek and Kallis stands up and tells me that something has come up and he must go. His face is grave; I assume they have found something important.

'Someone will be along later to question you,' he tells me. 'You wait, please.'

'Here?' I ask.

'No, you can go to your room, but you don't leave the resort, OK?'

'OK.' I nod, a slither of unease running down my spine at what they might have found. It seems increasingly likely that Em's son's death is suspicious and not the accident I'm still praying it might be.

If I am right and a murder took place here last night, I need to speak up about what I know. But I have a horrible feeling that, when I do, Em will know I was the one who told the police.

Chapter Four

Day Three – Monday

I woke at 6 a.m. on our second morning on Ixos. I wasn't sure what disturbed my sleep but I was suddenly jolted awake and pulled out of my dream. We had left the door slightly open during the night because James didn't like the intermittent burr of the air conditioner and so there was a faint breeze drifting into the room and a sliver of light coming through the gap in the softly billowing curtains.

At home I would have rolled over and tried to get back to sleep but instead I found myself reaching for the water beside my bed and getting up, heading for the door. The sun was already rising and the air was warm as it touched my bare arms and legs. I didn't want to waste the morning in bed and so I pulled on a sundress and the White Sands branded flip-flops and stepped outside, quietly pulling the door behind me.

Briefly my mind flicked through memories of the evening before: our second meal at the buffet and the wine that had been drunk in copious amounts. I had allowed James to order a second bottle, watched him scanning the menu as if he knew what he was looking for. It was an alien moment, my husband carefully selecting wine when over the years he'd only had the occasional glass. It troubled me, though I couldn't explain why.

Our conversation, inane chatter buoyed along with wine, should have set me at ease, but it was lacking. There was no depth, no substance to it. It felt, I realised, like I was on a second or third date and we were trying to get to know each other but weren't making any headway.

The next morning, certain I was overthinking things, I tried to focus on the moment instead of dwelling on last night's worries. The heat of the rising sun was warming me and my breathing was a little lighter than usual. I found myself noticing my surroundings – the lavender that lined the paths, its scent coming to me in bursts. The occasional tweet of a bird but otherwise a silence that for once I didn't fear. I had never been good at meditation in the few yoga sessions I had attended in the hope of calming my body and mind. I'd always found it impossible to stop myself thinking, but on this holiday there were times when I was beginning to relax.

The path wound round until it eventually reached the pool area where our waiter, Jonas, was busy behind the bar. '*Kalimera*,' he called out. 'Lovely morning!'

'It really is,' I said.

'You're up early.'

'I am. It's too nice to stay inside.'

'Yes,' he laughed and waved as he picked up a tray and walked off towards the restaurant.

I went over to the pool and slipped off my flip-flops, dipping my foot over the edge and into the water. It was perfectly still save for the occasional ripple that concertinaed across the surface.

I wanted to plunge in. To be the first person to break the surface of the water and submerge myself, but instead I pulled my foot back, picked up my flip-flops and allowed my inhibitions to control me as they always seemed to these days. I walked away and towards the steps that led down to the private beach, where I sat on the grass and stared out to the sea beyond.

It was emerald green and merged into crystal blue the deeper the water got, yet it was so clear that even from where I sat I could see the sand stretching out beneath its surface.

I was a million miles from home. Though I was lucky enough to live near the beach, I had never been able to shake off the dark cloud that hung over me these days and rid myself of the worries that plagued me. I no longer liked to stroll along the shore and collect shells the way I used to.

Even as an adult, and when I first met James, I would collect them in my pocket and take them home to make them into a picture or just save them in a bowl in the bathroom. But then I had always imagined myself doing it with my children and so as the years passed and my hopes became bleaker I stopped doing all the things that once made me happy.

I breathed deeply, letting the salt air fill my lungs. A moment later my thoughts were back there again, caught up in grief and longing, a thick black snake that coiled itself tightly around me. It had a habit of doing this whenever I tried to forget. It reminded me how imperfect my life was, that I shouldn't ever dream it was anything but. No matter how much I tried to focus on forging a life for me and James, it was not going to be an easy ride.

But then I had to accept that it couldn't ever be, not when my want for a baby had turned into a need and then an obsession. I needed to give myself some time, as my mum had told me. 'Things aren't going to change for you overnight,' she'd said when I revealed I would no longer plan for children.

I was impatient. I always had been. Impatient for things to happen straight away. You would have thought that five years of IVF would have helped me overcome this, but still I wanted to feel immediately 'OK' about my latest decision.

Mum was right though. The longing for a child wasn't something you could suddenly switch off. I had spent years plotting temperatures and peeing on sticks, having injections and forever waiting on calls from fertility specialists who'd inadvertently given me hope before charting its decline with each conversation through the small number of eggs collected, the fewer fertilised, even fewer that were growing until, finally, there was only one that was good enough to put back in.

The drugs pumped into me changed me, too. Maybe irrevocably, though I don't know for sure the blame lies entirely with them. James does. This is what he had said the evening he told me he couldn't do it any more. 'You don't need to keep doing this to yourself, Laila. It isn't helping you. It isn't *you*.'

He pointed it out to me, as did Claire, and then my parents. Had I been the only one not to notice that I was constantly moody and snapping at everyone around me for the slightest thing? No, of course I knew, but I had always ignored it.

'I've lost my wife,' James had said to me. 'And I want her back again.' He'd taken my arms in his strong hands and looked at me imploringly. There was something in his eyes that looked like fear. I knew then that however hard it might prove, I owed it to him to give him his wife back.

We were to hire kayaks today. I had relented, knowing James would not suffer a second day by the pool, but I drew the line at a jet ski, which James had lined up for himself first.

After breakfast he wandered down to the beach with a pocket stuffed full of euros in case the jet-ski man in his gazebo didn't take cards, while I ambled off to the pool, asking for the same two loungers we'd had the day before. Knowing that this afternoon I was being dragged out in a kayak, I wanted to make the most of a morning doing nothing.

Em was already lying on a sunbed on the other side of the lagoon. Behind her, her husband was pacing, on his phone. Five strides one way before he turned and paced in the opposite direction. His voice carried over to me, but only faintly. Even so, I could tell from his tone that whatever he was discussing was important to him.

Em didn't look up at him once, even when his pacing got faster. Every so often he'd stop right behind her sunbed, placing a hand on the back of it. Perhaps she was used to him working on holiday, or she was trying not to show her annoyance, but then she didn't look particularly annoyed. There was nothing readable in her expression at all.

I wondered whether he would interact with his boys any more than he had done the day before. From what I had seen, she was the one who had the relationship with them. Maybe that was the downside of being able to afford holidays such as this; in return you had to relinquish your husband to his mobile office.

Now the newlyweds were approaching the pool behind me. I heard him before I saw them. 'Rosie, over here,' he called out, pointing to two beds. His tone was brusque and snappy, as if she had annoyed him already this morning.

Ignoring her protests, he strode over to the ones he was pointing at, and she reluctantly followed.

'I want to be where we were yesterday,' she whined.

It *was* a whine too. A proper childish one. She didn't look like a Rosie. In my head Rosies were natural and bubbly, whereas she had dark eyebrows and lips that had had too much filler in them, and generally looked far too sombre, especially for a honeymooner.

I stifled a grin as her new husband sat down and his shorts rode up to reveal a brilliantly clear line separating red and white just above his knees. Today his shorts were much higher, which he must have chosen on purpose even though they made the stripes on his legs look ridiculous. As he tugged them down, failing to hide the line, I imagined how frustrated he likely was about having got sunburned.

Rosie swung her large bag onto the sunbed as her husband called one of the porters, who scurried over with an armful of towels that he took time laying on the loungers, carefully picking up her bag and replacing it when he was done. As soon as he had gone the husband stared at Rosie, who made a show of ignoring him as she rifled through her bag.

I wondered at the odds of them making it to the end of their honeymoon. I didn't fancy their chances.

By ten thirty I was restless. I got up to stretch and with James still gone I called over a waiter and ordered the Aperol I had wanted mid-morning the day before. There was something more relaxed about having a drink when he wasn't around, because I was becoming all too aware of how much he was drinking. It wasn't that it was too much, more that it was out of character.

The newlyweds were up now, pulling clothes on, tipping phones and sun creams into her bag. I watched as they ambled past me, his arm slung over Rosie's shoulder. It was the first contact I had witnessed between them and noticed how his arm didn't look right the way it hung limply. There was something about the looseness of it, and his hand that was clenched at the end signalled pretence.

I imagined them sitting opposite me on a therapist's couch, me with a notepad as I tried to help them get to the bottom of the issues they so clearly had. Beneath his arm I could see how stiff she was, how much she wanted to slip out from under it. For once she didn't have her sunglasses on. Under heavy black lashes she glared at me as she went past, a cold hard stare that showed no other expression on her petite face. I tried to read it as I smiled at her, more out of discomfort than anything else, but she looked away quickly.

What is it you're hiding? I would ask her. *What makes you flinch when your husband touches you?*

My mum had always told me that we never knew what problems people had, and I was a prime example of that. Yet there was something so amiss with Rosie that I would have loved to be able to put my finger on it.

He, on the other hand, turned in my direction and said hello. 'Did you find your watch?' he asked.

'No. I didn't.'

He stopped, which forced her to stop as well. 'You need to ask people if they saw anything.'

I nodded, subconsciously glancing over at Em. Isaac was just arriving at the pool, but there was no sign of Theo.

Rosie's husband turned to look at them too. 'Their kids were here yesterday,' he said. 'You think it might be them?'

'No,' I said hastily, embarrassed that this was exactly what had gone through my mind. 'No, I'm not suggesting it was anyone in particular.'

He shrugged and eventually turned to carry on walking. She followed a moment later but not before she had raised her eyes to me, no trace of any expression on her face, but it was a look that made me wonder what she was capable of. That made me think there was something about her I didn't trust. *What's your game?* I wanted to ask. *What were you thinking, marrying a man you so obviously don't want to be with?*

But with them gone my attention drifted back to Em, who had now spotted Isaac. She looked up at him and smiled, removing some things from the bed next to her and patting it as her husband continued talking into his phone behind her, seemingly unaware of his family.

My heart contracted at the sight of her small gesture. It was clear in the mum's smile how happy she was to see her son and how much she must love him.

He chatted to her animatedly, waving his arms about and making her laugh as he sat down next to her. Eventually, when he broke off, he scanned the pool, his attention drawn to where Rosie was hovering at the edge of the bar and his gaze rested on her.

He liked her. But then, despite the fact they were a world apart, he here with his parents and she with her new husband, there could only have been a handful of years between them, if that.

But then Isaac had turned back to his mum and their laughter rang out across the pool. I wondered what the two of them found to talk about, what they shared that made them laugh out loud, and I felt that familiar twinge, reminding me this was something I might never have the chance to experience.

It was odd because I had often noticed mothers with children in various stages of growing up and felt a pang of want, but never before had I experienced the same empty need watching one with older children. And right then I realised I had missed something else – the prospect of having children who grew into young adults, wondering what might become of them, who they might be or what their dreams were.

Em and Rosie couldn't have been more different but in that moment I would be lying if I said I didn't envy them both. Em for everything she had and Rosie for the fact that she was just starting out with her twenties ahead of her, plenty of time to make mistakes and then realise her dreams before it was too late.

My mum always said that envy would eat you up. I knew she was right because it had been doing that for years. On this holiday I was supposed to be finding my happiness in a path without children but with every moment it was becoming harder not to fixate on other couples who had what I so dearly wanted.

I ordered another Aperol and fought the urge to tell Rosie to either cheer up or leave him, and to tell Em that if all she had to moan about was that her room with a pool didn't have any sun after midday, then she clearly had a lot to be grateful for.

Day Six – Thursday

I was losing myself in the other guests in the first few days of the holiday. I think from the outset I realised that I was doing it to avoid confronting my own problems and the growing realisation that my husband and I had drifted too far apart.

After last night I keep wondering whether I should have made more effort to concentrate on us rather than everyone else, but I know that in the end it wouldn't have made any difference. Whatever happened yesterday to prompt our fight wasn't about us, of that much I'm sure. If only I had some idea what it *was* about.

James appears by my side as soon as Lieutenant Kallis leaves, his face contorted with annoyance and confusion. 'What was all that about?' he asks.

I long for the James I used to know to return. The one who would have been caring and attentive to my needs.

This one has been wound up since yesterday and his mood is getting progressively more agitated.

'They just wanted to ask me questions,' I say. 'I have to wait at the villa for them.'

'Questions? About what? What do they think you know? What's happening, Laila?'

'I don't know what's happening.'

'Well they must have told you something. What happened to the kid? Do they think it was an accident or did he jump?'

'You mean did he do it himself?'

'It's possible,' he said. 'Sadly, I mean statistically—'

'He didn't jump,' I say adamantly, as if I know this for sure, but of course I don't.

'Why are they talking to you, though?' James asks as we start walking back towards our room. 'They seemed pretty keen to.'

My mind shoots back to when Kallis found me twenty minutes earlier. He asked me what I was doing standing outside Em's room, and instead of just coming out and telling him I had information, I fumbled my response. No wonder he's suspicious.

'The detective saw me taking a walk so he stopped to question me,' I say. 'They're talking to everyone at the hotel.' There was a time when I would have told James everything, confided in him and asked him what I should do and we would have worked it out together. But I can't. Because then he would ask me how I know, and I would have to tell him what I did yesterday afternoon when he wasn't around, how I took it upon myself to find out if my theory about Theo taking my watch was correct.

I went too far and heard things I shouldn't have heard, and now I worry that I must have been seen.

For now I'm not saying anything to Kallis – or James. How can I, when I don't know how my husband will react?

It's obvious James doesn't trust me. He made this clear last night, albeit about something else entirely. 'I know what you've done, Laila,' he said as we walked to dinner. 'I know what you've bloody well done.' It's clear there are too many issues of trust and secrets for us to resolve right now. I wonder if, like me, he has no idea where we start.

'So where *did* you go this morning?' my husband asks me now.

'What do you mean?' I ask, though I know full well.

'The second time you went out for a walk, where did you actually go? I mean, I'm pretty certain you didn't go back to the pool. Or at least I hope to God you didn't. You didn't, did you? You didn't go back to see what was going on?'

'No!' I cry. 'I didn't.'

'Then where did you go?' he hisses, lowering his voice as we pass another guest, a man who is dressed in chino shorts and an open shirt that billows as he walks.

'Awful news, isn't it?' he says, pausing to talk to us.

'Horrendous,' James answers. 'Have you heard anything more about it?'

The man shakes his head. 'Just that we have to wait for the police to question everyone.'

'Yes,' James replies. 'I guess they want to know if anyone saw him.'

'Or what anyone saw,' the man says. He eyes us both. 'I mean, what if someone here killed the lad?' He gestures his hand about, looking at us knowingly, as if it's exciting that there could be a killer prowling the resort.

James narrows his eyes. 'Do you think that's possible?'

'It's what people are saying.'

'James,' I mutter, tugging on his arm. 'Come on, I just want to go back to the room.'

'Jesus,' James says as we walk away.

'What?'

'What do you think? You can already see what it's going to be like here now, the gossip and everyone making out they know more than they do. We need to get out of here, Laila. We'll wait until they come to speak to us, but we need to find somewhere else to stay. I'll look again when we get back to the room. I just need to see when the ferry is running, but I can't get any information online and reception are being particularly unhelpful. And on top of that there's you acting all secretive.'

'James, don't be like this with me, please.'

'Like what?'

'Angry.'

He has a hangover. I can see it in the redness of his eyes and the creases of his skin that are more accentuated than usual. He didn't get enough sleep because I'd woken him at six fifteen, but that isn't the only thing making him prickly. It's the aftermath of last night's fight that we haven't addressed.

We pass Rosie and her husband's bungalow. The doors are wide open and I peer inside. Their queen-sized bed has been split into two singles that have been pushed apart, leaving a wide gap in the middle. I suppose it should no longer surprise me, having watched them for the last five days, but it's hard to believe that a young couple on their honeymoon are sleeping in single beds by choice.

'What are you staring at?' James says.

'Nothing.' I stopped talking to, and laughing with, James about the other guests when one evening he accused me of becoming obsessed. I have no desire to start again now.

We carry on walking and eventually reach our room. Our bed is still unmade though I doubt anyone will be bothering to clean today. James's clothes are lying in a heap on the floor where he must have dropped them last night, apart from the shirt that he was still wearing when I woke him this morning. I pick them up and shove them into a washbag while he makes himself a coffee.

We need to talk about last night. About how he left me sitting at the table on the beach on my own as he stormed off. About the words he had thrown at me and the ones I'd hurled back in return.

But a boy is dead and, as significant as our problems are, there are other people suffering way more right now. Like Em. The woman I'd mentally chastised a few days ago for having nothing more to worry about than the sun on her decking – and now look at her.

On occasion I have thought of my own failed pregnancies as lost babies but this – this is a new and incomprehensible level of grief. Knowing your child for all those years, giving them life and watching them grow. This I could not even begin to imagine.

'You still haven't answered my question,' James says, his hands wrapped around a small cup as he wanders over to the bed where I am sitting. 'Where did you go this morning?'

When I don't answer, he says, 'You went there, didn't you? To her room?'

I open my mouth to protest but no words come out.

'God, Laila,' he sighs and shakes his head. 'You *are* obsessed. This is what I said, you let yourself get too—' He breaks off and clicks his fingers before finishing: 'Consumed. You've done it with her. And that young married one you keep on about.'

'That is not true,' I protest, my eyes filling with tears.

James rolls his eyes, like he doesn't believe me as he storms out of sight and into the bathroom.

He is right. We need to get out of here. I had gone to Em's villa to talk to her this morning but I didn't get the chance, and maybe that is for the best. I go over what I know in my head. I know that there was an argument yesterday and her son was threatened. And I am sure that when I crawled out of my hiding place I was seen, watching, listening.

James reappears in the room. 'You're right. Let's get out of here,' I say. 'I don't want to hang around any more.'

He says nothing, presumably assessing why I've had a sudden change of heart, then tosses his phone on the bed. 'Yes, well, it would help if I could get hold of the ferry company, because until then we can't go anywhere. We'll end up stuck here,' his voice rises into a panicked crescendo. James is as desperate to get out of here as I am. 'And it feels like there's nothing we can do about it,' he finishes.

Chapter Five

Day Three – Monday

James was taking his time on the jet ski. I had expected him to be back by now but there was no sign of him on the beach or even out to sea when I went looking for him. I knew he was too fidgety to spend another day around the pool but I was ready to give up my sunlounger so we could spend more quality time together, and not just when we were drinking our way through dinner.

When it turned out he was nowhere around, and I was two full days into the holiday without having seen much of the resort myself, I took out the map that he had given me when we arrived and went to explore.

I stopped at the spa and contemplated the menu of treatments they offered, all of them promising to either restore, relax or rejuvenate. When a therapist appeared in the doorway and asked me if she could help, I booked a de-stress massage and a seaweed wrap in three days' time.

I passed the games room with its pool table, alongside an AstroTurf pitch and tennis court that I couldn't imagine anyone using in the heat. We had already checked out the Greek restaurant that we were allocated two visits to and, given what the therapist told me, I booked us a table for dinner that night.

On I went, following the map. It seemed the path I was on would take me to the swim-up rooms, with their own private pools set apart from the main resort and cocooned in their own privacy.

Out of interest, I had looked up the cost of the swim-up villas on White Sands' website after I'd overheard Em at reception. Her two-bedroom villa with its own pool cost £7,500, and that was only for the week. I wanted to see for myself what kind of luxury such money afforded you.

There were only four of these villas on the resort, each spaciously built into their own area and divided by walls of shrubs. Four sunloungers were arranged either side of the small pools that backed directly onto the patio. Outside the last one I came to was Em's wicker bag that I had seen her carrying the day before.

So this one was theirs. An epitome of luxury that caused her to complain about its lack of sun, and consequently spend little time in. She appeared to have it all, at least as far as money was concerned, yet that age-old question popped into my head: *But are you happy?*

I thought she looked like she was, though already I had begun to see tiny cracks. Like the fact her husband spent more time on his phone than he did talking to his kids, and her relationship with her boys seemed a little off balance in that her attention was mostly lavished on Isaac. And then of course there was Theo. The youngest son, whose misplaced smirk disturbed me enough to think he might have stolen my watch.

I drew a deep breath as I glared at their villa with its two sets of bifold doors leading onto the patio. Was my watch in there? Could someone with the amount of money they likely had, be the type to steal? Of course, I thought. Anything was possible.

I was back at the main pool within ten minutes. Just for a short moment it had been fascinating to see what people like Em got to experience. What it might be like to be her.

Here she was, beckoning over a waiter for a drink, all the time listening intently to whatever Isaac was telling her. I couldn't imagine how you could spend so much money on such luxury and choose not to use it. It seemed frivolous, a waste. It was, in my mind, the attitude of someone who didn't realise how good they had it.

Now Theo was arriving at the pool, joining his parents, his head lolled and he was in the same sports top he had been wearing the day before. I looked for the likeness to Sam again, but Theo didn't have any of the cheekiness my ex had. He bounced his ball relentlessly on the ground and I had a sense he was trying to be irritating as he stood behind his brother's sunbed, thumping his hand repeatedly on the ball.

But then as Theo looked up, his eyebrows rising into a point and his mouth turning up in the corner, I saw the similarity again and it was something I didn't like. I shuddered as I looked away from him and back to Em. A shard of a memory I didn't want had come into my head. However cheeky and endearing I may once have found Sam, it was a relationship that didn't end well. He had wanted to control me while he was free to do whatever he pleased.

Em now turned at the sound of his ball and held up a hand in a wave that came across as more dismissive than welcoming as she swiftly turned back to Isaac, reaching over and ruffling Isaac's hair, leaning into him as she spoke. There was no space next to her for Theo and she made no move to find room for him. I wondered if her youngest noticed this, whether his incessant ball-bouncing was a cry for attention. Eventually she stopped again and gestured to a sunbed that the younger boy needed to drag over towards them until someone rushed to assist.

Theo didn't help the man who was hauling the lounger and unnecessarily apologising, most likely for the fact he hadn't foreseen that they might need another bed. The teenager didn't bother to thank him when the job was done, though his mother did so automatically and without glancing up, as if she knew any show of courtesy would fall to her. Even Isaac looked up and held up his hand in thanks, their dad still absorbed on a phone call.

I had never really thought before how much a mother's relationship might differ between her two children, but then perhaps it is rarely the same. To me, it seemed very much like Em had a better connection with Isaac, who reminded me of a peacock the way he caught his mum's attention.

Finally Theo stopped bouncing and slumped onto the bed that had been pulled alongside Isaac's and I watched their dad, who was a different story again. When he eventually put his phone away he stopped behind the beds and regarded his family for a moment without them knowing, watching the intimacy between his wife and oldest son.

What are you seeing? I would have asked him if I was their family counsellor. *Because it isn't pride, is it? Are you jealous of your wife's relationship with your son?*

I was so preoccupied with the question of whether a man could be envious of his wife and son that it took me a while to realise James still wasn't back. Even with my limited knowledge of jet skis I thought he'd only have been off on a fifteen-minute trip, but nearly an hour and a half had passed since I'd arrived at the pool.

I was hot. An unattractive slick of sweat was gathering under my bikini top, which I wiped away with my towel. I stood up and fiddled with the parasol, unable to push its centre up high enough to feed the plug through to hold it in place. With no one rushing to my aid, I let it ping down again. The nearest shade was in the bar, so I strolled over and sat on one of the bar stools, a waiter appearing swiftly to ask what I wanted to drink.

The Aperol from earlier had long ago worn off and the heat had left me with a slightly fuzzy headache, but what the hell – I was on holiday, and James wasn't back, and if you can't have a cocktail or two in the morning on holiday, when can you? I ordered myself another and hadn't even noticed anyone else's presence at my side until they asked the waiter a question.

When I turned I was surprised to see it was Em. Without thinking I blurted, 'Oh, hi,' as if I already knew her, because it felt, by now, that I did. We had seen each other enough times since the coach journey for each of us to be familiar to the other, yet she turned to me and frowned and appeared utterly confused, as if she were trying to place me. 'Hi,' she said back, smiling but already turning away again.

'We were on the same coach here,' I ventured.

'Oh, right, yes,' she replied.

She was dismissing me. She hadn't noticed me like I had her. I wondered if she'd noticed anyone else around the pool. Maybe it was of no interest to her to look at the other guests she'd be spending the next week or so of her holiday with. I didn't know which of us was the odd one. Maybe it was me for my interest in people; perhaps her lack of curiosity stemmed from her contentment with her lot. Then again, maybe there was an air of superiority to her too.

'Are you enjoying your holiday?' I persisted.

'It's amazing, isn't it,' she replied. She wasn't inviting a response; she had no interest in what I thought.

'I've never been anywhere like it,' I told her.

'Oh?'

'My husband's been to Greece before, though not Ixos. Or at least, I don't think he has,' I murmured.

'We have been to White Sands' resorts before, just not this one,' she said as she looked over her shoulder at her family.

'You must like them.'

'We do but …' she hesitated, 'I don't know, same with anywhere, I suppose. Every time it's a little less …' she broke off again, waving a hand as she looked for the word but then maybe chose to ignore it as she said, 'Perhaps it's just that the boys have outgrown it.'

'I'm Laila.' I held out a hand.

'Em.' She glanced at my hand before shaking it.

'So those are your boys?' I asked, gesturing to her sons like I didn't already know.

'Yes. Isaac and Theo.'

'They look like they're enjoying their holiday,' I said, more for conversation than because they did.

Em glanced back at them again, screwing her eyes up as maybe she considered this. 'I suppose they are, but then they're teenagers so you never can tell.' She raised her eyebrows as she looked back at me. 'Do you have children?'

'No. No, we don't.'

Em smiled again and, as that always seemed to be a conversation closer, she said, 'Well it was nice to meet you. I'll no doubt see you around. It's not as if you can get away from anyone in this place, is it?'

'No,' I muttered as she took a water from the waiter and walked back to her sunbed. She didn't look back, didn't tell any of the others she had met someone at the bar, like I would have done if James had been here. Our conversation was of no consequence to her and weirdly it left me feeling flat. Maybe it was because I was so much keener to speak to her than she was me, needier perhaps. It was apparent how much of my time I spent watching other people while the subjects of my interest were happily oblivious to the world outside their own family. I didn't resent them for it, but I did crave that contentment.

I sat at the bar and finished my drink and was back on my lounger when James finally appeared.

'Hey.' He grinned. 'Sorry I've been so long.'

'What have you been doing?'

He stripped off his T-shirt and threw it onto the sunbed. 'Well after the jet ski, I went out on one of the ringos,' he said.

'Oh! I wish I'd known. I could have taken some photos.'

'Last-minute decision. And then I got chatting to the guy who's going to take me out on the boat on Wednesday.'

'Fishing?'

'Yeah. We leave at nine.'

'You're definitely going then?' I didn't know what I would do with a whole day on my own. I may have passed the morning quite happily today, but this wasn't how we were supposed to be spending the holiday. This wasn't reconnecting or getting to a point where we were moving forward.

'You're all right with it, aren't you?' he said. 'You said you were.'

'Yes, I just . . .' But he was busy searching for his goggles, pulling them over his head and getting ready to jump in the pool, as if he wasn't particularly concerned with my answer either way, and so I didn't say anything.

'I'm going for a dip,' he said. 'Coming?' I shook my head as he dived into the water. It made me tired just watching him. There was something frantic about him, I thought, as he leapt from one activity to the other.

The night James told me he didn't want to try any more he had said to me, 'I'm not a husband to you any longer, Laila. All I am is someone for you to try and get pregnant by.' He had looked so sad as he said it, as if he had given everything to me and all I had done was take.

I told him this wasn't true. I had loved James with every bit of my being, as he had me. I wanted to give him what he wanted, but I didn't feel like he was reciprocating, at least not on this holiday. Two days in and it wasn't turning out to be the break for us I had been promised.

Or was I looking too deeply into it, as I was often guilty of doing? If I told James I didn't want him to go fishing, would he immediately cancel the booking, hurt at the thought that I was upset?

It unnerved me that I might not know my husband well enough to predict his reaction.

Day Six – Thursday

'This is all too far-fetched,' James snaps. He is pacing up and down our room as we wait for Lieutenant Kallis to arrive and question us, taking our instruction not to go anywhere literally.

'What is?' I ask. I wish he would stop moving about, just for a moment.

'That one of the guests is dead. It's like something from a TV drama.'

I am taken aback by how heartless he sounds as he strides across the floor. He doesn't know what to do with himself. I don't either, but my thoughts are filled with Em and how she is coping. I wonder what she is doing right now and how she must be feeling. How she was told and who was given the unimaginable task of knocking on their door this morning to break the news that her son was dead.

James's focus is on us and getting us out of here. He is wrapped up in our immediate problems and though I want him to sort it so that we can get out of White Sands, it feels like it leaves no scope to talk about anything else. Which means last night's fight and the dilemma that is eating away at me continue to hang like a black cloud.

He stops in front of me, staring into my eyes as if he can find the answer to his questions in there. 'What do you reckon the police are thinking?'

'How would I know?' I say quietly.

'I mean someone couldn't be murdered here, could they?' he says in disbelief. 'It doesn't seem possible.'

'Does it ever seem possible?' I say.

'You know what I mean,' James snaps. 'I just ...' He hesitates. 'I don't believe it,' he says before walking away.

I can't believe it either, but it has happened. I saw the body with my own eyes and while I wish more than anything for the best outcome right now, which is that it was an accident, I cannot help thinking this wasn't the case.

James has never been one for watching the news or the crime dramas I soak up. He shies away from anything unpleasant; it was one of the things I found so charming about him. There was a time when he caught me crying over a story of an abandoned puppy and he whipped my phone away and asked why I even read such stories. I tell myself that this is why he is so keen to get away from White Sands.

'The pool will be closed off for the rest of the day,' he says, seemingly apropos of nothing. 'No one will be able to go near it.'

'When do you think they'll reopen it?' Not that it is important, but it crosses my mind it could be days.

James shrugs. 'I've no idea. Surely by tomorrow? But then hopefully we won't be here if I can get a bloody boat booked.'

If they are treating the pool as a crime scene, how likely are the police to open it for everyone to start enjoying? No doubt there'll be forensics crawling all over the place for days. Besides, who in their right mind would want to sit around a pool knowing that someone has just died in it?

A sudden rap on our door makes me jump. James opens it and there are two police officers standing on the other side. I am surprised Lieutenant Kallis isn't one of them.

'Mr and Mrs Burrow?' the taller of the two asks, tracing his finger down a list and looking up to check he has the right people.

'That's right,' James says.

'We are here to talk to you about an incident that has happened this morning.'

'That's fine,' James says. 'We know what it's about.'

'OK. Good.' He nods. 'Maybe we could start with you, Mr Burrow?'

'You're not talking to us together?' James asks, as I say, 'You haven't come to talk to me?'

The officer looks from me to James before answering: 'We speak to you one at a time. Starting with you, Mr Burrow, please.'

I'm confused. I'd have thought that after Kallis had begun interviewing me they might have wanted to speak to me first, but I tell them, 'It's fine, I can go and wait. I'll be outside whenever you're ready.' I start to walk to the door as the officers step inside.

As they pass me, James catches hold of my wrist. 'Laila!' he says.

'Yes?'

His eyes meet mine and I can feel his fingers twitching against my skin as he loosens his grip. 'It doesn't matter.'

'What is it?' I say.

'Just that last night,' he starts, 'after I left you and we didn't come home together—'

'Mr Burrow?' one of the officers interrupts. 'Please?' He gestures to our sofa and waits for James to nod and take a seat, and for me to leave the room.

Chapter Six

Day Four – Tuesday

I woke at 6 a.m. again, or possibly just before. Once more too much alcohol had been drunk the previous night at the Greek restaurant, where the food had been delicious but we should have stopped at one bottle of wine. There had been no need for James to order another so quickly.

Conversation had become hazy after that point and it meant I woke a second morning in a row with an underlying notion that I wasn't sure where we stood. The days of our holiday were passing and, if anything, it felt like we were drifting further apart.

James was splayed on his front beside me on the bed, one arm hanging over his side of it. I had a rapid fluttering in my chest that I likened to a butterfly, just a soft one, but enough to make my breath catch as I watched my husband sleeping.

Perhaps I was putting too much pressure on us, I thought as I quietly swung my legs out and slipped on a sundress. Maybe I just needed to let everything take its course.

I padded out of the room, closing the door behind me and stepped out into the warm glow of the Greek sunrise. This time I took the path that wound away from our room and towards the main areas of the resort, and instead of going to the pool I headed down the steps onto the private beach below. Slipping off my shoes I walked barefoot across the sand and sat down on one of the sunbeds nearest to the edge of the sea.

Ahead I could make out a cluster of small islands in the distance that James had pointed out to me while we were kayaking yesterday. He had told me most of them were uninhabited.

In return I had pressed him about how well he knew the area. His face had clouded over and he'd shaken his head as he said, 'Not well.'

From the outset we'd agreed we were more comfortable in the present than the past and so on the whole our exes didn't surface. I wouldn't have minded telling James about Sam though. In some ways it might have been cathartic to explain how, if James hadn't given me his all from the start, I might have found it hard to trust him. Because Sam had definitely made it hard for me.

But James had thrown himself into our relationship head and heart first, always telling me how he felt, never leaving me to wonder when he was going to reply to a text or making me read between the lines about what he meant. There were no games. I never had to ask myself if he loved me. And so I'd taken his steer and brushed over Sam and Stephanie's existences. They were no longer important.

Except I didn't believe that. I knew that we were all shaped by our histories and by the people that came into our lives. Wasn't it one of the first things counsellors addressed? Wasn't it what made us into the people we became?

It was funny that I only began to think in that moment on the sunbed as I stared at the tiny islands on the horizon that for someone who wanted to become a counsellor I had never been able to get my husband to open up about his past.

I knew the bones of his life before me. James's mother had died after a short illness ten years before I met him. He had never wanted to join his father's construction business and so in his early twenties he'd flitted around aimlessly from job to job, with a girlfriend called Addie who eventually went off with a plumber who had come to fix their toilet.

He met Stephanie in a bar and later followed her on her travels around Europe. I asked him once why they broke up – it was probably not long after I had found her photo in the book and I was desperate to know more. I remembered

James's frown as he'd considered his answer, and the feeling of unease in my stomach as I waited to hear what he might say. I'd expected him to admit she had finished with him and left him heartbroken to return to the UK alone. It was a surprise when he revealed, 'I realised I was living her life and her dream. I was following her around and knew it wasn't actually the life I wanted.'

I must have accepted that the life he wanted was to end up working at his dad's company, even though I knew this was not the case. James's heart wasn't in construction, he hated working for his father, under the shining light of his brother, Carl. And so how could this have been the truth?

What was the point of me hoping to counsel strangers if I didn't even understand my own husband? I was spending my holiday mentally digging into the lives of the other guests while my own marriage was beginning to feel too fragile to touch. But then maybe that was the point, I thought. Maybe it was easier not to look too closely at yourself.

I sighed as I shuffled to the back of the lounger and flicked on my phone to take a photo. It was a picture-perfect view, and had I been an Instagrammer or had any desire to post on Facebook it would have undoubtedly attracted 'likes'. But I had long ago given up social media, I had no interest in sharing my life with anyone.

Sitting there on the empty beach, I no longer felt the peace and happiness I'd had when I arrived fifteen minutes earlier. Thoughts of James and Stephanie, and the puzzle of why my husband was still working for his father in a job he hated, had left me feeling troubled.

I found myself turning to the only place I knew where people understood me: MyFertility, the forum I joined two years ago. I went straight to the support group thread, scanning the recent posts. I had gone cold turkey six weeks ago, disappearing from the site like I have watched other members do over and over again. There were so many women whose journeys you travelled alongside them, until one day they dropped out of sight leaving you wondering what had become of them. Were they one of the ones celebrating a happy outcome they didn't feel they could share with an audience still struggling, or, like me, had they endured one failure too many?

I started tapping out a post of my own.

Sorry for my absence, I began. *But my OH and I decided not to try for children any more.* I used the lingo that I'd casually picked up, OH referring to my other half, my unnamed spouse. *In truth OH decided not to try,* I wrote.

I deleted and started again. I didn't want to confess the decision we had made, even if these were the only people who understood me.

I am on holiday and surrounded by mothers, I said instead. This wasn't true of course, but I was making some kind of point. *And I find myself wondering why none of them seem to appreciate the gift they have been given. It makes me sad.* I paused. Sad wasn't the right word, and this was one place I could be anonymous and therefore truly honest. I deleted the last word and typed *angry. I know it is wrong and I hate feeling like this, but I am. I am angry and really bloody sad too.*

I was beginning to realise that, as much as I'd been telling myself and those closest to me that James and I could move forward, I didn't know if we could.

Eventually I did what I always do and picked myself up, figuratively and literally, and walked back to our room. James was already out of bed when I got there. The toilet flushed as he appeared around the dividing wall. 'Hey,' he said. 'You been out for an early walk again?'

I nodded. 'Would you like a coffee?'

'I'll do us both one,' he said, making two and pulling back the curtain as we sat on the end of the bed.

'Was this hotel here when you came to Greece?' I asked him. Though I already knew the answer it was a leading question.

'What?' he turned, surprised. 'No. It wasn't built till . . .' He waved a hand in the air but didn't answer, instead frowning at me.

'You've been to Ixos before, haven't you?' I said. I didn't know how I knew, I just did. Perhaps it was the way he'd been last night when I had questioned him. Though he'd insisted he didn't know the area well, I had known he was lying.

'Once,' he admitted. 'Just once and I didn't stay long. Maybe one night.'

'With Stephanie?'

James nodded.

'Why didn't you tell me?'

'Because I didn't think it mattered. I don't know, Laila, we stayed in the village, nowhere near here. It was years ago. Why? Hey.' He grabbed my free hand and tugged me round to face him. 'It's not important, you're not upset, are you?'

'No. Not upset.' I wasn't sure if I was or not. 'I just wish you'd mentioned it. You made me think this was all new to you.'

'It is!' he laughed. 'My God, *this* is all new, I didn't go anywhere else on the island, I didn't stay in places like this. I promise you. I stayed one night, that was it.'

'OK.'

'OK?' he repeated. 'Are you sure it's OK? Because I'd rather you tell me now if you're not happy.'

'No.' I shrugged. 'It's fine. Honestly.' I smiled and sipped my coffee and convinced myself that it really didn't matter if James had spent one night in the village with Stephanie. I fought the niggling image of him standing on the roadside as we waited to board the coach, rubbing my back as I felt sick, looking around for the place they once slept in. I told myself it didn't mean anything.

The pool was busy and we'd ended up on sunloungers on the other side from our usual spot, tucked away in the greenery and close to Em and her family. James had already pounded back and forth in lengths of the pool and now he was perched on the edge of his bed, fiddling with a bite on his ankle that was an angry red and much larger than it should be.

'It looks infected,' I told him. 'You should get something to put on it.' I wanted him to stop picking at it; I couldn't imagine what people must be thinking if they were watching him.

'It's fine,' he said, giving another big scratch until it started to bleed.

I shook my head and turned away from my husband, pulling my sunglasses down and facing Em the other side of me.

In contrast to James's incessant scratching, her own husband was lying on the lounger next to her, one arm draped across her sunbed, his forefinger lazily running up and down his wife's arm. Later he got up and she called out 'Rob!' to him, and as he came back he leant over and kissed her slowly on the forehead, lingering, like he didn't want to let go as she told him whatever it was she wanted.

Their body language was loving and intimate and yet it didn't feel like a display. Em and Rob had no idea there were others around them, that anyone could possibly be watching. They didn't care, but why should they? After that many years of marriage and rearing two teenage boys, it was enviable that they still had so much love for each other.

Isaac, who was the other side of his mum, lay face down on his lounger, head hanging over the top as he held a phone in his hands. Every so often he dropped it and rolled over to talk to her, which he was doing now. In return Em was on her side too, facing her son so that when Rob came back with drinks she didn't notice him.

I had a clearer view of Rob's face than I'd had the day before, as he watched the two of them together. He was a good-looking man, dark hair cut short, gold-framed Aviators that looked like they'd been made for his face they fitted so well. He pushed them on top of his head as he stood by his wife's bed, revealing a frown that creased his forehead as he looked from her to Isaac. Then he raised his eyebrows and blew out a breath and I thought to myself that I was right, he seemed jealous of their closeness.

For a moment he stood beside her, the glasses of drinks on the tray rattling against each other, and still she didn't look up as she laughed along with Isaac at a joke they were sharing. 'Your drinks are here,' he said, a little loudly, but not enough to raise suspicion it seemed as Em rolled onto her back and smiled at him. And then the frown was gone, and Rob appeared relaxed again as he sat down next to her and Isaac went back to his phone.

Don't you see it yourself? I wanted to ask her. *Don't you see what your husband sees?*

I laughed to myself then, because who was I to talk? And the more I thought about it, the more I wondered if I was cut out for counselling, but at the same time I couldn't bear to think that I might lose another dream.

After a while I went back to watching Em and pondering the glimpse of exasperation from her otherwise loving and attentive husband. I wondered if it meant that his smile was an act. Regardless, something was off for sure, enough to throw my thoughts of their marriage off-kilter. As always, my interest was piqued when something didn't make sense, relishing the challenge of piecing it together.

People like Em and Rob were harder to dig into because on the surface they were the perfect family of two plus two, but there can always be something lurking, even in the most model of households.

Maybe I was looking for it. In two days' time I would be asking myself this over and over. Had I imagined all those little signs? Or had I been right to suspect that all was not as it seemed?

It was a while later when Rob sat up on the lounger and asked where Theo was. 'When's the last time you saw him, Em?' he said.

'I'm not sure.' She lazily reached for her watch. 'Nine-ish?'

Rob frowned. 'Don't you think we should check what he's up to?'

'He's probably still in the villa.'

Rob stood up and pulled a T-shirt over his head and told her he would check. He seemed anxious as he pulled his glasses down, and looked around behind them. Too worried for the safety of a fifteen-year-old boy, I thought as he caught my eye.

If Em answered him I didn't hear, but neither did she look up. Isaac had her attention again, he was showing her something on his phone and now Rob was staring at them again. He gave a mild shake of his head before he reiterated, 'I'm going back to the room, so I'll see if Theo is there. Do you want anything?'

'No thanks,' she replied cheerily.

I watched Rob walk off. Whatever issue he had with his wife and son – and I was almost certain there was one – it didn't bother Em in the slightest. It was an interesting dynamic that I couldn't quite get a handle on. They seemed so comfortably in love, judging by the way they held hands on the coach and how he stroked her arm as they sunbathed, yet there was definitely something troubling Rob.

A sudden movement in the bushes behind me made me jump and I shot upright, looking over my shoulder to see Theo emerge. He brushed down his arm as he stepped into the sunlight and bumped the back of my bed, looking down at me as he did so. I waited for him to apologise, but he said nothing, his deep brown eyes just staring at me, eyebrows pinched together so that I wondered if he was amused at surprising me.

I thought he had the look of an obnoxious kid who didn't care. In every respect, Theo was the opposite of his brother. He carried on past my lounger and threw his rucksack down on the end of Isaac's bed, who in turn kicked it off as I resisted the urge to call out, 'Don't worry, I'm fine.'

'That's got my iPad in it,' Theo snapped.

'Then you shouldn't have dumped it on my feet,' Isaac retorted.

Em didn't say anything to either of them as she sat up, leaning forward to pick up the rucksack and place it on Rob's vacant lounger, tapping it, getting Theo to come and sit the other side of her where her husband had been only moments before he went off looking for Theo.

Theo didn't move and instead stripped off his top and dived in at the end of the pool, landing with a splash and sending water flying out right next to where James was pulling himself out after his latest swim.

James looked back at him and pulled a face. 'Idiot.' He scowled as he came to get a towel. 'Kids like him don't care about anyone else.'

He was right, but it wasn't just Theo. I saw it in the family's aloofness, Theo's lack of apology and the way Em didn't tell her son off. The way they were totally absorbed in themselves.

'You still think he's the one who took your watch?' James asked as I stared at the teenager.

'I don't know,' I muttered. I had little evidence other than a gut feeling there was something about Theo I did not like.

Momentarily I was distracted by the newlyweds, whose arrival at the pool was announced by Rosie screaming, 'Spencer! what are you doing?' as he tipped a glass of ice down her back.

She stood up, shaking the ice off, her face aghast while her husband laughed. I grinned myself as he held his hands up in mock surrender.

A member of staff was immediately at her side, offering her a towel, which she went to take, but Spencer waved him away. 'She's fine, it's a bit of water,' he said, loud enough for us to hear, as Rosie slumped back down onto her bed, turning away from him and catching my eye.

She was holding a hand over her stomach protectively. It was only brief, before she rapidly pulled it away, but I knew the sign.

'She's pregnant,' I murmured. It was a fact that made their relationship all the stranger.

'Hmm?' James looked up from his phone. 'Who are you talking about?'

'Rosie, the one on her honeymoon who doesn't appear to like her husband.'

'Right,' he answered with complete disinterest. 'I need to be at the beach at nine a.m. tomorrow.'

I turned to James.

'For fishing?' he said as if I hadn't remembered. 'It's only me going, so it's more money than I'd thought but ...' He threw his phone down, not bothering to finish his sentence.

'James, I wish you weren't going,' I said.

'What?' He looked surprised.

'It's a whole day, and the thought of being here on my own feels odd, and ... I don't know, I just wish you weren't going, that's all.'

'Laila,' he sighed, shaking his head.

I hadn't told him not to, I'd just said what I felt and it was up to him now. Perhaps, I thought, if he told me he wouldn't go, I would tell him he should. I think I just wanted to know how he would react.

'It's too late now,' he muttered. 'I can't cancel it. I'm going to get a beer. Do you want anything?'

Irritated, I shook my head as he got up and walked off to the bar. As I watched my husband, Rob returned to find Theo's rucksack on his sunbed. Though now when I checked the pool there was no sign of Theo. Every now and then I had a sense of someone behind me, but each time I looked over my shoulder I couldn't see anyone.

Em and Isaac were perched on the end of their loungers, playing cards, their heads almost touching. It was the two of them that I couldn't take my eyes off. If anyone asked me, I'd have said Em's life was perfect because of the relationship she had with her son. Not her husband, however in love they still appeared; it was the mother and her eldest son who intrigued me the most.

Rob was still the other side of her, flicking through his phone, every so often glancing over like he wanted to be a part of the game that no one had invited him to. And then Theo reappeared and tossed his phone beside Isaac. 'Dad's called you again,' he said.

The energy changed then. Em stiffened and the game was over and I looked at Rob from a different angle. Was that the reason he looked like an outcast when Em was with Isaac? Was it because he wasn't the boys' father?

Day Six – Thursday

Isaac is dead. Yesterday I had been watching him laughing and joking with his mum beside me at the pool. This morning I have seen his body face down in the water, being dragged out by hotel staff. There was no saving him by then. At some point during Wednesday night he drowned. We still didn't know whether he fell in or was pushed, and either way Em must be in agony, desperate to know why.

I am sitting on the grass under the shade of the tree just outside our garden while James is inside, being interviewed by the two police officers. The snake is back inside my stomach, wrapping itself around and around, tightening its grip until I fear it will suffocate me.

I must tell them what I know. As soon as the police officers have finished questioning James, I have to say what I heard yesterday. In any normal circumstance I would have told them already, but the fact is I should never have been listening, because I should never have sneaked into Em's villa in the first place. But I did, and now I have information that could hold the key to Isaac's death, and they need to know. *Em* needs to know.

I am snapped out of my thoughts by a voice. I open my eyes to see Rosie hovering above me, a long white floating dress hanging off her waiflike body. 'Sorry, I disturbed you,' she says.

'You didn't, I – actually I'm just waiting for the police to finish speaking to my husband. I take it they're questioning everyone in the resort.'

She nods and sits on the grass beside me. She is prettier closer up, I think, as she lets out a sigh. 'It's tragic, isn't it?'

'It's awful,' I agree. It is the first time she has spoken to me and I am taken aback by the conversation, but then tragedy can bring people together.

'I can't believe it. I mean, you hear about these things, don't you? You see them on the news, like when someone has fallen off a balcony on holiday or something, but you don't imagine it'll ever happen to you. I mean not to you, but you know what I mean. Where you are. That boy just fell in the water and drowned.' She looks at me. 'Do you think he was drinking?'

'I really don't know,' I say, wondering the same thing myself as I think back to the previous evening. I had seen Em and her family at their table, and Rosie and her husband too, but I had been too absorbed in my own nightmare evening to be taking much notice of any of them.

'Spencer thinks he might have been drunk,' she says. 'He says maybe that's why he drowned.'

'Spencer is your husband?'

She shrugs awkwardly and mutters, 'Yeah,' and then says, 'I had to call my mum.' Rosie holds up her phone and the closer I look at her, the more I can see there are tears in her eyes. 'I just wanted to speak to her.' She laughs shortly, then looks away and blinks the tears back.

'Are you OK?' I ask; a stupid question when she obviously isn't.

'Yeah, you know, it's all just . . .' She waves an arm as she tries to come up with the right words.

I feel for her now. Her tears and her loss for words, and the fact that she had to call her mum. It reminds me how young Rosie is. She can't be much more than twenty-one. Behind the plumped lips and overdone eyebrows she is barely an adult, yet she is already married to a man who must be ten years her senior.

'But maybe I should be asking if you're OK?' she says.

'How do you mean?'

'After last night . . .'

'Oh. Right.' I feel my cheeks redden as I remember the way Rosie had been staring over at us the night before. Many people on the surrounding tables must have heard us arguing, however hushed we tried to make it. 'It was nothing,' I say hurriedly, the creeping flush of embarrassment bleeding into an unwilling need to explain myself. 'It was just a row – we'd had too much to drink.'

Rosie nods slowly. She knows as well as I do that it wasn't nothing. She, along with most of the other guests, would have seen the way James left me on my own last night. Eventually I'd had to walk back to our room alone. I have no idea where he went or what time he returned. And now there is something he wants to talk to me about before the officers speak to me, and why he couldn't have done it earlier I have no idea.

Chapter Seven

Day Five – Wednesday

Before he went on his fishing trip, I sat across the table from James at breakfast, watching him picking at his food. He had a bread roll on his plate and a pile of ham and cheese, but apart from prodding at the ham he had barely eaten any of it. 'Aren't you hungry?' I asked.

'Not really.' He dropped his fork and pushed his plate away. It had been an even later night than usual the night before, he hadn't wanted to go to bed. We had finished dinner and sat in the bar while a man hammered out show tunes on a piano. Bottles of wine had been ordered and drunk, then cocktails. I had wanted to go to bed but James wasn't in the mood for sleep.

'Are you feeling OK?' I asked.

'I'm fine.' His tone was clipped but, then realising he had snapped at me, he hastily added, 'I'm fine, I just need to get to the beach for this fishing trip.' He looked at his watch and then pushed his chair back. 'You coming down there with me?'

I looked at my own half-eaten breakfast, not sure what all the rush was about, but figured I could come back and get more to eat when he was gone. There was still another hour and a half before the restaurant closed.

He extended his hand, willing me to take it as I got to my feet, and we walked back to the room hand in hand as we had done every day.

We were doing all the right things like holding hands and linking arms. We had even had sex the night before, although I couldn't help feeling there was something missing. That every one of these gestures was an act that didn't reach much deeper. That neither of us were *feeling* it.

That morning James's hand felt stiff against mine and he seemed distracted as he swept around our room, picking up whatever he thought he might need for the day. His kiss against my cheek was brusque as he said goodbye.

I followed him back as far as the steps where he waved at me and descended to the beach and then walked over to meet the boat driver who would take him out on his private trip. After that I carried on to the pool, not bothering with going back for more breakfast now that my own appetite had faded too.

I felt alone. Lonely even. Not a good feeling to have when you're in a luxury resort surrounded by couples and the odd family. I felt like I was part of neither, our decision that it was right to move on childless yet happy together waning fast. I would turn forty next month; there was no denying that my chances of conceiving were depleting. Only a matter of weeks ago I had convinced myself it no longer mattered what age I was. I could accept that I was growing older and no longer needed my body to reproduce.

But it did matter. I couldn't keep denying it. I didn't want to feel anger towards my husband even though I undeniably did. I had been trying to suffocate the rage but it kept raising its head. I was angry with myself too. As an aspiring counsellor, I should have known better and my problem was that I hadn't addressed it.

That morning neither Em and her family nor the newlyweds were by the pool, so I picked up my book and flicked through a few pages, but I couldn't concentrate. By mid-morning they still hadn't appeared. I didn't know what they could be doing when they were all usually there. It was a funny feeling, lying on my own, knowing my husband wouldn't be back until the end of the day, and not even having people-watching to occupy me. I liked losing myself in the other guests' interactions, and without that I was restless.

I ate lunch on my own at the pool bar, and wandered back to the room twice. It was only 2 p.m. when I checked the time on my phone and got up, pulling a sarong over my bikini, to go for another stroll. I needed something to do, and so I ambled down to the beach, one eye on the sea for my husband, though of course there was no sign of him. I wandered along the shore, the cool water lapping my feet, to the end of the cove and then back again, eventually returning up the steps, not much else to do but aim for the pool until it was time to get ready for dinner, and of course hopefully by then James would have returned.

I had my head down and it wasn't until the last minute that I looked up and caught sight of two figures off the path, just tucked around the corner, standing by the bushes and looking out to sea. One of them was Rosie, in a floaty dress that hung just above her knees; even from where I stood I could see the other wasn't her husband. They were a few feet apart from each other but the figure next to her was much taller than her, much skinnier. It was only when I took a few more steps in their direction that I realised it was Isaac.

There was nothing in it, I presumed. An innocent conversation, nothing more. They weren't standing all that close together and I was certain Rosie wouldn't be so brazen anyway, pregnant and with her husband nearby, but it was funny how the two of them looked so much more like a couple with only a handful of years between them. I even heard Rosie laugh, her head rocking back as she did so.

I was intending to ignore them and weave off to the left, towards the pool, until I saw that I wasn't the only one to have spotted the two of them. At the edge of the greenery, trying to keep out of sight, was Theo. He was leaning back in a wicker dome chair, legs and arms crossed and feet on top of a small glass table, almost hidden by the bushes that surrounded him. His sunglasses nestled into his bouncy mass of dark hair as he glared at his brother across the grass.

The scowl that shone through his eyes beneath the frown of his thick eyebrows made it clear that Theo wasn't happy. Perhaps it was nothing more than jealousy that his brother was talking to the youngest and most attractive girl in the resort, but I could see that Theo was a boy who didn't like not getting his way.

As soon as he saw me his mouth pinched, his eyebrows meeting in a point as he glared at me. The boy was only fifteen and yet his look sent a chill through me, the same feeling I'd had in the reception lobby when he was lurking behind the potted tree.

He got up, taking a step in my direction before stopping again. His hands were clenched at his sides. There was something so aggressive about him, like he was warning me off and I found myself turning on my heel and scrabbling off towards the pool, where I threw my bag on the sunbed, clocking Em on the other side, oblivious and relaxed as she flicked through a copy of *Hello!* magazine.

I tried to make sense of why Theo had this effect on me, why he managed to shake me. Perhaps it was nothing more than the way he felt so casually sure of himself, how he could put me in my place with a look, the way Sam also used to be able to. *You don't belong here,* I could imagine him saying.

I hated that I'd let a teenager get to me, and hated Theo for the way he managed to make me feel so powerless. How easy it was for boys like him to be superior when they came from money as he did. He must have grown up his whole life thinking he could get his own way just because of what his family had.

He appeared at the further edge of the pool now, lolloping around it, not looking over at me as he wandered towards his mum. I just had to ignore him, stay out of his way I thought as a voice behind me said, 'You ever find your watch?'

I turned to see Rosie's husband dropping a rucksack onto a spare lounger, pulling his cap off his head and rearranging it.

'No.' I shook my head, wondering if he knew where his wife was right now.

'Sorry to hear that.'

I nodded a thanks, turning back to Theo. There was no reason why, coming from such a wealthy background, he would need to steal a watch, but then it wasn't always about money. Sometimes it was just about doing it because you could, and because you could get away with it. But in that moment I was determined there was no way he would.

Day Six – Thursday

By the time James appears in the doorway to our room, Rosie is gone. I have been going over what the police might have asked him. I assume they must be the standard questions but then I cannot help my mind running wild, as surely anyone would when their husband is being questioned about a death, even though I know they are speaking to every guest in the resort.

'What happened?' I ask him quickly. 'What did they say?' His expression is unreadable though I try to see past it.

'What you'd expect,' he says. 'When I last saw the boy, that kind of thing.'

I wait for him to go on and when he doesn't, I ask, 'When *did* you last see him?' I realise then that it's odd that we haven't discussed it between ourselves. It hadn't even occurred to me to ask James when he last saw Isaac, and whether he noticed him last night. Surely other couples are dissecting the situation in minute detail, trying to piece together what they might know, like we would have once done. This in itself seems to underline how distanced we have become.

'I don't know,' he says. 'Probably at dinner. I wasn't really noticing anyone else last night.'

If this is a jab, I choose to ignore it.

'Anyway they just wanted to know if I knew anything more and obviously I said no.' He runs a hand across his chin that is stubbled from not shaving this morning. I think it makes him look slightly wild; James has never gone more than a day without a shave.

'Are they are treating it as suspicious?' I think about what Rosie said to me, how her husband suggested Isaac might have been drinking. If it was an accident, maybe I don't need to tell them anything at all about what happened yesterday. I don't need to admit that I'd crept inside Em's villa.

'They didn't say …' He pauses. 'But would they be asking all these questions if they weren't?'

'No. I don't suppose they would.' After a moment I add, 'And that was it?'

He frowns. 'What else is there?'

I hesitate but I need to ask him. 'Did they want to know about us? Did they say anything about the fact we were arguing last night?'

James frowns and glances over my shoulder, away from my gaze. 'They brought it up. Someone must have told them. Was it you?' he asks, turning back to me. 'When you spoke to the detective earlier?'

'No – God, of course it wasn't.'

He stares at me. 'Then someone else has. Like it was of any importance.'

Not of any importance? I think. But then of course he means in relation to the case and not to our marriage.

'What was it you wanted to say to me, James?' I ask him. 'You wanted to talk about last night.'

James shrugs. 'It's not important.'

I hang my head, wondering what he is holding back. 'What did you tell them happened then?' I ask, thinking of the way James left me.

'I told them the truth,' he says plainly. 'You went to the room and I was half an hour behind you.'

It is this that fills my head as I follow the police officer inside. My mind is racing back to the point I eventually got up from the dinner table last night.

James had left me, though he'd done it subtly and that in itself had angered me: the way he'd nonchalantly wandered away, not wanting to bring attention to the fact he was leaving me at the table alone. It almost made the whole situation seem worse. It certainly made me feel more pathetic.

To anyone else it might have looked like he was going to the toilet, but I knew he wouldn't be coming back. The way he'd gritted his teeth as he pushed his chair back, hands curling round the edge of the table. His eyes penetrated me with a dark stare. He had never looked at me that way before. Yes, there have been occasions when he's been angry or disappointed, but never so cold and empty. I didn't know if it was hatred but there was certainly no love.

'This evening's been shit, Laila,' he had hissed in my ear as he walked away, up the steps and out of sight. I'd glanced over my shoulder, trying to keep it subtle so I wouldn't draw attention to myself. Out of the corner of my eye I saw Rosie looking over and so I'd snapped my focus back to the sea, its calmness a sharp contrast to the turmoil inside me.

I stayed for long enough that it wouldn't look odd. Or that's what I was attempting to do in my drunken state. I was certainly conscious of the other guests glancing in my direction as I sipped the remainder of the wine.

It didn't taste nice any longer. It was leaving a sharpness in my mouth that I couldn't swallow, and my hands were trembling against the glass. James was right. Our night had been awful and I wanted to erase it, go back to the beginning and start again. I wanted James to come back to me, tell me he was sorry and that he didn't mean any of it. But, like I said, I had never seen him so full of rage before and it scared me. I didn't know what to expect.

He had made it clear how angry he was with me for what he had found out, and I knew I had been in the wrong, but I also knew his reaction was unjustified.

I couldn't be sure how much time passed before I got up to leave. Possibly it was only five minutes, but it felt longer, as excruciating as it was. I slung my bag over my shoulder and as I started walking back to the room, tears stung my eyes.

By the time I reached the room I had no idea what would be better: finding James in there, waiting, or finding it empty so I wouldn't have to face him. I couldn't look at him any longer, but at the same time I dreaded the idea of not knowing where he was or what he was doing.

The room was in darkness, our curtains still open. I pushed the door open and stepped inside. I have never been one to sleep easily if I was expecting James home, even at the best of times. And this was the worst of them. He wasn't there, and as far as I could tell he hadn't been back.

I undressed and climbed into bed and told myself not to be stupid. He wasn't going to be far away, he wouldn't leave the resort. I fell asleep pretty sharply, dragged into an alcohol-induced slumber, and didn't wake until a little after 5 a.m.

'You are ready?' the officer asks as he gestures for us to go out to the back of our room, where his colleague is already sitting on one of our loungers. I am conscious of my swimming costume drying over a chair, of bottles of sun cream discarded beside it from where I tipped my bag out yesterday.

'Yes, I'm ready,' I say.

'We would like to ask you some questions,' he says. 'About Isaac Lawson. His body was found in the hotel grounds this morning.'

I nod, my thoughts a jumbled mix of seeing his body floating in the pool and the image of Isaac yesterday, so full of life and laughing with his mum like he had no cares in the world.

'When was the last time you saw him?'

'It was at dinner last night,' I say firmly, answering the question Kallis had already asked me, which made me think our earlier conversation had not even been discussed. 'He was with his family. They were a few tables away from us.'

'And was there anything out of the ordinary you saw at dinner?'

'No, I don't think so.' For once I hadn't paid them much attention. My focus had been on my life, not theirs.

'And what time did you leave the dinner, please?'

'I'm not sure. I think it was about ten or ten thirty ... Wait – I can tell you exactly.' I pick up my phone and bring up the forum's web page, scrolling down to the post I had written at the table. It was another cry for help from the friends I have never met and never will, and one that I had intended to delete this morning but never got round to.

'Oh, it was later than I thought.' I scrunch my eyes up, taking in the time. I posted at eight minutes past eleven, but as I scroll down the responses I realise I had replied to some too. 'I guess it must have been quarter past eleven or around then,' I say, putting my phone away.

'So at eleven fifteen you leave the dinner. And what do you do next?'

'I walked straight back here. To the room.'

'On your own?'

I nod. I assume they already know this.

'And did you stop anywhere, or see anyone else during the walk to your room?'

Yes. I did see someone. 'One of the guests. His name is Spencer.' I watch the way his colleague, who has remained silent, glances down at his pad, presumably checking for the name. 'I didn't speak to him. I don't know if he saw me, he was walking on his own. Back towards the restaurant and the pool.'

'And what time did your husband return, please?' he asks.

'I don't know,' I admit. 'I fell asleep straight away, but I don't think it was long after.'

'OK. Thank you.'

I am relieved when it appears they are finished with me. That they have no more questions to ask. I can leave it here and walk away, not mention anything about what I was doing yesterday in Em's villa. And yet it is the thought of her that won't leave me, of her need for answers, however hard they will be. I cannot say nothing. Whatever the consequences, that is not the right thing to do.

I take a deep breath. 'Actually, there is something else,' I say.

PART TWO

EM

Chapter Eight

Day Six – Thursday

The woman is outside their villa again. She is just standing there, looking in, though surely she cannot see beyond the thin curtains that are drawn across the window. She seems to be forever watching her, yet now, of all moments, you would think she'd have the decency to stay away.

Em's hands shake. It feels like all the breath has been taken out of her body, leaving her a shell. Rob keeps talking to her, trying to encourage her to come away from the window, needling her to have a drink and something to eat. She ignores him. She needs him here, but she also wants him to leave her alone.

Her legs don't feel like they are attached to her body, yet somehow they are keeping her upright.

'Em?' He is speaking to her again, but she carries on watching the woman and doesn't answer him.

What is she doing? Her name is Lila or Lola or similar. They'd spoken at the bar three days ago, but Em wasn't listening properly when she'd introduced herself. She has always been bad at doing that and then it gets to the point it's too rude to ask.

The woman tried talking to her again yesterday after lunch, coming over to her sunbed to strike up a conversation, but Em has never been one for making friends on holiday. Holidays are about family time, not speaking to strangers.

'Em, please eat this toast,' Rob urges.

'I don't want anything,' she mutters. The thought of putting food in her mouth, chewing it and swallowing, is too much to contemplate, and anyway what is the point? Why eat when she has nothing to live for?

She has told Rob this already within the last hour. 'Em!' he'd exclaimed as his eyes flicked to Theo.

Her son was white as a sheet, staring blankly back at her. He reminded her of the little boy he once was – Theo at seven, the way he used to stand with his teddy hanging loosely from one hand, looking at her imploringly.

She had closed her eyes so she didn't have to look at her son, because when she did she saw Isaac too. Most people can't see much resemblance between her sons, but as a mother she sees them differently. People have told her the boys couldn't be more unlike one another in their mannerisms, the way they are, and she supposes this is true to an extent, but not wholly. As a mum you know more about your children than anyone else possibly can, or at least this is what she has always thought. Now she isn't so sure. After the questions that the police officers are drilling them with, Em wonders if there was something she didn't know about her oldest child. She wonders if Isaac was keeping something from her, but she cannot fathom what.

She wishes Rob didn't feel the need to remind her that she has another son to live for. Right now such practicalities are not what she needs. Right now she actually wishes he would allow her to crumble and dissolve into nothing, because she cannot imagine how she will ever step outside again. Put one foot in front of the other, carry on living and breathing and surviving. She doesn't know how and she doesn't want to.

'Mum?' Theo's voice rings out and she snaps her head round. He needs her and so she beckons him over, brings her son into her arms and holds him close against her chest. Her tears continue to run down her face, dripping onto Theo's warm face. She does know she has another son to live for but she also knows it is no longer enough. And it breaks her heart into more tiny, guilty pieces to admit it.

This is why Em would rather watch the woman outside her villa. It is easier to look at her and wonder what she is doing here, yet again. Just for this moment Em can force her mind to idle on something other than the raw pain that is eating her up.

She doesn't even feel angry with the woman. She did the other day when she spotted her outside, but she doesn't today. Em doesn't know anything about her, though she did watch with mild interest and a little embarrassment as the woman's husband had started shouting at her last night. She and her family had stopped mid-conversation. Most people had stopped talking, to be fair. Their argument was loud enough to catch the attention of the guests on the tables nearby. However much the husband tried to keep his voice down he was neither quiet nor discreet.

She also noticed how he left her at the table on her own and didn't return. 'God, if you ever did that to me,' she'd murmured to Rob.

'I'd be better off dead,' he had joked. She had laughed at the time but now the comment chills her.

'Em?' Rob's voice is more urgent now. 'Come away from the window. Please.'

But if she comes away and stops watching, her head will be filled with Isaac again. Of the son who has been ripped out of her life. And if she thinks of him, if she thinks of Isaac, then she will never be able to breathe.

They'd told her Isaac was dead at six thirty-five this morning. There had been a loud knock on their glass door, waking her and Rob from sleep.

'What the hell is that?' Rob had said, leaping out of bed.

She had glanced over at the boys' bedroom. The door was closed. All Em hoped in that moment was that the disturbance didn't wake them too.

Rob answered the door and she heard him talking but couldn't work out what was being said. When he came back in his face immediately told her something was wrong.

'Who is it?' she asked. She couldn't fathom what problem there could be, because if something had happened to her parents she would have got the call on her mobile. But the man who'd followed Rob into the room started telling her he was a police officer and so she knew that something was very wrong.

She got out of bed, stood beside it, her gaze flicking from him to Rob, wanting an explanation from one of them.

'Mrs Cross?' he said.

She nodded, glancing at Rob again.

'Maybe you could take a seat, please.'

'What's happened?' she demanded. 'Just tell me.' All the while her heart was hammering. This wasn't good. Whatever they had come to tell her, it wasn't good.

'Mrs Cross, I'm afraid we have news. It is about your son.'

'OK?' She shook her head, looked to the boys' door. Now she was thinking, what had they done? Had one of the guests complained? Was it serious?

'I'm afraid we found the body of your son this morning.'

Maybe it was his broken English, the way his words didn't really seem to go together as they should that made Em laugh out. 'What do you mean, you found his body?'

Her sons were in the room next to hers. They had the wrong person.

'Isaac Lawson.'

'No.' She still didn't believe them. Even though she'd heard the words and her heart was thumping, she didn't believe him because Isaac was sleeping in the room next to hers. What the police officer was telling her was just ludicrous. She pushed past Rob to shove open the boys' door. Theo was nearest, curled into a ball, his legs and arms tightly scrunched together. His eyes were open, he must have heard the knocking and the voices. At the sight of her he sat upright and asked her what was wrong.

But she didn't answer because she was looking past Theo to the empty bed. 'Where's Isaac?' she yelled.

'I don't know.' Theo looked frightened by her screaming as he turned to look at the bed too.

'Where is he?' She turned back to Rob, who was standing right behind her. The police officer behind him was regarding her anxiously.

'Em,' Rob said softly, taking her arm, 'I don't know what's happened but it seems there was an accident last night.' He tugged on her arm, pulling her back into their bedroom.

The thumping in her heart was getting heavier, vibrating through her body, making her ears ring. She held her hands over them to make it stop, shaking her head as the police officer started talking again.

'I am afraid your son was found this morning. In the swimming pool. I am very sorry, Mrs Cross, your son—'

'Don't tell me,' she screamed. 'Whatever you're going to say, don't say it. I want to see Isaac. I want to check he's OK.' She turned back to Rob. 'Come on.'

'Em, the officer is telling us Isaac has—'

'No,' she cut him off too, but she was crying now. Tears running down her cheeks in streams, taking her breath with them. She held a hand against Rob's chest. 'No, don't tell me that.' She started running through the door, the officer and Rob following her, Theo presumably following them.

If they didn't tell her, she wouldn't hear the words. It wouldn't be true.

At 7.30 a.m. Lieutenant Kallis arrived and told her he was heading the investigation. Em, Rob and Theo were back in their room, all three of them suspended in a prison of disbelief. They had given her something to calm her down. Em, who usually hated taking paracetamol, had allowed Rob to press a pill into her hand and had swallowed it with a glass of water. She had no idea where he'd got it from or what it was.

Kallis entered their room and sat down with them. 'I know this is hard, Mrs Cross, but we need to work out what happened to your son.'

Em was sitting in a basket chair, a soft grey blanket wrapped around her. A glass of water and a mug of tea untouched on the table that Rob had pushed in front of her.

Her head was pounding. It was the first time she had sat still in forty-five minutes, the first time she had stopped crying. How did that even happen? How did the tears dry up? She wondered if it was the pill.

Kallis was there to go through the details. When did they all last see Isaac? What was his mood like last night? Rob took them through the evening, the fact they all came back to the room together at 11.30 p.m. Isaac was with them. As far as they knew, he hadn't left the room again.

Rob led Kallis through the door to the boys' room. Like Em and Rob's room it had its own en suite bathroom and glass bifolds that opened up onto the decking which led to their private pool. There was another door to the villa, which opened into Em and Rob's room, but the only way the boys could leave, if they didn't come through their mother's room, was onto the decking and past the pool.

Kallis wanted to know how Isaac was at the end of the night. Was he chatty? Did anything seem unusual?

Rob carried on answering him. There was nothing, he replied, nothing at all that seemed odd or different. He probed Em for answers, though she guessed what they were getting at.

'He didn't kill himself,' she said. 'Isaac would not do that.'

Kallis didn't respond.

'We were laughing together.' They'd been faintly amused by the woman and her husband who were arguing loudly at their table. Em had felt sorry for her too, but Isaac was making her laugh with his imitation of the man and the dramatic way he had left the table, pretending it was nothing when they all knew it was. 'There was nothing wrong with Isaac, nothing at all.'

But the police had nonetheless taken his phone and had gone on to talk to Theo. Theo had been the last one to see his brother. They shared a bedroom. Theo must have known what time his brother walked out again. Possibly even why.

'Can you talk me through what happened last night when you got back to the villa, Theo?' Kallis asked him.

'We just went to bed.'

'Isaac too?'

Theo nodded.

'And what time did he go out?'

'I don't know. I fell asleep.'

'So you didn't hear him?'

Theo shook his head.

Kallis looked perturbed. 'So you didn't know your brother went out again?'

'No. He must have gone out later.'

'And did anything else happen before you went to sleep?'

'Like what?' Theo said.

'Did Isaac have a call from anyone or a message?'

'I don't think so.'

'Did he say anything to you that sounded odd, or was he worried about anything?'

'No.'

'Did your brother tell you he might go out?'

'No.'

'Has he done so any other night?' Kallis persisted.

Theo shook his head. 'I don't think so.'

'Did Isaac have any reason that you know of to leave the room last night?' he tried.

But Theo just shook his head.

He was of no help and the police weren't getting anything from him.

'Is there anything at all you can think of, Theo,' Rob said calmly, trying to help the detective. They all knew that Theo was their best bet for understanding Isaac's movements.

'Like what?'

'Like did he talk to you about anything, even in the day? Was there something upsetting him?'

'Why do you keep asking this?' Em cried out. 'Like you think he did this himself. If there was anything to know, I would have known. Isaac would have told me.'

Rob nodded. Only once, but he would have known this too. If Isaac was going to talk to anyone in the family it would be her. As close as her boys were, or at least had once been, Isaac wouldn't have likely shared anything with Theo. But did that mean he would have told her?

'Someone else must have seen him,' she said, turning back to Kallis.

'Of course. And we will be asking everyone at the hotel.'

'We don't even know when he left yet, do we?' she went on. 'It could have been just after his brother fell asleep or he might have woken early this morning. I mean, that would make more sense wouldn't it?' Em wasn't sure how it made more sense, only that she was clutching for something. 'He could have gone out for a walk early or—' She stopped abruptly. Nothing went in any way towards explaining why Isaac had left the room and *nothing* could explain how her son had ended up dead in the swimming pool.

'Mrs Cross,' Kallis said calmly. 'We will find out what happened. I promise you this. I will make sure you know what happened to your son.'

Em nodded, closing her eyes as she took in a deep breath.

'I will not stop until I know,' he told her. And he sounded so sincere that she chose to believe him.

Chapter Nine

Theo has left her side and is now sitting by the pool. He is hovering beside it, one leg hanging over the edge. Both her boys can swim well. She made sure they were taught at an early age, just as she had been herself. They are both confident and strong in the water, so how the hell has Isaac drowned?

The thought jolts her because she can't see how it could have been an accident. So what does that mean? Were the others right to imply her son could have taken his own life?

She must yell out in that moment because Rob is suddenly beside her, panicking. 'What is it?' he asks.

She is staring at Theo.

'He's OK,' Rob says, as if she's worried he might fall in too. 'Theo's OK.'

She stares at her husband. 'He's not OK.' She breathes out the words. 'How is he ever going to be OK again? He's lost his brother. He's lost his best friend.'

'I didn't mean that ...' His words fade out.

'Why didn't I know where Isaac was?' Em asks Rob. 'I thought he was sleeping. I slept through everything.' She holds her hands against her chest. She should have felt it in there. In her heart. How did she not have the instinct that something was dreadfully wrong? 'Why did he go out in the middle of the night?'

Rob shakes his head. 'I don't know. I can't imagine why. It doesn't make any sense.'

Nothing makes sense any more. Em turns back to the outside world again. Past the decking and their pool and the wall beyond, she can see Lieutenant Kallis. He has returned with another officer and they are speaking to the woman, no doubt asking her why she is standing outside Em's villa. Em does not have a clue what excuse she is giving them for being there. Finally, Lieutenant Kallis walks away and the woman follows him. He has managed to move her on and hopefully she won't come back.

As soon as they are out of sight, his colleague, who has been left behind, walks through their front area, around the pool, and approaches their door. He taps on the glass and pushes it open, as if along with losing her son she has lost all rights to privacy too.

'Mr and Mrs Cross? Can we speak, please?'

'Yes.' She gestures to an armchair by the dresser that he sits on. Rob perches on the end of their bed and holds out his hand for her to join him, but she stays where she is.

'We are still waiting for a full pathology report,' he says.

Em nods.

'But there are some obvious injuries.' His eyes crease, she notices, as if it is paining him to give them this information. 'Isaac has a fracture at the back of his skull.' He touches the back of his own head as if she might not know where he means.

'What does that mean?' Em asks.

'He could have slipped and hit his head when he fell into the pool, but . . .' He pauses again. 'There is also sign of a broken rib.'

She shakes her head. 'I don't understand.'

'The combined injuries suggest he didn't fall into the pool.'

'What are you saying?' Rob chimes in. 'That he was pushed?'

The policeman takes his eyes off Em and glances at Rob, who is now standing by her side. 'Possibly. But he also could have sustained these injuries before.'

'Before? Like when?' she demands.

'What I am saying is that there is a chance Isaac could have been seriously hurt and then, somehow, he ended up in the pool. This is what we work on now. This theory.'

'You're telling me that someone did this to him?' Em cries. 'This is what you're thinking? That someone hurt Isaac and then what – pushed him into the water?'

'That is what we will find out,' the officer says. His words are calm amid the storm that is brewing inside her. They do not fit or make any sense.

She shakes her head vigorously in response. 'Who would hurt him?' she yells. 'No one would. Everyone likes Isaac.' This is true. Her son has never made an enemy as far as she is aware, he is likeable and kind to everyone, which is evident in the number of friends he has. 'He wouldn't hurt anyone, so why would anyone hurt him? That doesn't make sense.' Her body is shaking. Ripples course through her, juddering her arms and her legs. She could not still herself if she tried. Em had thought there was nothing more they could tell her. But the thought that Isaac has been murdered ignites an altogether different level of grief.

The officer bites down on his lip. 'Mrs Cross, can we speak alone?' he says.

She looks at Rob. What do they want to speak to her about that her husband can't hear?

'I would like to ask you some questions,' he says, as if he's trying to give her an explanation.

'I'll wait outside with Theo,' Rob says, and when the officer nods, her husband leaves the room and pulls the glass door closed behind him.

She watches him go. He joins Theo, who is still sitting beside the pool. Since they last questioned her son she has come to her own conclusions about what Theo does and doesn't know. As soon as Kallis left earlier she turned on Theo herself, begging him for answers, pleading with him because he has to know something. They were sharing a room.

She had watched Theo carefully with every answer he gave and came to the conclusion that he might not know *why* his brother left their room last night but that he knew that he did. She is certain Theo must have woken as his older brother had crept out.

She has instilled in her boys from an early age that it is wrong to lie. But Em isn't naive enough to think there aren't times when they do. What she'd like to think is that she's become adept at knowing.

Perhaps Theo thinks he will get in trouble. Possibly he saw the rawness of her pain and thought that if he dared say anything that suggested he might have at least tried to stop Isaac walking out in the middle of the night, then she would never forgive him.

She would of course, she would forgive either of her sons anything. That is what a mother learns the day her child is born. There is nothing your child could do that you would not forgive, not someone you love with all of your being.

'I would like you to think about last night again,' the officer repeats when they are alone and there appears to be no chance of anyone else overhearing. 'Anything Isaac said to you or did that doesn't make sense, that seems out of the ordinary perhaps. Please, just take your time.'

Em lets her mind wander to the gala evening. Theo and Isaac had got ready for dinner quietly, as always. They manoeuvred around each other as they showered and dressed, all of them taking it in turns for the bathrooms. They weren't the type of brothers who have a laugh together, but that's the way it's always been.

As they were about to go, Isaac had appeared in the doorway to her bedroom wearing a pair of trousers and a shirt he hadn't worn before. She had previously told him to change out of his shorts, and when he'd reappeared she told him he looked nice. He had grinned. Now she thinks about it, he was slightly coy with her, turning away as he caught his reflection in the mirror. She hadn't pursued it, though she had noticed, and there were times when he was like this that Em knew she wouldn't get anything out of him.

But it was nothing, a small reaction, and then she had walked with him to the dinner on the beach. Theo and Rob were behind them. She tells the officer how they talked about his university applications.

Em closes her eyes as a lump forms solidly in her throat. Every memory brings with it a fresh wave of grief as she thinks of all the things her son will no longer do. 'He wanted to study law,' she says. 'He was going to London.'

'And what happened at dinner?' he asks her.

'The same,' she says, trying to think if there was anything at all that made her think something was wrong. But there wasn't. Not a thing. 'He just chatted, made us laugh. He was in his usual high spirits.' Possibly more so, but then he'd had a couple of beers with dinner.

'Did he leave the table?'

'Once, I think, to go to the toilet.' Em can't really recall.

'And after the dinner, you went straight back to the villa? And Isaac was with you all this time?'

'Yes. All the time.'

The officer purses his lips and leans back in his chair before saying, 'How is your son's relationship with his stepfather?'

'Rob?' Em screws her eyes up at the question and glances outside again. This is why he wanted Rob out of the way. 'Good,' she says. 'They've always had a good relationship. Why are you asking me this, you can't surely think my husband knows anything?' She turns back to the policeman.

'I am just asking the question, Mrs Cross. We want to find out what happened to your son. That is all.'

'Rob is a good stepfather. The boys have always got on well with him.'

Though this isn't strictly true, she thinks. It was less than three and a half years ago when she met Rob, and in the early days both of her sons were apprehensive of him in their own ways, but then considering what the three of them had been through, that was hardly surprising. It had been a year since she and their dad, Charlie, had separated and she had gone to a very dark place. She wasn't looking to meet anyone, or even particularly wanting to. But then a friend had introduced Rob to her and he just kind of came into their lives. It was like one day he wasn't there and then he was.

Isaac was fourteen and Theo twelve. They were at tender ages for another man to come into their lives and neither of them had completely got over Charlie's betrayal of their family. Well, certainly that was true for Theo. Isaac was more accepting of the situation, she supposes. His focus was on school and sports and his mates, as it should have been. She wouldn't have wanted it any other way but sometimes, in the years since, she'd wondered how his father's leaving seemed to wash over him. He certainly hadn't been scarred by it and it didn't take long for Isaac to accept Rob.

She may have made herself ill after Charlie left, but her mother was there to scoop up the tasks that needed doing, making sure the boys were fed and had clean uniforms. Isaac was kind to her, gentle too, he just didn't wrap himself up in the blackness that had swept through the house.

Theo was a different story. He was the one who closed in on himself along with her, mirroring her grief. Who, at eleven years old and having just started secondary school, felt the betrayal of his father stronger, and who had a bigger issue with Rob coming into their lives.

And so there is absolutely no reason for her to bring any of this up with the police officer when Theo was the one who withdrew even further, because Isaac had always been polite and well mannered and made Rob feel welcome.

Isaac never gave her any need to worry, but as the officer watches her carefully she suddenly wonders if it was possible she missed something.

'So as far as you know, Isaac and your husband did not have a disagreement yesterday?'

'No!' she exclaims. 'Of course not.'

'And did your husband leave the room at all for any reason last night?'

'What?' she cries again. 'No!' She shakes her head, vehemently. Her heart is racing. She can feel it pounding harder with every question. Do they know something she doesn't?

Em looks out the window again to where Rob is crouched down next to Theo, talking words she cannot hear. He is good with her boys, patient. Rob is a kind man. If anything, she has sometimes thought of him as so good he could be a little dull. It's a thought that's always made her feel guilty, but it's the truth. He has never excited her like Charlie used to, but Rob is solid. He would never hurt her.

She keeps telling herself this only because the police officer has sown a seed that she cannot now ignore. Was there a chance Rob could have left the room without her knowing?

No, she cannot go there, and besides, he is moving on already. 'How did Isaac get on with his brother?' he asks.

Em feels the question burning inside her. 'They got on fine,' she says, 'and you're looking in the wrong place. My family are happy, we were happy. We were just a normal happy family and that's why—' Em breaks off as tears flow down her cheeks. 'That's why this is impossible.'

What good this interrogation will do Em doesn't know. Nothing he wants to know about her family matters, because neither Rob nor Theo would have been responsible for killing Isaac. It is simply not possible. And so she will not get into the intricacies of her family life for them to pull apart because it is no one else's business but theirs.

All that matters is that her son is dead and, from what they have told her, someone caused it. She will never again be able to hold Isaac or speak to him, and she wasn't even with him in those final moments. Someone out there has taken that away from her and that is the tragic truth of it.

Chapter Ten

The police officer eventually leaves but he lingers outside their villa, talking to a colleague who has just arrived on the path. The doors are open and Em can hear their voices, speaking in Greek and so she cannot understand what they are saying.

She turns to look at Rob, who is by the pool with Theo. In contrast to the policemen, they are talking so quietly that Em cannot hear them even though they are closer. But Rob looks up and sees Em watching and so stands and beckons her outside as he walks in. 'You need to talk to him,' he says. 'Just be with him for a moment.'

She feels like she is drifting above the ground as she goes. Like her feet don't touch it. Everything about her is numb though there is a scream rising inside her that she wants to let out. When she starts she might not stop and so she suppresses it, pushing it down deep as she sits on the edge of one of the loungers.

Unable to find the words to start a conversation, Em reaches out for her son and pulls him up next to her until he is curled tightly into her side. When he was little he used to roll himself in a ball and suck his thumb when he needed comfort and she would wrap her body around his like a cocoon.

Neither of them speak, but they don't need to. She and Theo never have. He feels warm against her and she presses her face into his hair and lets the tears start flowing again.

Theo has always been her baby, the one who can be sorted out with hugs. When he was young she struggled to get much out of him, and often had to beg him to talk to her, to 'use his words' from an early age. Often Em was told he was too dependent on his brother to do the talking for him. Em fretted, but then her mother put her mind at rest.

'He doesn't need to speak,' she had said. 'Look at the way Isaac does everything for him. It's like he second-guesses what his little brother needs and talks for him.'

Em knew she was right, although she hadn't seen it for herself before then. But Isaac always understood Theo in ways no one else had ever been able to. 'He wants that, Mummy,' her oldest would say, and she would give it to Theo, curiously, and would always find that Isaac was right.

As he grew older, Theo spoke more, but they still had nothing like the conversations she had with Isaac. Like the ones they'd been sharing on holiday.

She thinks back to yesterday, to the way she and Isaac had been laughing by the pool. Why didn't she ask him if he was all right? Why didn't she check that there was nothing worrying him? She didn't because there was no need to. Her son, as far as she knew, was happy, but now there is a niggling thought in her head, that maybe there was something she didn't know.

Isaac has always been one of those children who floated through life without giving her any cause for concern. When he was in year six the teachers told her Isaac would have his pick of schools, which was lucky because it meant he would get into the grammar. The state option wasn't high on her list and there was no way she and Charlie could have considered private. Isaac was popular and kind. He didn't get into trouble. She never had to use Google to try and understand him better.

Theo was a different story. Don't they always say you worry about one of your children more than the others? This is what she and her friends agree, and for her, without a doubt, it has always been Theo.

Theo found it harder at school. He was quieter and didn't like to speak up in class and ask questions. 'He's shy,' she would tell everyone when he was in reception, talking for him, allowing her son to stand behind her as she excused his need to respond. Later she would wonder if she was making it worse and that if she forced him to respond to people he didn't know, then he might have been more confident. The truth was she had no idea what was right. How do you tell your children to be stranger aware and then prod them in the back to reply to a woman they don't know who's asking him what his favourite subject is. Even Em could see that was madness.

Often Em has wondered if the reasons for his shyness were her fault. It was soon after he was born that she first suspected Charlie of cheating on her, though at the time she never found out for sure. The first few years of Theo's life were a blur in some ways and while Isaac thrived happily regardless, Em suspects she didn't concentrate on meeting Theo's needs enough. She had one son who liked sport and running around the playground in a superhero costume with a big gang of boys and assumed the other would be the same. She didn't realise that Theo didn't like the big birthday parties she threw upon him until he was six years old when she wondered if the damage had already been done and she'd pushed him further into himself.

Em would say she'd never change either of her children for the world, but if she was honest, really truthful, then perhaps the one thing she would do is give Theo some of Isaac's confidence. Just for a day she would have loved for her youngest to have walked in his brother's shoes, to have seen what it was like for things to feel so effortless.

Now, she thinks, he has no one to be compared to or to compare himself against. Now he is just Theo. The boy she loves so much for who he is.

And so they hold each other and cry together, like he is still a part of her, and maybe one day Rob will press her into making Theo see a therapist, and possibly she will have to also, but for this moment they don't need to do anything but cry.

But Em can't stop thinking about the conversations she will never again have with Isaac and it is a thought that burns through her, making her choke as she sobs into Theo's curls. He pulls away and looks up at her and she shakes her head to convey it is OK, when they both know it is anything but. So she draws him closer again, trying to squeeze out the thoughts she cannot deal with. Like the thought that her oldest son, her young gentleman, is gone.

When Kallis returns he tells her and Rob that his team are questioning every single guest and member of staff. He assures her they will be told if there is anything to know, that he and his team will be piecing together timelines of everyone's movements. She thinks he is overly confident that within the next couple of hours they will know if anyone saw Isaac out during the night. As soon as they have information, he advises her, they will let her know.

In the meantime Em dissects their last few days further, carving up the memories of their holiday in the hope that she will suddenly remember something that might help her understand who could possibly have hurt Isaac.

She plays out last night's dinner over and over in her head, trying to make something click into place. She recalls

Rob getting up to take a call midway through the dinner and Isaac commenting that he couldn't let his work go. Though she agreed with her son, she made an excuse for Rob. 'We wouldn't be here if it wasn't for the amount he works,' she reminded him. Her salary from her job at the bank certainly wouldn't extend anywhere near a place like White Sands.

It is 11.30 a.m. when Lieutenant Kallis returns. He tells her that they have now spoken to 80 per cent of the guests and that there is something he wants to talk to them about. He asks Em and Rob to come outside so they can all sit in the shade on the decking, where there is more room for the four of them than in the bedrooms.

'What is it?' Em says. 'Has someone told you something? Did someone see Isaac last night?'

'No this isn't it,' Kallis replies. 'But there are a couple of things I would like to clear up.'

'Clear up?' Rob asks. 'How do you mean? Haven't we told you everything we know already?' His hand is resting on her arm as he sits beside her. Em knows it is intended for support, but she wants to shake him off.

'I'm not sure?' Kallis poses it as a question, as if he is saying, *Have you?*

Em shifts herself on the seat and Rob stiffens beside her. He has worded it wrongly. He should have told the detective that they *have* told them everything they know, because it has given Kallis a chance to make it sound like they are keeping a secret from him. And all of a sudden Em feels a shift that makes her wonder if he is no longer on their side but opposing them.

She doesn't trust herself to speak and so she waits for Kallis to go on although the silence is interminable and in the end it is Rob who says, 'I think we have.'

Kallis nods but then asks, 'Yesterday afternoon: could you run me through your whereabouts again.'

'In the afternoon?' she says. 'I was at the pool. We all were.'

'All together, all the time?'

'Well yes, I mean – well no, not all the time. The boys went off for a bit and then Rob came back to the villa for half an hour.' She looks to Rob and then back to Kallis, confused.

'Just to pick up my charger,' her husband says. 'My phone died, I was waiting for a call. From the office.'

'Was anyone else here when you got to the villa?'

'No. Why?'

'And can you tell me what time this was, please? Just for my own notes,' he assures them, although nothing feels reassuring any more.

'I'm not sure, three o'clock? I don't know. Why?' Rob asks again.

'And what about you, Theo?' The detective shifts on the lounger as he turns to her son. 'Did you come back to the villa at all yesterday afternoon?'

'Yes.' Theo shrugs. His eyes are wide with something that resembles fear. This must be so excruciating for him, Em thinks. Answering questions when he is trying to deal with his grief. 'I came back to change.'

'And were you on your own?'

'No. Isaac was here.'

Em glances at her son. She doesn't know if he had told them this earlier, but she cannot see how it matters.

'And can you tell me what happened, when you and your brother were in the room yesterday afternoon?'

'Nothing happened.'

'Are you sure about that, Theo?'

'I don't know what you mean.' His eyes flick to Em's and she catches a look of uncertainty in them.

'Did you have an argument with Isaac yesterday afternoon in your room, Theo?'

'No.' Theo shakes his head adamantly. He looks like he is close to tears.

Em sees her son tense. She clocks the way his leg muscles tighten and his fingers curl into balls. She knows then that something happened between her boys yesterday afternoon, but she tells the officer, sharply, as she keeps her eyes on Theo, 'I don't see what any of this has to do with Isaac's death. There's no need to keep questioning us like this. I want you to go. I want to be alone with my family.'

Chapter Eleven

Lieutenant Kallis nods his head gravely as he stands. 'I understand, Mrs Cross. But we need to piece together what happened yesterday. It is important we gather up everything Isaac did before he died. If he had an argument, it helps us to know.'

'Even if they did, brothers argue. It's what siblings do. So questioning my son about some supposed disagreement that took place won't help.'

Theo isn't looking at her. His gaze is focused on a spot straight ahead, and she knows that Kallis has caught this by the way he is watching Theo out of the corner of his eye. She wills her son to say something, to explain what might have happened between him and Isaac yesterday, if anything. All he needs to do is put her mind at rest, but then it's just like Theo to clam up when he feels like he's being pressured.

But she can guess what the detective is thinking: that Theo looks cagey. Em would be thinking the same thing herself if she didn't know him inside out. 'He's just lost his brother,' she says. 'This isn't the time.'

Em gets up and goes to Theo, reaching out to hold his hand and squeeze it tight. She wants to tell him he doesn't need to talk about anything right now, but Rob is speaking.

'They're trying to help Isaac here,' he's telling her, his eyes never leaving her as she paces back and forth across the decking. All his words are in that calm manner he's been able to maintain all morning. 'I think we should go through it, Em.'

She flashes Rob a look of what she hopes will portray irritation but fears could come across as hatred. Or worse, that she is silently telling her husband to shut up. She imagines Kallis analysing every one of their mannerisms and drawing conclusions that might harm them. How everything has so quickly changed from earlier this morning when he was assuring her he would do everything he could to help her.

'How is this even happening?' she cries. 'How can you be questioning my family? We all love Isaac. What are you accusing us of?' The horrifying thought comes to her that it is always the family they suspect first.

Em wants to throw up. Her hand is shaking as it grips onto Theo's. Is it any surprise they are turning on them if they have no other clues? Possibly this has been their intention all along.

'Em, I don't think that is what Lieutenant Kallis is doing,' Rob pipes up.

She swings round to face him. 'Whose side are you on?' she screams.

'Em!' He holds up his hands in surrender as he stands too. 'I'm on your side, you know that.'

'Then act like it!'

Rob doesn't answer. He looks taken aback and mortified. She wonders what is going through his head with the luxury of being able to look at the situation a few steps further back than she can. The boys aren't his own, and as attached to them as he has become over the last few years he can separate emotion and reason in a way she cannot. He will feel grief for Isaac, but it will never match hers. And he will be able to look at Theo and wonder what he might know that he isn't saying, without having the gnawing pain of hoping he does not know a thing.

'I will go now,' Kallis says, 'but, Mrs Cross, we do need to understand the facts. And Theo, if you remember an argument you had with your brother it could help us rule out some questions.'

'Theo?' Rob leans around Em as if he is trying to stop her from blocking them all out again. 'They want to help us.'

'I ...' Theo hesitates, and Em doesn't breathe in the silence that follows. 'I don't know what we argued about. It was nothing.'

She feels her heart sink at Theo's sudden about-turn. He had adamantly told Kallis that he and Isaac hadn't argued, only now he is admitting they did. She dreads to think what the detective is putting together right now.

Kallis isn't speaking, just waiting for Theo to go on. Eventually her son caves in and says, 'We were talking about our dad.'

'Your dad? What do you mean?' Em asks him.

Theo shrugs. 'Just talking about him.'

'Well there you go then,' she says to Kallis. 'Their father is a constant source of dispute, so it's no surprise they didn't agree if the subject was my ex-husband.'

Kallis raises his eyes and asks Theo some more questions which appear to be futile, for eventually he seems to accept there is nothing more to enquire about. He says he will go now and that he's sorry to have disturbed them, and concludes, 'I will be back again as soon as there is any more news,' then heads to the door.

'Wait!' Em calls after him. 'Who told you about my boys?'

'I am afraid I cannot answer that.'

If anyone heard them they had to have been lingering close to her villa, which isn't on a path to anywhere else in the resort. 'It was that woman, wasn't it? The one who was outside this morning?'

'I am not able to say.'

'You don't have to,' Em says as he opens the door. 'I know it was her. That woman has been watching me since we arrived. So what the hell was she doing here in the first place?'

The lieutenant stops at the door and turns back to her.

'Why was she even here?' Em repeats.

He gives a small nod as if he's considered the question, and then tells her he will be back shortly.

When he is gone, Em releases her son's hand and sits down beside him. Theo has pulled his legs up onto the seat and wrapped his arms tightly around his knees, leaning his head into them so she cannot see his face.

She leans back in the chair and lifts her head to the sky. She wants to tell him it's going to be OK and that it doesn't matter if he and Isaac argued about their dad. She knows well enough how strained Theo's relationship with Charlie is. She also knows that Isaac wouldn't have been any support to him. They were never on the same page over the divorce, Isaac drifting through it as if it wasn't the destructive presence she and Theo had felt.

Of course she knows as well as anyone that you shouldn't bring your children into your marital problems, and the fact that Isaac came out unscathed is a blessing. But Theo didn't. And other than her, he has no one else he can talk to about it. And he doesn't even really talk to her.

So perhaps they could have argued about their father, but at the same time Em isn't convinced. Perhaps the topic of their father was something Theo managed to construct in the 'time out' he seemed to take when Kallis was speaking to him. Because otherwise why didn't he just admit to a row in the first place?

Theo looks even paler than he did earlier.

'What was all that about?' she asks softly.

Theo pulls his head up so she can see his face. Her son's eyes are filled with fear and she holds him again as she tries to make his pain go away. Her arms ache to pull him to her but something stops her, because she wants to know. 'Why did you say you didn't have an argument when you did?'

Theo shrugs. 'I didn't think it was an argument.'

She doesn't believe him.

Em sighs, her mind returning to that woman, eavesdropping on her sons. She hates the thought of her watching her family, no doubt desperate to make herself crucial to Kallis's investigation. Em knows plenty of women like her, always wanting to be involved in everything and at the centre of what's going on. There were many parents like that when her sons were at primary school.

Now she is back to thinking about what Theo is keeping from her, because she is sure there is something. When the boys were young she once told her friend, Stacey, that she knew Isaac better than she did Theo. 'I don't always feel like I get him,' she had admitted, and immediately felt guilty for it, because actually she wondered if it was true. Just because one of her sons talked to her more it didn't mean she knew Isaac better. Most of what they talked about was sports or mates at Isaac's schools. It was nothing in depth. Certainly in the latter years she has been closer to Theo.

She might have laughed with Isaac like she never could with Theo, a wonderful relationship to have with a seventeen-year-old, but when she told Rob and the detectives that if there was anything to know about Isaac then she would know it, Em doubts this is actually true. There could have been plenty of things Isaac hadn't told her about.

She tries to shake the idea that there was something troubling him, because right now it is Theo she needs to get through to. She has to find a way to get him to open up, to believe what he tells her, to trust him.

'Was there more to it?' she asks. 'Because if there was, this is the time to tell me.'

'Theo?' Rob prompts him when he doesn't answer.

Theo is playing with his hands in his lap and she feels her gaze drift down to them. One folding over the other, again and again. She looks back up at his face and feels herself crumple. She wants to be there for him but at the same time she knows there is something he isn't telling her and so as desperate as she is to hold him she forces herself not to. It is the hardest feeling, pulling away from your child when they need you more than ever, but if this is the only way to get Theo to talk—

'I didn't do anything, Mum,' he cries out, his body deflating, bending in on himself as if someone has just punched him in the gut. They may as well have, she thinks. She feels bruised herself. 'I didn't do anything,' he repeats.

Christ, do they think he did? Surely the police aren't going there? Then again, what other leads do they have to go on? Theo was the last person to have seen his brother and now they know the two boys argued earlier in the day. Is her son their main suspect?

She shakes her head, ridding it of the idea that Theo could be in any way responsible. She is his mother and she knows what he is and isn't capable of. Her son is no killer and he would never harm his brother.

LAILA

Chapter Twelve

'You were a long time,' is the first thing James says when the officers have left. I watch them walk up the path and make a call once they are out of earshot. Every so often they glance in my direction. I may not be able to hear what they are saying, but I'm almost certain they are talking to Lieutenant Kallis and telling him what I have just told them.

James walks inside and shuts the door behind him. I cannot make out the look in his eyes as he trails his fingers over the desk. It is more than just quizzical. It is like he is wary of me, or he doesn't trust me.

I suppose he has every right to be curious, in that while I told the officers what I overheard yesterday between Isaac and Theo, James still knows nothing of it. Now all I can think of is that someone will head straight over to Em's villa and question her son about what involvement he may or may not have had in his brother's death. That he will know it is me.

Oh God, what if I've done the wrong thing? I have pointed a finger at Theo. The police officers were enthusiastic to hear my story, taking down copious notes. Someone would be along later to take a proper statement from me, they said. For now they just wanted all the grit of the argument I'd overheard. Did I know for certain it was Theo and Isaac arguing? they asked.

Yes, I was sure about this.

Could I tell them word for word what I heard?

I relayed it in as much detail as I could.

'But this might not mean anything,' I said to them. 'I mean, just because they had an argument, it may not be anything more than that.'

'Of course this is correct,' one of them said, nodding at me knowingly, like we all must surely be in agreement that an argument between two brothers just before one of them ends up dead means *something.*

I feel sick at the thought of what I have done. Em is suffering enough right now and I have single-handedly made it worse for her, and there is nothing I can do to take it back.

The police officers wanted more details from me, the question I knew would be coming. What was I doing there? Where was I when I heard this argument?

I lied. There was no way I could tell them the truth, that I had found myself outside Em's villa, that the doors were wide open and the cleaner was just leaving and I seized the chance to sneak in and look for my watch, because by then I was certain Theo had taken it.

I'd intended to be in and out in five minutes. Entering with trepidation, I'd briefly stopped to glance at Em's room, her clothes hanging neatly from hangers instead of strewn across chairs like some of mine were, and her dressing table that looked like a counter in Boots. Who took three bottles of perfume on holiday?

I didn't chance snooping for long, I was too nervous, but it was only moments anyway before I heard the brothers' voices and saw them approaching the glass doors as they walked around their pool, leaving me no choice but to quickly hide in the wardrobe and pray they couldn't hear the hammering of my heart which seemed to thud through my chest.

I didn't tell the officers any of this; instead I said that I was outside, on the path, that I had been walking past when I heard raised voices and that the brothers were inside their room. That I could hear their argument because their doors were open.

James is waiting for me to answer and I know I should tell him, but I don't want to. I don't wish to give him the satisfaction of pulling apart what I have said because I fear that is what he will do. The husband who has always been stoically by my side is no longer the man standing in front of me. We have somehow managed to tear down what we had built together and I no longer feel like he would tell me I have done the right thing. And right now, I don't know that I have either.

In the end I say, 'They just asked me the same questions they did you, I guess. When I last saw him, that kind of thing.'

James nods slowly. 'And that was it?'

'Yes, that was it.'

'And what did you tell them about last night?' he goes on. 'You know, when we both came back separately.'

His fingers have stopped trailing over the desk and now his middle one is tapping on it, thudding rhythmically.

'I just said I came back and fell asleep, that I don't know what time you got in.'

His finger stops tapping.

'Because I don't, James. I was asleep. But you said it was half an hour later?' I question.

'It was. I know. I just didn't like the thought of them interrogating us about our night that was all. I don't want them picking at our personal business,' he says.

'Well they didn't,' I tell him.

'Good, that's good,' he says, and he turns away and disappears into the bathroom, leaving me to think that it is anything but good.

It is a little after midday when James tells me they have opened up the Greek restaurant for lunch, and that he wants us to go now. I can't fathom how he is already hungry, I only picked at my breakfast and have no desire to eat, but then I have never known James's appetite to wane.

We walk over there together in silence, the events of last night and this morning hanging over us precariously. There are too many things that we haven't addressed, and the more time that passes, the harder it is becoming to bring them up.

I want us to speak about our fight. We need to confront it and work out where we go from here. But what makes it worse is there are patches of last night that are crystal clear and others I cannot recall. I remember the start of the evening with surprising clarity, the part up to when James told me, 'I know what you have done, Laila.' But later, it is hazy.

We should also confront the fact we are dancing around each other today. I know I am keeping things from James, and I am certain he is keeping things from me as well. I am sure something happened on his fishing trip yesterday to induce such a bad mood in him, and he was wary about me speaking to the police about the end of our night.

I decide it is this I need to bring up first as we walk to the restaurant. 'James, were you really home only half an hour later than me?' I ask.

'Oh my God, Laila,' he mutters. 'What is this?'

'I'm just asking,' I say. 'You wanted to talk to me before I spoke to the police. I thought it could be about that.'

'Are you saying you don't trust me?'

'No. That's not what I'm saying,' I reply.

'Because it's the other way round, isn't it? I think you proved last night that I couldn't trust you.'

I sigh and look away. The supposed heart of our fight had been because I had betrayed James.

It is true, I have gone behind his back. I have done something I should not have done. All the same, the more I piece together about last night, the more I think that this is a convenient distraction from whatever James is hiding from me.

It was seven o'clock by the time he finally returned from fishing. I had already showered and was drying my hair, a dressing gown wrapped around me over my underwear. My evening dress was hanging on the wardrobe door and I'd chosen the jewellery I was going to wear. My make-up was applied, shimmering gold eyeshadow that complimented my tan, and a pink gloss that sparkled on my lips.

James was back two hours later than expected and by the time he walked in, my hopes for the evening were already tainted. I'd got myself all worked up over why he was late, wondering whether he'd had an accident and how I might find out when both times I had tried his mobile it went straight to voicemail. By the time he appeared I was both relieved and annoyed.

'At last!' I'd said. 'I was wondering where you'd got to.' I poked my head around the dividing wall and waited for his apology and explanation. Only there was something off about his body language, his arms hung tensely by his sides and his fist was clenched around his phone that as far as I knew wasn't even switched on.

He didn't respond or say he was sorry for being so late or that he hoped I wasn't worried, as he usually would. I feared I was losing my caring and attentive husband and I genuinely couldn't understand why. Since it appeared to be up to me to turn this around, I said, 'Did you have a nice time?'

James grunted. 'Yeah, it was fine.'

'You're later than I thought.'

'Yeah, I know, we went further than I expected,' he said.

I nodded. 'Did you catch anything?' I tried.

'No. And I'm going to have a shower.' He swept past me, leaning into the shower cubicle to switch on the water and then closed the door as he waited for it to heat up. My cheeks burned when he caught me watching him in the mirror; he looked at me as if I was spying on him, and so I turned away and left the bathroom and wandered outside to sit in the evening sun.

By the time he came out I was dressed but he didn't comment on my outfit. He gave me a cursory glance and shuffled through the wardrobe for something to put on. Everything about his movements was uncharacteristic, and maybe that was what troubled me the most. There's nothing scarier than someone you know and love as well as I do James acting so out of character.

'Is everything OK?' I asked. I had no idea what could be bothering him.

He stared at me in response. Actually, he stared through me like he couldn't even see me, and I don't recall him answering as he pulled out the first shirt he found and slipped it on.

He didn't hold my hand as we walked along the cliffside path in silence, as he had done on previous nights.

'James,' I said as we reached the top of the steps to the beach. 'What's the matter? Is everything OK?'

'Yep. Everything's absolutely fine.' He turned to me and smiled, but I could see it was more of a grimace, like he wanted me to know it was an act.

It dawned on me then, the only thing I could think of that could have changed his attitude to me, causing him to disappear from me gradually over the last few days. I had tried telling myself it was in my head and yet I knew it wasn't. This had something to do with Stephanie.

Fear gripped me like a vice. Was there a chance he could have met her?

I should have called him out right there. At least then we could have gone back to the room to resolve it. I didn't though, and maybe that was down to the sight of the beach below us. The tables were spread out along the sand and the twinkling fairy lights danced in the breeze, white bulbs hung in a canopy. Murmured conversation and laughter sprinkled the air and on the far side of the cove three members of a band were setting up their instruments for later in the night. It was perfect, save for my husband's foul mood.

The scene and the appeal of a glass of wine carried me forward. Our minibar hadn't been restocked, and so the beach held my best chance of getting a drink before I confronted him. And confront him was what I intended to do.

As we reached the sand a waiter stood, a beaming smile across his face. 'Where would you like to sit?' he asked. I glanced over the tables. The ones nearest the sea were already taken. Em and her family were seated around one of them in a prime spot. I pointed to another at the edge that was laid up for two.

As soon as we sat, James asked for a beer and a bottle of the Sancerre we had been drinking most nights. He didn't ask me if I was happy with his choice as the waiter ambled off, and I didn't comment. It felt easier to let it slide as I waited for the chance to start talking.

Now I look back and wonder why I wasn't angrier with him in that moment. I think I was fearful of what he might tell me more than anything. I was frightened by his drastic change of behaviour, and so I didn't come straight out and ask him if this had anything to do with his ex. Instead I said, 'I know something's up. Please, James, can you just tell me what it is?'

His reaction was unexpected as he slowly reached into his pocket, where he had put his phone, and laid it out on the table so carefully that it drew my gaze. Only then did I see that it wasn't his phone James had been holding, but mine.

My breath immediately balled in my throat, but at the same time my head whisked through the possibilities of what he might have seen and I couldn't come up with anything. I didn't send inappropriate messages to male friends or colleagues, none of the jokes I'd copied could ever offend James, I didn't even text my friends about my marriage or anything remotely private. There were no photos he would dislike and no websites—

Oh, but of course there was one. Although he would only have come across the infertility forum if he had been looking for it. Could he have read my posts? He wouldn't have had time to look through them tonight – he had been in the shower and getting ready and had barely been back in the room before we left again – and even if he had, would that explain his mood?

James watched me as my thoughts raced. 'I wasn't looking for anything, before you start on me for going through your phone. It was ringing when I was in the shower.'

I thought back and realised I had left my phone in the bathroom when I'd gone to sit outside and then get dressed.

'OK,' I said cautiously. He didn't know about the forum, but who could have called me?

'Well, aren't you going to ask me who it was?'

'Who was it?' I said. I was on edge, my heart fluttering because I didn't like the game he was playing with me and neither did I like the look in his eyes.

'A Mrs Laurier.'

'Oh.' That same fluttering heart now sank, because I knew who had called him and what she might have said.

'What the hell have you done, Laila?' he said, leaning across the table towards me.

'I didn't—' I stumbled.

'You went behind my back.'

I shook my head, but of course he was right, and clearly he knew it.

'I'm sorry,' I said, 'I wanted to tell you.'

'And when were you going to do that?'

'On this holiday,' I said. I had intended to, at some point.

'After everything I said to you, and then you had a go at me about booking this holiday. How much have you spent, Laila?'

'I don't – I'm not—' I felt completely flustered.

'You don't what? You don't know?'

'I *do* know.' I just didn't want to tell him.

'Because it's more than what I paid for ten days in Greece isn't it?'

'Yes,' I admitted. 'But James, that's what the money was meant for.'

At this moment the waiter appeared with James's beer and a bottle of wine. 'Beautiful evening, yes?' he said. 'Very romantic,' he went on, oblivious to the fact it couldn't have been less so. He spent an age opening the bottle and pouring a drop into James's glass for him to try, which James flapped his hand over, rudely signalling for him to keep pouring. It was all I could do to smile at the waiter so he didn't sense an atmosphere.

When he left, James leant forward across the table and hissed, 'No it wasn't, Laila. Not any more.' He shook his head. 'I cannot believe you did this.'

It was our best chance, or at least that was how I saw it. It was only a couple of weeks before James told me he couldn't go through any more IVF that I'd come across a post on the forum. A woman called Molly36 enthusing about a clinic she had visited in New York. After five attempts in the UK she had finally had treatment that worked. Yes, it might have set them back over £20,000 with flights and accommodation and the price of the treatment, but as she had said in her own words, 'It would have been worth it at double the price.'

I booked it. Only I didn't tell my husband.

'You must have spoken to them and decided on your own that we were spending the money,' James had persisted last night.

'It's what it was for,' I said again, an insubstantial excuse possibly, and yet it was the truth.

'I told you. I told you, Laila, I don't want to go through it any more. It was not your decision to make, and it was not your money.'

I reeled. That stung.

It was *our* money, we were married. Right from the beginning we used a joint account and James had always told me everything was ours. I was grateful we had managed to buy our house mainly because of an inheritance left by his mother, and James's salary, which far outweighed mine, afforded the lion's share of our treatments, but I had always ploughed every penny I could of my own into our savings.

He drained the last of his beer and poured a slug of wine into his glass, leaving me to top up my own. He was drinking too quickly already, and maybe I was too. I knew at that point the night was going in one direction and I should have taken a hold of it there and then, but I didn't stop. I made it worse by tipping my own glass of wine back and pouring myself another, my eyes goading him as I did so. I think even then I knew what I was doing but I didn't care. Maybe if I had stopped drinking in that moment and if another bottle of wine hadn't been ordered so readily before we had even been served our starters, we could still have salvaged the night, but that wasn't how it panned out.

I brought up Stephanie, later on, at a point when I was almost beyond caring what he told me. By then James had asked me how much money we could get back, what I could stop.

The truth was I didn't want to stop. I had realised over the last few days, watching Em with her boys, seeing Rosie, pregnant, I didn't want to give up my chance of having children. Only now I no longer knew if I wanted to do it with James.

'Did you see Stephanie today?' I had blurted out.

'What?' James had looked at me, incredulous, like he couldn't believe I could ask such a thing. His eyes were wide as he slammed his glass on the table, wine sloshing over the top of it so that it ran down the edge of the table and onto my dress. 'No,' he yelled at me. 'Christ, no. I have not seen Stephanie.'

I have to be honest, I think he was telling me the truth.

Chapter Thirteen

The midday sun is beating down as we stop outside the Greek restaurant, nowhere to hide from its rays as we wait to be seated. The restaurant isn't big enough to host all the guests at the same time, so the waiters are asking the party of three in front of us if they'd be happy to come back later.

They don't want to, at which the waiter politely nods and says, 'Of course,' as he leads them over to the corner. Clearly what he really wants to do is tell us all to piss off back to our rooms and stop harassing them for food when a young boy has been found dead in the hotel.

It is surprising how many of the tables are already taken. I wonder if panic has set in and the guests are suddenly worrying how they will get fed. Tragedies can bring out the very best but also the worst in people.

I pull on James's arm. 'We should just come back later,' I say.

'We're here now, we might as well see if they can fit us in,' he replies, and turns to one of the staff I have seen every day who is usually tucked behind one of the buffet counters, and whom I am sure doesn't speak much English. 'Is there any chance of getting a table please?' James asks. 'There are only two of us.' He holds up two fingers as he gestures to me and then back to him.

The man appears flustered as he scans the scattering of tables. 'We can come back later,' I say again.

But James remains persistent as he ignores me and waits for the man to find a spare table. I'm actually pleased when we sit down because at least that's one less thing for him to get annoyed about.

It is so quiet, the mood so sombre. All around us guests are engaged in either a low murmuring of conversation or none at all. Surreptitious glances are being thrown about, no one quite knowing what to do with themselves. I focus my attention on the menu. James has already chosen a steak and is now flicking his thumb against his phone screen.

'I've found another hotel,' he says out of nowhere.

'Where?'

'By the harbour in Crete. It's bigger than this one but cheaper.'

'Great.'

He looks up at me. 'You do want to leave, don't you?'

'Yes I want to leave,' I say. I do, desperately. I want to get away from White Sands and Ixos as soon as possible, but I don't want to spend another five nights in Crete. I want to go home. What I actually want is to see my mum and dad and close their doors behind me and pretend that none of this ever happened.

'There's a pool there too. And water sports.'

'James?'

'What?'

'How can we possibly enjoy the rest of our holiday? I saw a dead body this morning. He was only a child.'

'I know that.' He frowns. His thumb tapping against the side of his phone. 'I do know that.' He leans across the table. 'That's why we need to get out of here. It feels like this place is closing in on us, what with the police questioning us and half the resort closed off.'

'Don't you think we should just get flights home instead?' I suggest.

'Is that what you want?'

'Yes. I think so.'

'Yeah, maybe that's for the best.' He blows out a breath and leans back in his seat, his gaze wandering around the restaurant.

'How quickly do you think we can leave?' I ask. 'Do you think they will let us?' I've watched enough *Death in Paradise* to know we must all be suspects right now. Even after what I've told them about Theo. For all I know he's got an alibi that proves he couldn't have been anywhere near his brother last night. And then what? Not only will he and Em know I sent the police in his direction, but there's still a murderer among us? We could be trapped here for the next five days. Possibly even longer.

James glances at me as if the thought hadn't occurred to him that they might now allow us to go. '*Can* they keep us here?' he says, and then, 'Surely not. They haven't even told us a crime has been committed. As far as we know it was an accident. No.' He shakes his head adamantly. 'They don't have the power to hold every single guest in the hotel just because we were in the vicinity of where a body was found. That's not how it works.'

'How *does* it work then?' I ask.

But he doesn't have an answer to this, and so we fall into silence. The waiter delivers us a bottle of water and I pour us both a glass as a man on the next table leans over to the couple next to them, who he appears to know, and says, 'The police been to see you both yet?' I glance over. He's a large man who I've seen around the pool a few times. His belly is squeezed in between him and the table and he doesn't make much effort to keep his voice down.

I can see that James is listening too by the way his head lifts up, his face drawn in concentration.

The other man is in his mid-fifties, dressed in a smartly pressed white polo shirt and chino shorts. He looks slightly awkward as he replies, 'Yes. Of course there was little we could tell them. I didn't even know who the poor lad they were talking about was.'

'Makes you wonder though, doesn't it?'

'Wonder?'

The large man's wife appears to be cowering into her seat. She must be used to her husband embarrassing her by now; he certainly seems the type to speak out often. 'The fact any one of us could be responsible.' He waves his arm about the restaurant.

'Harold,' his wife hisses, leaning forward.

'What?' he replies. 'I'm sure it's what they're thinking.' Harold gestures at the couple next to them, who look appalled.

James's face is ashen. I can only think that it's because he loathes conflict that he looks like he wants to get up and leave. Nearby another couple appear to have stopped their own conversation to listen in too.

Harold is continuing, talking to his wife now, but at a volume that suggests he's quite happy for those of us around him to hear. 'Some young lad's been killed and we've had the police questioning us this morning, which I assume everyone in the restaurant here has too. So I don't know why we're pretending it hasn't happened.'

His wife looks stricken, she can barely look him in the eye, her gaze flicking nervously around the restaurant. I dip my head away when she catches me looking.

The woman on the table next to them speaks now. 'How do we know it wasn't an accident? I haven't heard anything to the contrary so I don't think you can start implying someone killed him. It all sounds very macabre.'

'It wasn't an accident,' Harold replies. 'You can tell that by their questioning, the way they're combing over the grounds around the pool. Have you seen how far out they've got their forensics teams looking?'

'What does that mean?' the woman asks. Her hand is tapping her fork against her plate as if she can't stop it from shaking.

'It means ...' Harold pauses for what I think is effect, ' ... they likely believe the body got moved.'

'Oh God,' she replies, and I glance at James, who is watching the charade in horror. His eyes are wide with shock as he pushes his glass around in circles, making the water splash precariously close to the rim. He is fidgety and anxious and any minute I expect him to leap out of his seat and leave the restaurant.

'They know more than they're letting on,' Harold says

'And how exactly do you think you know all this?' Polo Shirt asks.

'Because I'm ex police myself,' he says, if possible puffing his chest out even more.

At this a silence falls across the restaurant, only the minimum of clatter from knives and forks. Because here is a man who professes to know about criminal procedures such as this and seems happy to share his knowledge with anyone who wants to listen.

I, for one, want to know more and I lean across our table and say to him, 'You think the body was moved? What do you mean by that?'

'Well,' he says, shifting around in his seat so he can face me, clearly pleased he has an attentive audience. 'In my experience it's likely the boy was killed somewhere else and then pushed into the pool afterwards. This was no accident,' he says. 'Like I say, they already know more than they're telling you.' He says *you* in a way that implies this doesn't include him.

'Like what?' Polo Shirt snorts.

'Like they know what time it happened.'

'And when was that then?'

'Some time just after midnight.'

'How do you know this?' Polo Shirt asks in disbelief.

'Because I had a conversation with one of the police officers earlier. They think the body was there a few hours. And I also know they have a witness.'

'What do you mean a witness?' Polo Shirt's wife asks.

Harold nods as he turns to her now. 'One of the waiters saw something after the gala dinner. Someone acting oddly at the pool bar.' He shrugs. 'It'll all be out soon.'

'Surely if you're ex police you should be keeping these opinions to yourself,' James says abruptly. 'Isn't there some kind of code against it?'

I agree with him, but Harold screws up his eyes. 'Would you rather not know what's going on?'

'I'd prefer the facts,' James says bluntly.

Harold grunts and shakes his head as a waiter appears with our meals, hovering anxiously like they don't know whether they should step in or come back when the conversation is over. They must be feeling worried themselves; most likely every one of them has been hauled in by the police too. One of them might have been the person who found Isaac early this morning, or part of the party who had to drag his lifeless body out of the pool. We have forgotten the staff in the midst of this horrendous situation.

The waiter shuffles in between the tables and puts the plates down hurriedly.

'As far as I see it there isn't anything we can do but sit and wait for the police to carry out their jobs,' Polo Shirt says. 'In any case, there's a family here who have just suffered unbearable loss.'

'Exactly,' I say. There is nothing more important right now than Em's grief and I shouldn't have piped up when I did. When I turn to James he is looking at me oddly and I try to read his thoughts: what is it that is going through my husband's head? For the first time in my ten years of knowing him, I no longer have any idea. I am certain he didn't meet Stephanie from the way he reacted, yet he is keeping something from me for sure.

We finish our lunch quickly and by the time we set off for our room it is just before 1 p.m.

'What are *they* doing here again?' James says as we round the path and our room looms into view, along with Lieutenant Kallis and the officer who questioned me earlier. They have their backs to us, facing our door as if they have just knocked and are waiting for it to open. 'We've told them everything we know, what the hell are they doing back here again. Laila?' he questions me, his voice low as he grips my arm.

'I haven't a clue,' I say. I sense James doesn't believe me, but it's the truth. I don't know.

'You didn't say anything earlier?' he asks.

I shake my head, refusing to meet his eyes.

But he grips my arm and stops me in my tracks, making me twist round to face him. He knows something is up, I am sure of it, but I don't know how. Though we haven't spoken about what I did yesterday afternoon James's expression is one of more than mild curiosity.

I don't have a chance to ask him what's bothering him because Kallis and his officer have turned now and are walking away from our door as Kallis calls out to us. 'Ah, good timing. Mr and Mrs Burrow, could we speak?'

James lets go of me. We have no option but to go over to meet them. They wait patiently as James searches his pockets for our room card and eventually finds it and presses it against the keypad on the door to open it.

'There's something more we would just like to ask please, Mrs Burrow?' Kallis says as they step inside and James closes the door behind them.

'Oh?' I reply, feeling James's eyes on me.

'About what you saw yesterday afternoon.'

James walks around and stands in front of us so I have no choice but to glance at his confused expression.

The officer with Kallis, who questioned me earlier, makes a show of getting his notepad out as he starts to speak. 'You say that you were outside the room of the deceased when you heard the argument.'

I nod, mutely. I can feel the intensity of James's glare but I daren't look at him.

'And that the two brothers were inside their room when it happened?'

'Yes,' I say quietly.

Kallis pipes up now, 'We were there this morning,' he says. 'And I stood on the path where you tell us you were.'

'OK.'

'And it came to me that the path is actually a long way from the room. Because the swimming pool and their – what do you call it? Veranda? Is between you, yes?'

'I suppose.'

'And so I asked my colleague to go inside and raise his voice. But I couldn't hear a thing.'

'Laila?' James is now stepping forward and I can feel the blood draining from my face. 'What's all this about?' he says, and as Kallis turns to him, hanging his head quizzically, I can see realisation dawning on him that I haven't told my husband any of my story.

'Mrs Burrow,' he says. 'Are you telling us the truth about what you heard yesterday afternoon?'

EM

Chapter Fourteen

Kallis and his team have been in and out all morning, at one point loitering on the path outside though they have left again for now. Em doesn't know what they've been doing, she's just relieved they're gone. Only now she isn't certain how to get out of this circle that they have found themselves in. She is watching Theo, waiting, anticipating him saying something – anything that will help her understand more about his argument with his brother yesterday. In return Theo is watching her, presumably willing his mother to believe him with 100 per cent of her heart. God how she wishes she could.

Em knows Kallis is unsure about something – he and his colleague were debating outside for a while – but she does not know what. It's as if they've forgotten that she is the victim here. Her family are the victims, but in the last hour she has started to feel like they are all suspects.

For now she is grateful the police officers have gone; hopefully that means they will start questioning the right people. Someone must have seen Isaac in the night. Someone must know something. And even if Theo knows more than he is telling her, she is certain that the solution to her son's murder is not going to be found within these four walls.

Rob is outside on his phone, though to whom she has no idea. It is just her and Theo in the room when she asks him, 'What was your argument about, Theo?'

'It was nothing.'

'You said it was about your dad?'

Theo shrugs.

'Has something happened with him? You said he was in touch yesterday.'

'No. It was nothing. It was a stupid disagreement. I don't know why they're even bringing it up with me. I've told you that.'

'I know you have.'

She closes her eyes, willing her heart to stop fluttering so wildly. It is making her breaths short. Isn't it enough that her precious son is dead? Now she has to look at her other one and wonder what he knows that he isn't telling her.

The police have made her feel this way, barrelling in and firing their questions at Theo, making her look at her son with the same suspicions they have. That woman has done it too with whatever she has told them. Watching her family's every move like some freak. If the police don't tell her what she said, Em will need to find out for herself. She will speak to the woman.

She stands with renewed purpose as Rob finishes his call and wanders back into the room. 'Can I get you something to eat?' he asks, his phone hanging out of his hand at his side. She is sure he has been on a call to work, updating someone, telling them of her tragedy that means they must leave him alone for now.

She shakes her head.

'You need something,' he says softly but urgently.

'I'm not hungry.' Will she ever feel hungry again?

Rob looks at her helplessly, but she is grateful for his solid, calm presence. After a messy divorce with Charlie, he was her light at the end of the tunnel. When her marriage collapsed she didn't think there was a way out of the deep pit she'd found herself tumbling into.

She was the one who should have left Charlie. Her mother had told her only three weeks before their wedding he wasn't good enough for her, but who listens to their mother? Em was angry with her for leaving it until the eleventh hour to announce that she had grave doubts about her future son-in-law. 'And what is it you don't like about him?' she had spat.

'There's just something I don't trust, Emilia. I don't know what it is.'

What was so awful was that this was completely out of character for her mother, who had always liked her past boyfriends, and so while Em toughened her armour and fought against her mother's opinions, a glimmer of doubt managed to slither its way into her mind.

After they were married, the tiny seed of doubt grew. The years blessed her with her boys and drove her focus away from being Charlie's wife to being a mum too. After Theo was born, and the seed grew again, the idea of pulling her family apart seemed too hard to bear and so she shut it out, focusing her energies on keeping them together.

Perhaps she was wrong to do this. Maybe if she'd confronted Charlie years ago it might have been better for her and her boys in the long run, but that is something she will never have the answer to.

Instead she never opened up and admitted to anyone that her husband rarely came home from work on time, or that she couldn't put her finger on why but she suspected there was something about the girl in the office, Sasha, whose name sent a shard of ice into her every time it was mentioned. She didn't do that because she didn't want to admit that her mum might have been right. Pride was a funny thing. It often led to Em making decisions she'd later regret.

In the end her world fell apart at a time when her boys were going through big changes themselves. Theo had just started at the big comprehensive down the road and was finding it hard to settle, already lost in a year group of almost two hundred. Her mind was on him and how this wasn't the right school for him and so she hadn't noticed what was going on right in front of her until she came home early to find her husband in bed with one of her oldest friends, Mel.

Despite the warning and niggles over the years, the shock she felt was palpable. Charlie later admitted he had had a brief affair with Sasha as she'd suspected. Ironically he seemed relieved to finally get everything out in the open.

Em fleetingly toyed with the idea of forgiveness, of taking him back. *For the sake of the boys*, she told herself. Charlie had begged her but his promises were lacklustre. The following day he suddenly admitted he wanted to be with Mel.

Time has softened her feelings. Nowadays she can see Charlie for what he is, what he was, the good bits too. In fact some days, and she would never admit this to a soul, she misses those times.

Em slips on her sandals as Rob grabs hold of her arm. 'Where are you going?' he asks, concerned.

She toys with not telling him the truth because she knows he will try and stop her but in the end says, 'I need to know what that woman has told the police.' She utters this in a low voice, hoping Theo on the other side of the room won't hear.

'You shouldn't do that,' Rob says to her. 'You mustn't get involved.'

'Not get involved?' she cries out.

The sound of her mobile alerting her to a text cuts their conversation sharply. She picks it up and reads it. 'It's from Charlie. He's got a flight but it gets in late. He'll have to get a boat to Ixos first thing in the morning.' She sighs as she drops her phone on the bed.

They have spoken three times this morning and now she just wants him here. She has learnt to talk to him without bitterness and with some acceptance, and right now she wants someone who understands even a part of the pain that is eating away at her from the inside, until she is certain it will kill her completely.

Rob is devastated, she can see that, but his grief does not touch hers. Charlie would understand that she needs to talk to this woman. He would not try to stop her.

God, she misses Isaac. She craves him. The pain is so raw, too deep to make sense of, but between them all they aren't allowing her to grieve for her son wholly, not when Rob is telling her what she shouldn't do, and when she is filled with dread that there is more that Theo knows.

Yet she realises with a gut-wrenching twist that her priority right now has to be Theo. Her surviving son. Although how it can be when her priority is also Isaac and getting to the truth of what happened to him? Because the truth is what she needs, even if Theo—

No. She will not go there. She cannot. Theo does not know more about his brother's death than he is telling her. He does not know why Isaac left their villa again after they had gone to bed. This is what he has told her and this is what she must believe.

Theo has gone outside and Em follows him. She sinks into a chair in a corner of the decking, the other side of their pool to her son. 'I need you to tell me everything that happened last night,' she says to him.

He looks up at her, his brows furrowed as if to ask why. Like he thinks he has said enough already, when in reality he has told her nothing. But she wants to move on from the argument. She wants to discuss the evening and the fact that, as far as they know right now, Theo is the last person who saw Isaac alive.

'I need to hear it, Theo,' she tells him.

He shakes his head, only a glimmer. He does not want to go through it again.

'Baby, what happened? Was there something going on with Isaac?'

Theo parts his mouth. *Yes,* she thinks. *There was.* But at the same time she can see that Theo doesn't want to tell her.

'What was it?' she persists. 'This is important, you're not in trouble, I just have to know.'

She holds her breath as she waits for him to tell her, but when he eventually says, 'I don't know what it was,' Em wants to scream.

It is there. It has risen inside her. Building like a fire as it ravages everything in sight.

But this is her son and she knows Theo. She has to push it down. Screaming will send him running and she cannot afford to lose him. There has to be a reason he doesn't want to talk.

'So tell me about last night,' she says. 'When you went to bed. You must have heard him leave again? There must be something you can tell me.' Can he not see how desperate she is to understand what must have been going through Isaac's head? 'Why would he leave the villa after we had all come home?' she adds.

'I don't know why. I was asleep.' Theo shrugs, his eyes wide as he watches her.

She can feel the tears pricking the corners of her eyes. She is almost certain he is lying but she doesn't know what about. Is it nothing more than a white lie, because he was still awake when Isaac left, or is it something much worse?

Em pulls herself out of the seat and strides alongside the pool. She feels Theo's eyes following her.

The truth is she has been purposefully spending more time with Isaac on this holiday because she barely sees him these days as he flits in and out of the house, seeing his mates, playing for various sports teams, hanging out with people whose names she's often not heard before.

She's been using the holiday to reconnect with her seventeen-year-old.

Theo's the one who's always been happiest at home. She hasn't had to worry about who he's with or what he's doing, her concerns are more centred around wishing he'd go out more. After Charlie left them, it was Theo who inadvertently saved her when she took to her bed for a few dark weeks, depending on her mum to cook them meals every night, iron the boys' shirts for school and make sure they had lunch money and the right books.

One night Theo had crept into her darkened room and sat at the end of the bed. She had thought it was the middle of the night. 'Have you had a bad dream?' she murmured in a haze.

'No,' he replied. 'I wanted to know if you were coming down to eat?'

'Hmm? What time is it?'

'Five o'clock.'

She couldn't believe she had slept the entire day.

'I'm scared, Mum,' Theo had said, with an honesty she didn't normally get from her eleven-year-old.

'Scared? What about?'

'That you're not my mum any more. You don't look like her or smell like her. You don't do the things that mums are supposed to do.'

Her son was shaking, she noticed as she reached over him for her glass of water and knocked bottles of pills onto the floor. They scattered like marbles out of their containers and it was all she could do to watch them bounce across the carpet.

In the mirror on the wardrobe she'd caught her reflection looking back at herself, and saw what everyone could. She was thinner and paler, her cheekbones were too accentuated and her shoulder blades poked through the T-shirts she had been wearing for the last few days. Theo was right. She was a fraction of the woman and mother she'd once been.

This is why she needs to tread carefully with him now. He carries all their hurt and is hurting too. Although the thought that Theo saved her once, and yet she couldn't save Isaac this time, makes Em let out a wail so loud that Rob comes rushing through the doors. 'What is it?' he shouts.

The police have told them it was no accident, and neither did Isaac jump. His injuries tell them this much. Someone else did this to her son and she will find out who.

Chapter Fifteen

Rob is fussing around again, asking Theo if he can get *him* something to eat now, though Theo is point-blank refusing his stepfather. Her son has always had a healthy appetite, so she knows this is odd, but she doesn't know how Rob can possibly expect either of them to want food.

Em gets up and walks past him back into the bedroom, feeling like a prisoner trapped inside this villa, even though she cannot imagine walking outside of it ever again. At some point she will have to. They will all have to leave and go home, a family of three.

She is trying to make sense of what she knows. She is certain Theo wasn't asleep when Isaac left the room last night. She can tell by the way his eyes flick away from her when he speaks. Had it been Isaac sitting in front of her she would probably have shaken him until he'd told her the truth. But with Theo she has to keep the channel of communication open for him to speak to her when he is ready.

She can only hope this is not too long, and still she reassures herself that whatever Theo has to tell her, it is not going to help lead them to knowing who hurt her son.

It is the thought that someone out there could have done this to Isaac that she cannot get her head around. How could someone have wanted him dead?

Her two sons had loved each other as young children. They'd wanted for no one else, or at least that was the case with Theo. He looked up to his brother constantly, like Isaac was the only person on the planet. Em has often wondered if he never felt the need to make loads of friends when he always had his brother to play with.

She can remember them as two little boys as if it were yesterday, the holiday in Majorca they went on when Isaac was seven and Theo five, in their matching swimming shorts, their excitement. They never used to argue, not properly like some siblings did.

Em realises in that moment that there is someone who can answer one of her questions: Charlie. Why didn't she think of it before? They supposedly argued about their father so he might know why.

He picks up on the first ring. He must be expecting more news. 'Hi?' he says urgently.

'The police have been here again,' she tells him. 'They think Isaac was pushed.'

'Oh God.'

'It wasn't an accident and he didn't do it himself. So someone killed him.' Her words break. 'Who? Who could have done that to him?' she cries.

'I don't know.' His words are short and breathless, a mixture of grief, anger and disbelief. 'But we are going to find out, Em,' he promises her. 'We won't stop till we do. Did you get my text? I have to go to Stanstead but the flight doesn't leave until nine p.m.. I'll stay in Crete and get a boat over in the morning.'

'OK.'

'It's just me coming,' he tells her. Not the new girlfriend that he mentioned earlier. Who she had told him not to bring, who had only met the boys on two occasions.

'Right.' She is glad of this, but she doesn't want to give him the satisfaction of knowing. 'Charlie, did you call Theo yesterday?' she asks.

'Yeah. I tried Isaac a couple of times but I couldn't get hold of him so I spoke to Theo.'

'What did you want to talk to him about?'

'I just wanted to catch up, see how the holiday was going.'

'What did Theo say?'

'Hardly anything. You know what he's like. Why?'

'He says they had an argument about you.'

'About me?' Charlie sounds surprised. He's silent for a moment. 'Why would they argue about me?'

'I don't know, but someone heard them arguing in the villa yesterday afternoon and they've told the police. They came to question Theo but he lied about it at first, and then later admitted it was about you. He won't tell me any more than that.'

'I have no idea,' Charlie says. 'I don't see why they'd have argued about me.' He seems genuinely confused.

'So nothing was said between you and Theo that he might have taken the wrong way?'

'No. It was a short call. I asked him how his holiday was and he said, "Hot." I asked what he'd been up to and he said, "Nothing much." So I asked him to get Isaac to call me. Only he never did.'

'And that was it?'

'Almost word for word.'

'I don't get it then,' she says.

'No, nor me.'

Em is silent for a moment as she thinks what this means, but there is nothing there. 'Do you remember that holiday we had in Majorca when the boys were seven and five?'

'In Alcudia?'

'Was it?'

'Yeah, that place with all the slides.'

'That's right.'

'Why are you remembering that?' he says.

'There was an incident one day with that kid in the pool.'

Charlie doesn't answer.

'Do you remember it?' she presses.

'Em?' he questions. 'Why are you bringing that up?'

'Tell me what you remember about it.'

'God. I don't know, it was ten years ago. I *can't* remember it really,' he says, though she knows he can.

'I wasn't there. I was having a massage or something, but when I came out some kid was screaming about Theo.'

'Jesus, Em, why are you bringing this up?'

'Because I don't think I ever knew exactly what went on. You played it down but something happened, didn't it? The other mother said he had hurt her kid.'

'Yeah, but it was an accident. Theo was five years old and besides, Isaac said it was an accident too.'

'But the mother swore blind it wasn't. And Isaac always stood up for him, you know he did. They always stood up for each other.'

Charlie sighs. 'I have no idea if it was an accident or not. I didn't see Theo do anything. What's this about, Em?'

'I don't know,' she admits.

'You're getting at something.'

She doesn't know what she's getting at, really. There's just this shard of worry stabbing at her, the odd memory springing into her head. 'I don't like the way they questioned Theo, it's like they're looking at him.'

'Looking at him?' he says. 'You mean they think he might have done something?' Charlie's voice is rising into a crescendo so that he is almost yelling by the time he's got the sentence out. Him saying it out loud makes her realise how ludicrous it sounds.

She nods in response and then adds quietly, 'Surely not.'

Outside, Theo is shuffling on his lounger. He cannot sit still. He doesn't know what to do with himself but then none of them do. Rob is the other side of the pool and every so often he glances at Theo and then inside to where she is perched on the end of the bed on the phone. 'I don't know.' Em gulps back a sob. 'I don't know if they're looking into him seriously, or if they don't think any more of it. They probably just don't have anything else to go on right now. I don't know,' she says again.

'But you know he didn't do it, Em,' Charlie says. 'There is absolutely no way he is capable of doing anything like that. And not to Isaac,' he says. 'Not his brother.' She can hear the grief in her ex-husband's voice and it punches into her, folding her over as she sinks deeper into the bed.

'Em?' he snaps. 'You know that, right?'

'Yes of course,' she says. But she can no longer see what is true and what isn't.

LAILA

Chapter Sixteen

I can tell that Kallis is intrigued that I haven't told my husband any of what I have spoken to his colleague about. My lack of communication has only made it worse. Who wouldn't confide in their own husband about something so integral to a police investigation? Kallis must know my reluctance to talk to James is because I don't want to, and now he is no doubt trying to figure out why that is, while beside him James is doing the same thing.

'Laila, what's going on here?' he asks.

Kallis has just implied that I'm not telling them the whole truth, but I can't possibly admit that in front of the lieutenant. I tell James, 'I overheard an argument yesterday afternoon between Isaac and his brother. I thought I should tell the officer I spoke to earlier. That's all.' I shrug, trying to convey to James I think it's no big deal.

His eyes narrow quizzically and he clearly wants to ask why I didn't tell him this earlier, why I didn't mention it over lunch. But then he pulls himself back and nods his head slightly. No doubt he knows why I haven't. After last night we have hardly been on the best of terms.

But then the inspector reminds me why he is here. 'Your wife told my officer that she overheard the argument in the room outside the villa. Here' – he pulls a piece of paper out of his folder – 'let me show you.' When he unfolds the paper I see it is a map of the resort, similar to the one I have. Kallis reaches into his pocket for a pen and makes a circle in thick black around Em's villa. 'This is the villa of Isaac Lawson's family,' he explains, presumably for James's benefit.

My husband leans over for a better look.

'As you can see it is at the end of a path.'

'What were you even doing there?' James asks me.

Kallis straightens up and nods for me to answer. He's interested to know himself.

'I was just walking around the grounds, I didn't know where the path led,' I say.

'Ah, so you end up here. By accident?' he clarifies.

'That's right,' I lie.

Kallis nods. 'Yes this is what my colleague tells me earlier. And you also told him the doors were open, this is right?'

'Yes.'

'But you see here is where I have the problem. To stand on the path here' – he prods his pen at a spot on the map – 'it is a long way from the villa. And the brothers were in the room over here, correct?' He makes another circle around the boys' room.

'Yes.'

'As I say I stood there myself earlier today, and I asked my colleague to stand in this room and raise his voice, and even with the doors open I could not hear him. Maybe the odd sound, but certainly I could not make out any of his words.'

James's breathing is loud in my ears, but to give him his due he doesn't butt in.

'Mrs Burrow, I need to check your story. That there isn't anything about it you want to add or you have remembered differently, perhaps? That maybe you didn't actually hear what was being said?'

'No, I did,' I tell him. 'I've told you the truth, I heard exactly what was said.'

'Something doesn't add up for me. Maybe if you think about it and anything comes to you, you might want to let me know?' he says as he heads to the door. He opens it and James goes to follow him and to close the door behind him, when Kallis turns and says to me, 'And you say you didn't know where the path led, is that right?'

I nod. 'Yes.'

'Only, Mrs Cross tells me she has seen you outside her villa on occasion before. Do you remember this?'

'No.' I shake my head. 'No, I don't remember walking that way before. I mean, I might have done,' I fluster, 'I don't know, the paths all look the same.'

'Yes, I suppose they do,' he says, in a way that suggests he doesn't agree one bit and that he knows as well as I do that I was aware of whose villa I was standing outside.

As soon as Kallis finally leaves James closes the door behind him and says, 'What was all that about?'

'Oh my God, James,' I cry. I cannot keep it in any more. 'I don't know what I've done.' I sink onto the bed and cover my face with my hands, the memories of yesterday afternoon swimming about in my head. I'd hoped I could get away with the fact I was inside their room but already it's clear I can't, and right now the last person I want to confide in is the only person I have ever been able to in the past.

'Laila?' He sits on the bed next to me and prises my hands away. 'You need to tell me.' His voice is much softer than it has been all morning, his face no longer angry but concerned. I hadn't expected this reaction from him after last night. Somehow it is the old James looking at me, closely, and so I tell him the truth.

I could not stop thinking of Theo. It was the way he had stood in the reception, smirking, and the way he looked at me moments before. I couldn't get rid of the notion that he reminded me so much of Sam, and how that made me feel.

Em was on her own at this point, lazily stretched out on her lounger with Theo at the bar. I don't know what made me wander around the pool and stop to talk to her, it was nothing in particular. I wasn't planning to question her about her son, hoping I could somehow strike up a conversation and work in a mention of my watch. I couldn't bear her lying there, oblivious, while I was so bothered by the thought of him having stolen something so precious.

'Hi again,' I'd said as she turned to one side and held a hand over her eyes to shade them.

'Oh, hi.'

'Another lovely day.'

'Yes, isn't it?'

'How are your boys enjoying it here, are they finding enough to do?'

'Yes, they've always been able to keep themselves busy.' She smiled at me thinly, her words a contrast to how bored she was worried they might be, and I wondered if she remembered telling me that.

'My husband's off for the day,' I told her. 'Fishing. I have to be honest, I don't think I've ever heard him show any interest in fishing before. I think he's getting restless sitting around the pool.' I laughed, expecting her to join in.

Instead she replied, 'Oh. OK.' Her lips were pressed tightly together as if she were trying to smile but at the same time make it known she had no interest in speaking to me. The way she'd brushed over Theo's rudeness before, I wondered if Em was the kind of mother who, if she found out her son had stolen a watch, would try to cover it up. Would she stand by him and not dish out any punishment?

'I lost my watch the other day,' I said. 'I wondered if you'd seen it anywhere.'

'Oh?' She gave her head a small shake. 'I don't think so. What does it look like?'

'Thin gold bracelet, white face and Roman numerals.'

'No. Sorry.'

'It was a gift from my grandmother,' I went on. 'If I don't find it, I . . .' I pause, taking a deep breath. 'It's just important to me.'

'I'm sorry,' she said again. 'I'll keep an eye out.'

'Thanks.'

Em nodded and didn't reply and eventually I said goodbye and walked away, fuming. First her son and now her treating me like I was nothing.

I was certain I was right about him and I wasn't prepared to let him get away with it.

'That's why I headed towards their villa,' I say to James now. 'But I still wasn't planning to do anything.' Or I didn't think I was. But maybe I was fuelled by two glasses of Aperol and my own fury at being dismissed, and when I saw the cleaner emerging from their room I pretended it was my own.

'Don't tell me you went in,' James says. His mouth is hanging open in horror. 'Laila, you didn't?'

'I only meant to be five minutes and I was literally going to find the boys' bedroom and look for the watch. That was all. I thought it would be safe. She was by the pool with Theo, Isaac was on the cliff.'

'You broke into their room.' He is aghast.

'I didn't break in,' I cry. 'The door was open.'

'That's irrelevant, you know what I mean.'

'I know. It was wrong.'

James sighs. 'So what then?'

'I was inside and the boys came back.' I hear him groan but I carry on. 'It was a nightmare, I felt sick. I hid in the wardrobe so they wouldn't see me.'

'What if they'd stuck around and then she came back and found you in there?'

'Don't! It doesn't bear thinking about.' I shudder at the thought. 'Anyway, that didn't happen.'

'Yes, luckily for you. But it might have done.'

'It didn't, James,' I say. 'So can you stop and just let me tell you what did happen.'

He nods for me to continue. I try to read his expression but I don't know what I see. It still doesn't look like anger though and so I go on. 'The boys were in the room next door to me and they started fighting. I could hear every word they were saying.'

I began telling James what I'd heard. How one of them said he was going to tell Mum what the other was doing.

'No you won't,' was spat back with the pompous attitude I could imagine from Theo. Back and forth they went, volleying abuse at each other. One of them threatened to reveal a secret, the other got angrier, which made Isaac laugh.

He was mocking his brother, taunting him and pushing him to the edge. I could hear it in Theo's responses, the thud as one of them was pushed against a wardrobe.

'What would you do? Go on then, tell me, what would you do if I said anything to Mum?'

The response was muffled and I couldn't hear every word, but the anger was unmistakable. There was another shove against the wardrobe, a yell, and then footsteps retreating before the doors were opened and pulled shut so noisily I thought the glass would shatter.

I waited a moment before creeping out and scurrying through another door and hiding between the bushes. That's when I saw him there, Theo, and he was looking right at me.

James is watching me intently.

'Say something,' I beg.

He shakes his head in disbelief and then looks away. I can see the way his mind is working, whirring through what I've told him and what he makes of it. Of me.

'I don't trust him,' I say. 'I'm certain he took my watch. And he knows I was there yesterday and now I've pointed the finger at him . . .' I realise I'm shaking. 'Can you please just tell me I did the right thing in telling the police what I did, because at this moment it doesn't feel like it.'

'You did,' James says. 'Clearly the boy's involved somehow.' He doesn't add any more and eventually he gets up and wanders over to the coffee machine, popping a pod in and waiting for it to churr into action. He makes us both one and I follow him outside. The sun is burning and he moves our chairs into the shade so I can sit down next to him.

'Laila, we do need to talk,' he says.

'Yes.' I nod, 'We do.' I am pleased that he has brought it up and that we can finally address the layers of deceit and decisions that loom ahead. We shouldn't have let things get to where they have.

'We need to talk about what's going on with you,' he says.

'What do you mean, what's going on with me?' I ask, surprised, biting back at him because I don't want him putting this all on to me.

'I'm worried about you,' he says, and I realise I don't like where this is going. This is not the conversation I intended for us to have. James isn't looking at me as he stares straight ahead, his head tipped back so the sun reflects off his glasses. I was right about his sunburn, I think, my attention distracted momentarily by the patches of red on his forehead, a streak along his hairline that is already starting to peel. I focus on it, resisting the urge to rub at the loose skin. I should be asking him what he means again, but I have a sense I know where the conversation is going and if he is going down that road then he may as well just come out with it.

'You knew where her room was, didn't you? You didn't simply fall upon it by accident, which means you've been there before.'

'Only by chance,' I say. 'I haven't been stalking her if that's what you're implying.'

He chews on his lip. It's exactly what he's implying, I realise.

'James, don't even do this,' I say.

'You've become too focused on this woman and her family for some reason. It's unhealthy and—' He breaks off and takes a deep breath. 'I assume it's because she has a family. Is that what this is?'

'Don't, James.'

'Laila, you broke into her room.'

'We've been over this already. I explained how it happened.'

'I know, but the police aren't going to see it like that, are they? It's clear they don't believe your story, and as soon as that boy tells them he saw you it's not going to take long before they come looking for you. They'll twist it, make out you're lying because you want to get back at him. Shit, Laila, we're not going to get rid of them.

'Why did you do it?' he says. 'Why did you get so absorbed in that woman's family?'

'I didn't. *You* are twisting it,' I say, tears of frustration springing into my eyes.

'This holiday was supposed to be about us,' he says, 'and it hasn't been. None of it has. It's like nothing's changed.'

I open my mouth and go to tell him that it isn't my fault the holiday hasn't turned out how it was supposed to when James says, 'Can't you see how this is going to pan out?' He shakes his head. 'We have to get out of here. Some way, we need to get off this island. I can't stand this any more.'

EM

Chapter Seventeen

Confronting that woman is Em's only option now if she is going to get some truths. Rob makes a vague attempt to stop her leaving the villa again. 'You need to let the police do their job,' he says. 'You could make it worse.'

She stares at him for a moment before saying, 'How could anything possibly be worse?' Her son is dead and the police are asking her other son questions that he may or may not be answering truthfully. It could not get any worse and so she will do what she needs to, which is speak to the woman and ask her what she thinks it is that she heard yesterday.

Finding her is the issue, however. She has no idea where she might be staying, so her only hope is that the staff on reception will give out that sort of information. The woman behind the desk shifts about in her chair uneasily when she realises that Em is the mother of the dead boy, but Em stays calm as she describes the woman she's looking for and says she needs to speak to her urgently about her son.

The receptionist flaps about at first, saying she really doesn't know that she can give out guest details. She is only young, not even mid-twenties, Em thinks, which she uses to her advantage. 'She said she could help me,' Em says. Her hand is shaking as she places it on the desk. 'Please. Can you just try. Her first name is something like Lisa. Or Lola.'

The receptionist shakes her head as she pores over her screen. 'I don't have any guest here with those names.' She pauses. 'Could it be Laila?'

'Yes,' Em exclaims. 'Laila.'

'OK.' The receptionist frowns in concentration as she taps on her keyboard. 'Laila Burrow. She's staying in room 23.'

'Thank you. Thank you very much,' Em says as she scoops up a map from the desk and locates room 23 on the other side of the resort.

It doesn't take her long to find the room. Em doesn't hesitate as she knocks loudly. It takes a moment before the door is opened and the husband is standing the other side of it. His face drops when he recognises her, his mouth parts to speak though he is lost for words and so Em says, 'I want to speak to your wife.'

'Right. Er . . .' He looks over his shoulder nervously before he calls out, 'Laila?' He doesn't know what to do with himself, he must know why she is here. 'I'm so sorry to hear what's happened,' he says. 'It's – I can't even imagine.'

'No,' she says bluntly. 'No one could.' She looks over his shoulder to where Laila has appeared, her face mirroring her husband's as she realises Em is waiting at the door for her. 'I want to speak to you.'

'Of course,' Laila says hurriedly. 'Let me come out.' She pushes past her husband and steps out to join Em. 'I'm so sorry about your son. What's happened is tragic. I'm so sorry.'

Em ignores her and says, 'It was you who spoke to the police about my boys, wasn't it?'

'Yes,' she admits.

'What did you tell them?'

'I told them what I overheard yesterday, that's all. They were having an argument. I'm sorry, I really didn't want it to cause you any more pain.'

'What did you hear?' Em doesn't want her pity, she just wants the facts.

'I heard Theo threatening Isaac,' she says.

The sound of her boys' names rolling off the woman's tongue catches her off guard. How does she even know them? She is using their names with such familiarity that it makes her reel.

'That's why I thought I had to say something,' she is saying, trying to justify herself.

'Threatening him how?' Em demands.

'They were talking about telling you something. Theo didn't want you to know about something he'd done but Isaac was going to tell you. Theo got angry with him, but as I told the police I didn't actually hear the threat.'

'That's it?'

'That's what I heard,' Laila says. Her hands are shaking by her sides, Em sees.

She doesn't know what to do with the information. Her head is too full to process it. What has Theo done? But still. Still. Even if she knows that, it does not tell her why her son is dead.

She waits a moment for the woman to add more, but when it appears she isn't going to, Em says, 'What were you doing outside my room?'

'As I told the police,' she says, 'I was just going for a walk.'

'You knew it was my room. I've seen you there before.'

'Maybe—' She brushes the suggestion off quickly. 'I don't know. I didn't register it was your room,' she says.

'I don't believe you,' Em replies.

'I didn't, I don't – I'm sorry,' Laila says, 'I don't know what more I can say.'

Em turns and walks away. She cannot bear to look at Laila any more. Her heart is thumping so loudly it reverberates through her ears. She can't believe she has managed to hold it together during the confrontation because now she feels like she is going to fall apart. As soon as she is out of sight of Laila's room she grabs hold of a wall in an attempt to steady herself as she topples into it. Her whole body is physically shaking.

There is something about Laila that isn't right. Maybe it was her use of the boys' names, but it is also the way she has been so interested in Em's family that unnerves her. For all Em knows she might have made half this stuff up so she could get involved in the case. Either way, she needs to go easy on Theo. She will not push him too hard or she will lose him.

By the time Em gets back to their villa she has almost managed to convince herself the fight meant nothing. It is only what siblings do. They argue and say nasty things they don't mean. What's strange though, is that it's uncharacteristic of Theo to behave this way towards his brother. She has never heard him utter anything vicious towards Isaac. He's never threatened him like Laila suggested.

Em thinks back to the last time they were all together – last night. Isaac had been out by their pool when she had finished getting ready for dinner. She had breezed out with a glass of wine that Rob had poured for her, and sat on the sunlounger next to him. 'Are you really wearing those shorts tonight?' she had said to Isaac. There was a hole above the seam and he had been wearing them in the day, so she'd expected him to get changed.

Isaac's head was buried in his phone as he stretched his leg out and eventually turned his attention to his shorts. He shrugged. 'Do I need to get changed?'

'Well it's the gala evening tonight, everyone's going to be dressed up.'

He turned to look at her. 'You look nice.'

'Thank you.' She smiled at her son; he was always so attentive. She had on a new long, green dress that she hadn't worn before. It draped along the ground and her toenails, especially shellacked for the holiday, poked out beneath it.

'I suppose I should put something else on then.'

'I would.' She nudged him and waited for him to get up and disappear into his room.

He had been quieter than usual, though at the time Em hadn't noticed it, or at least hadn't taken any notice of it. But there'd been a frown on his face as he'd been scrolling through his phone and he'd barely spoken to her when he'd emerged in a different pair of shorts and a shirt.

He did later though. As they walked through the resort. And then at dinner when he sat next to her and diagonally opposite his brother. Theo had been his usual quiet self. Though later on in the evening, not long before the fight erupted rather loudly between the woman and her husband, Theo had said something odd to her.

She remembers it now, the look on Theo's face and his furrowed brow as he'd spoken to her. She tries to recall exactly what he had said. At the time it got overlooked because they'd all been distracted by that woman's husband's raised voice.

It was something to do with Charlie. Something like, 'You would never forgive Dad for what he did, would you?'

The question had come from nowhere and it had taken her aback. She thinks she told him the truth: no, she could never forgive him. She'd intended to add that it didn't mean she wasn't happy now, but she can't remember if she actually said that or not. What she does recall though is the way he was leaning back in his chair as he spoke, his eyes on his brother as he said, 'Thought not.'

The moment passed quickly as they all turned to see what was unfurling behind them and what the husband's yell was about. By then Em was wondering if he had meant to be so loud, because he looked sheepish as he hung his head in his hands. They had both had a lot to drink. Em noticed that much. She had seen at least a couple of bottles of wine being ordered and consumed, and more drinks arriving.

She unlocks the door to their villa and lets herself in. Theo is hovering by the pool. She needs to get to the bottom of whatever happened because as much as she tries to tell herself it is nothing, she cannot believe it. It drives fear through her that Theo might somehow be more involved than he is telling her.

LAILA

Chapter Eighteen

James has been inside our room furiously tapping away on his phone for the last fifteen minutes, searching for a way to leave the island, which appears to be futile as he says, 'I definitely can't get a ferry today, I don't even know when I next can.'

I wonder how long this means we are going to be here for.

'We could hire a private boat,' he says.

'You are joking?' I walk inside, noticing that one of our suitcases has been pulled out from under the bed. There is a pile of James's T-shirts inside it. He is looking at his watch as if we are on some sort of time limit. 'You've started packing?'

'Yes.'

'Don't you . . .' I pause. I don't know what to say to him. I know it sounds odd, but I no longer think I can leave. Seeing Em at our door scared the life out of me, but she didn't know anything more and Theo clearly hasn't said he saw me. All Em wanted was answers about her sons.

I hated to see her grief so raw and painful. It was etched onto her face that I could almost touch it. I played a part in making her hurt more, saying what I had about her boys, and now I wish I could take it back. But it is too late. The damage is already done. Only the thought of us leaving feels like we are running away, and I don't want to do that. It doesn't feel right.

In contrast, James can't get away quickly enough, already packing and prepared to throw money at a private boat to get us off the island.

'Don't you think it's going to look odd anyway if we suddenly go?' I say.

James has tossed his phone aside and is grabbing a pile of his shorts out of the wardrobe. 'Look odd?' he says.

'Suspicious.'

He lets out a laugh. 'Everything about what you've said to the police is suspicious. What must have gone through your head when the mother turned up at our room? It's only a matter of time before they find out you broke into hers.'

'It doesn't mean we run away, James.'

'We aren't running away.'

'That's how it feels. I don't think we should rush anywhere. We should wait and see what happens.'

'Laila!' he exclaims, waving his hands in the air. 'Do you even comprehend the gravity of the situation? The whole resort is a crime scene, what do you think you are actually going to do for the rest of the holiday anyway?'

'I don't know, but we're not paying for a private boat. How much would that cost?'

He looks up at me sharply and follows me to the basin. 'Does that really matter?'

'Yes, it matters.' I frown. 'It'll be hundreds. Or more.'

'Well we can use the money you intended to spend on the clinic. Have you cancelled it yet?'

I shake my head. 'Not yet.'

'But you will?'

'Yes, I'll cancel it,' I mutter.

James seems satisfied as he throws his shorts on top of his T-shirts.

'I don't want to leave,' I say. 'Em knows it was me who told the police about her boys. I feel like I have to stay.'

'*Em*,' he mutters. 'You talk like you know her. Plus, the fact she knows it was you is the reason we have to leave. You act like you think you're actually friends with this woman. I can see why it is you got infatuated with her – they clearly have a good life. He has money and they both have their looks, but we know it's more than that. It's her kids. The fact she has a family. Do you even realise that every night on this holiday all you've done is tell me about them in detail?'

I shake my head, but before I can speak he continues. 'I laughed along with you at first,' he says. 'Because I know that's what you do, you've always liked people-watching, I get that. But this was more than that.'

'It wasn't *more* than anything.'

'This is what worries me. The fact that you don't seem to have any idea what I'm talking about.'

'Don't patronise me, James,' I say, my teeth gritted. I am trying to steady myself but I can hear the wobble in my voice.

'It's the detail you get into, the way you integrate yourself into their life like you're actually a part of it. At first you joked about loads of people around the pool, including that pregnant girl, but then that stopped, and you only had one focus. The mother. Em. You became obsessed with her.'

'I am not obsessed with her.'

'You are.' He sighs. 'This is why I worry. I have done for a while.'

'I think your concern is misplaced,' I say snidely.

'That group you're always on. The fertility website,' he says. 'I've seen your comments.' He reaches for his phone again and I watch him scrolling through his photos until he stops on one. I can tell straight away it is a screenshot of a page on the forum by the distinct pink-and-blue logo at the top.

I can't see the words beneath it though or what post in particular he must have taken an interest in. My mind races through the very many comments I have made over the last two years since I first found the site. There are too many to choose from but it is the only place I have been confident enough to be totally honest about how I feel, and that's because everyone on there understands. We have all felt the same way at one point or another and we don't judge.

I only use my first name on the site and I don't have a picture of my face, just some random shot of the sea I must have taken once, but it wouldn't have been hard for James to find me, and especially not if he was using my phone to look.

'I wasn't checking it.' He gives a half-hearted attempt at an excuse, and not one that even hints at an apology. I would direct my feelings into anger at James's invasion of my privacy if I wasn't so hung up on what he has seen. It was the only safe space for me to air my views though now it feels like anything but.

Eventually he passes me his phone. 'I didn't even know you posted on sites like this,' he says, with what feels like contempt, as my gaze blurs over the screenshot. When it comes into focus I realise it's a post from three years ago.

12th March

12:54 Laila B
Hi
We have just been through our 3rd IVF and it hasn't worked. I don't know how much more I can take of this. I feel like a failure. Like I must have done something really bad in a past life. This morning I went out, having taken the test that was of course negative, and I saw a woman

with her little girl in a pushchair. The child was crying, calling out for her mum who kept telling her to shut up, and saying she was doing her head in. I was this close to going over and telling her she should never have had kids if she didn't want to spend any time with them. It makes me angry seeing mothers like that. It feels so unfair. Why should they have them when I can't?

13:04 Laila B
P.S. I know everyone tells you you should never say that, but it's the way I feel right now.

13:14 Maggie Moo
So sorry Laila B, feel comfort that you're not the only one to be suffering like this. I think we all must feel like this about bad mothers.

13:15 KC1987
I know how you feel. There are too many mothers who don't know how to look after their children.

13:17 Laila B
They should never be allowed them in the first place.

13:33 Stayingpositive
Laila B, try not to focus too much on anyone else right now, you need to stay strong for yourself. Sending healing vibes your way.

13:36 KC1987
Laila B, maybe next time you should say something. I reckon it would be cathartic.

I stop reading and look at James. 'So what? These are normal feelings. You can see how the other people agree with me.'

'There's more.' James scrolls through the screenshots and shows me another.

26th March

16:38 Laila B
On my last post I said I hated the way some mothers treated their children, like the ones who are always on their phones instead of speaking to their kids, or the ones that slap them or swear at them in the middle of the supermarket. But I have a confession to make. Sometimes it's the other ones that annoy me too. The good mothers. The ones who are pushing a buggy with a baby in and a toddler gripping onto the handlebars behind.

I've had a bad day, I can't lie about that. I was in town this morning and a mother came into the coffee shop looking like she had walked out of the hairdressers and her two girls were so beautiful and impeccably behaved, and she might have been genuinely happy and pleasant but I thought she looked so smug. And I couldn't bear this feeling that started rising inside me. It was unstoppable, like a jealousy and rage that this stranger had exactly what I wanted.

I know this makes me sound bitter and crazy but … please someone tell me I'm not alone?!

16:43 Candy

Laila B, you are not alone. We all have feelings of jealousy.

16:55 HG 87

We're all in the same boat. That's what I love about this group, we can all be so honest.

'I didn't mean anything by it,' I protest, but I know how it must look. That I can't control myself. That I'm jealous of every mother I see. But this is not the truth.

'I think you should start packing, Laila.' He takes his phone back and slips it into his pocket. 'I'm going to carry on seeing what hotels I can find and I'll try and get us out of here tonight.'

'James?' I question. 'What exactly do you think I have done?'

He doesn't answer me, but instead he mutters, 'We have to go. I'm doing it for us. For you,' he adds.

'What do you think I'm capable of, James?' I cry.

Chapter Nineteen

I cannot breathe.

I don't start packing as James requests. Instead I walk straight past him and out of the room. He calls me back but I carry on walking and don't stop until I get to the steps by the beach.

I need to get away from my husband. The way he looked at me made me feel like the walls were closing in. Every word an accusation, a stab at what I have been through, the things I have trusted him with in the past in terms of how I have felt and the parts I never did for fear of what he would think of me.

To my left the pool is in the process of being drained. There's a police officer standing next to it and another in it, the water only coming up to his knees.

Nearby they have cordoned off the shrubbery with red-and-white-striped police tape draped around the trees. The loud ex-policeman, Harold, from lunch had been right. That is where the activity is. Even from where I am I can see more officers raking through bushes, checking the ground. They are more interested in the area surrounding the pool than the pool itself.

As one emerges he looks over in my direction and I quickly turn and head down the steps, stumbling on the uneven rocks, though there is a small sense of relief when I feel the sand on my feet, having left the pool and its crime scene behind.

When I reach the sea I have an urge to keep on walking and not stop. Tears sting my eyes and I don't know how my legs carry me because they feel like liquid. Only when I reach the water's edge do I crumble and sink onto the sand, letting the sea lap over me.

I don't want to think about what James is getting at but I cannot stop myself. His eagerness to leave White Sands, as if this is somehow all my fault. Surely he isn't suggesting I had more involvement? Surely he doesn't think I could have had anything to do with Isaac's death?

No. I cannot imagine this, and yet he points out my so-called obsession with Em, his insinuations layered into the screenshots of what I once posted three years ago. The darkest depths of my mind.

If it wasn't enough that my husband ended my dreams by telling me he no longer wants to try for children, now he is throwing me to the wolves too.

How can he not know me?

But then, do we ever know anyone?

Claire told me once we never truly could. I remember the conversation, though I don't recall what started it, probably something trivial, but it had meandered and strayed as they do, and we had found ourselves in the realms of reactions, husbands and how well we know each other.

I had told her then that James and I knew each other inside out. I could trust him with my life I said, and he knew he could me.

'Crap,' she'd replied. 'We don't ever know anyone else one hundred per cent because we don't know ourselves that well.' When I looked at her oddly, she said, 'OK, so let's say Greg has taken Sonny out to the park on his own, I'm not with them. And Greg takes his eyes off Sonny and my boy goes missing.'

'Jesus, Claire,' I had laughed, the thought of her husband doing such a thing.

'No, go with it. How do I react? I mean, Greg is going to be mortified, he'll be beating himself up. I know he's made a mistake that I could have easily made, because let's face it I don't have eyes on Sonny all the time. And remember I told you about that one time he disappeared inside that tunnel and I couldn't find him for nearly ten minutes?' I nod, and she goes on, 'Or do I hands down blame Greg?'

'I don't know,' I say.

'Exactly. That's my point. You don't know how I would react and neither do I. Greg certainly wouldn't, which means we never really know anyone. Not totally.'

Is she right? Is my husband sitting in our room and wondering the same thing? But what about him, I remind myself? I know there is something he is keeping secret from me, and maybe he didn't meet Stephanie yesterday, but something happened, I am sure of it.

'Hey.' A voice pulls me out of my thoughts and I look up to see Rosie standing beside me like a ghost in her short white dress.

'How are you doing?' I ask her.

She shrugs. 'We tried getting another flight home from Crete but there isn't one for three days. Are *you* OK?' she asks, squinting at me.

I nod, wondering if this means we won't be able to get a flight home soon either. 'I'm fine.'

Rosie is wearing an oversized straw hat that keeps flapping in front of her face in the breeze. 'How did it go with the police?'

'OK,' I tell her. No one else needs to know that Lieutenant Kallis came back again. 'You?'

'Same. There wasn't anything I could tell them of course.'

'No,' I agree. I won't admit my own part, but then surely she had something to tell them? She was talking to Isaac only yesterday afternoon, with Theo watching them curiously.

Rosie purses her lips and I know that she wants to tell me more but instead she seems to have a change of heart when she says, 'I feel so sorry for the family. It's scary, isn't it? Not knowing what happened. I mean how do we know that it isn't one of the guests or the staff? That's what Spencer reckons. He thinks it was one of the staff who did it.'

'Why does he think that?'

'Well it has to be someone.'

'True.' I can only imagine the conversations that take place between Rosie and her husband and from what little I have seen of him it doesn't surprise me that he's readily accusing one of the waiters without any evidence. But then this is far better than whatever my own husband is thinking.

We fall into silence, neither of us sure where to take the conversation and so I find myself saying, 'You're pregnant.'

Rosie looks at me in shock. 'How did you know?'

'I can tell. I noticed it before, the way you hold your stomach protectively.' I have been known to do that myself and I have not even been pregnant. But in the days in between IVF and waiting for the test, I have laid in the bath and imagined the baby that might already be growing inside me, my hand protecting what might be in there.

But Rosie doesn't look happy that I have worked it out.

'I'm sorry, I didn't mean – I shouldn't have said anything,' I say.

'No. Don't worry, it's not your fault.' She looks away from me and out to the sea. 'It's very early. Only six weeks.'

'Well congratulations,' I say.

'Don't say anything, please – to anyone else, I mean.'

'Oh, no, of course I won't.'

'Spencer doesn't know,' she says.

'Oh. I see,' I say, though I really don't. How can that not have been the first thing she shared with her husband on their honeymoon? How has he not guessed?

'I mean I only found out right before I came out here and ...' She shrugs and doesn't finish her sentence as if she thinks this is reason enough not to have told her new husband they are having a baby. As if the mere fact of at least seven hours of journey time to Ixos and then five days on an island in a remote and romantic resort have stood in her way.

I can only assume Spencer wouldn't be happy about the news and I feel sorry for Rosie, who looks distressed at the subject. I change it and say, 'You were talking to Isaac yesterday, weren't you?'

At this her head pings up. She looks shocked that I had seen her, or that I have brought it up, and, I think, a little guilty.

'I saw you up there, that's all.' I gesture in the direction at the top of the steps. 'I didn't speak to him myself or anything and so I thought, you know, it must be harder for you having had a conversation with him.' My words come out in a rushed jumble, tumbling over each other without any thought. They were an attempt to make her feel less awkward but I can already see I shouldn't have brought this up either.

'I didn't even know his name until this morning,' she says, 'when the police told me. It wasn't a deep conversation or anything. We chatted for a bit while Spencer was out fishing. There wasn't anything more to it than that.'

'No, God, I wasn't suggesting there was. I meant the fact you actually had a conversation with him, it's like you know him a bit.'

'I don't,' she says quickly. 'I don't know him at all.'

'No. OK. I didn't mean anything by it.'

Rosie sighs. 'I know you didn't. It's just, someone must have told the police I'd spoken to him yesterday because they asked me about it. Was it you?' she says, as if having the sudden thought it might be.

'No. Not at all.'

'I don't know who it was then. I didn't like it. They started questioning Spencer too, like they thought it was really important. But I was literally chatting for like five minutes. Still, I suppose if *you* saw me anyone else might have too.'

'I suppose,' I say, but my mind was somewhere else. 'You said Spencer was fishing? Did he go out on a trip?'

Rosie nods, looking at me questioningly. 'He was with your husband,' she says.

'Oh. No, I don't think so, James went on his own.'

'No. They were definitely together. He said the other guy was called James and then he pointed him out to me last night.'

'But I saw your husband here yesterday,' I say. 'He was at the pool. I talked to him about my missing watch.'

'Yeah, he came back earlier. He got the guy to drop him off.' She screws her eyes up. 'You don't know any of this?' she asks, like it is of some importance.

'No,' I say, thinking of how late James was, and how he told me that the man had taken him out further than he'd expected.

'Right. Only …' Her words fade as she seems to be working out what to say. 'Only it was because of your husband that Spencer came back sooner.'

'What do you mean, did something happen?' I have a fluttering sensation in the pit of my stomach. James must have been telling the truth about Stephanie, but I was right to think there was more to yesterday's fishing trip than he's letting on.

'Apparently your husband wanted to get to this place. This island. Only the guy taking them didn't want to because he said there was a risk of getting grounded, the tides get really low or something. But Spencer says your husband was pretty insistent. To be honest,' she says, 'I wondered whether that was what you'd been arguing about last night.'

'I don't even know anything about it,' I say. 'Why would we be arguing about it though? I don't get it, what does it matter if James wanted to see an island?' Only it clearly did matter. I just couldn't fathom why.

Rosie shrugs. 'All I know is that Spencer said he got angry and frustrated when the boat guy wouldn't take him to this place.'

'Where was it?' I ask her.

'I don't have a clue. Some island, I don't know what it's called.' She looks as confused as I feel. 'Have I said the wrong thing?'

'Not at all.' I smile, a lacklustre one that tries to imply I'm not at all bothered, when really I have been handed a piece of a jigsaw, though one that by no mean fits yet.

I was right to think that James's mood hadn't started when he got back, when he'd taken the call from the clinic in New York. Whatever had happened to change my husband into the monster he was last night had started on the boat.

'I need to go,' I tell Rosie.

I need to confront James. He was pushing the blame onto me last night, inferring our fight was all about the clinic, and then again today, over my supposed obsession with Em, but he is the one lying to *me*. Only I have no idea what about, and whether it's even important. But I have a horrible feeling it could be.

EM

Chapter Twenty

Rob tells Em he needs to speak to someone at reception. 'Are you going to be OK if I go?' he asks. 'I won't be long, I can't get through to them on the phone at the moment.'

'That's fine,' she tells him.

He hovers by her side, not moving.

'It's fine,' she reassures him.

He nods and leans forward, kissing her on the forehead. She doesn't ask what he needs to go for; probably he wants to get away from them for a bit.

Theo is sobbing on his bed, curled up tightly in the shape of a peanut. She can see him through the open door and it reminds her of how he always slept when he was little, so tightly balled up, his thumb stuck in his mouth. Nowadays he takes up most of the bed he is so big, but it is uncanny how much she can keep seeing the young child he used to be.

He has always slept so differently to Isaac, who, in contrast, spread out like a star on the bed, arms and legs splayed, lying on his back like he had no cares in the world, barely moving through the night. Theo on the other hand constantly shuffles and fidgets as if he can never rest. Such simple differences that say everything about her boys.

'Theo?' She goes over to him now. He is in a single bed and so she crouches on the floor next to him and wraps an arm over his body. Only now does she see the other side of his bed and the pile of Isaac's clothes that are strewn into a heap on the floor. On top of them are Isaac's headphones.

'What have you done?' she gasps. She pulls her arm away from Theo and stands up suddenly, walking round to the pile where she sinks down next to them and runs her hand over one of her son's T-shirts. He has had this a year, she bought it for him last summer and it still fitted him. 'Why have you thrown Isaac's clothes down here?'

She lifts up the same T-shirt and holds it to her face, breathing in the scent of Isaac's aftershave as she closes her eyes and rocks her head back. Tears are running down her face in rivers. The pain in her chest is so searingly sharp and deep that she fears it will burn a hole right through her.

'Theo?' she shouts at her son, who is still sobbing on the bed in a ball behind her. 'Why have you done this? Will you please speak to me for once?'

'I can't see them,' he yells.

'What do you mean?'

'I don't want to see his stuff. It's everywhere in the room. His clothes are still hanging in the wardrobe like he's going to walk back in any minute. It's like he's still here,' he cries, his voice rising in pitch.

She looks about her and sees the same aftershave she can smell on his top sitting on the small chest of drawers next to his huge green washbag that he never unpacks. A toothbrush is poking out the top of it, its bristles flattened and splayed in all directions. Hadn't she bought him a new one for the holiday? She always has done so, every time they go away, she's done it since the boys were tiny.

'Then what do we do?' she cries. What the hell *do* they do?

'I don't know. Pack them up? I don't want to see them. I can't bear looking at it all.'

'Pack them up?' She thinks of folding his clothes into a suitcase, taking them home with her. Is that what they will have to do? Of course it is because she cannot leave them here. 'I don't want to pack them up.' She folds her arms around the pile, grabbing as much as she can as she holds it to her chest. Her son has only been gone hours, she isn't going to start hiding his things away as if he never existed. How can she do that?

'You have to,' Theo says. 'I don't want them around me.'

'Then come out of the room.' It's the only possible answer. 'You can stay in my room instead.'

She hears his sobs gradually begin to subside, until they are only a whimper. Only then does she haul herself to her feet and turn back to Theo. His eyes are ringed with bright red circles, they look raw from where he has been crying and rubbing them. His hair is matted in tangled knots that she wants to pull out by running her fingers through it. He hasn't allowed her to do that for years, but she used to sit with him and gently tease them out. Theo has never liked his hair, he always wanted hair like Isaac's that was poker straight like his father's and easy to cut short and keep smart. But she loves Theo's curls.

She is still holding Isaac's clothes but now she puts them down carefully on the other bed – Isaac's bed – and runs her hand across the top of Theo's hair and for once he doesn't flinch. Slowly she presses her fingers into the mess, separating strands that have formed small knots. He closes his eyes as he lets her.

'I need to know what happened last night, Theo,' she pleads with him.

Beneath her hand she feels her son tense, but his eyes remain closed and he doesn't pull away from her.

'Theo? You have to talk me through what happened when you went to bed. I can't bear this not knowing. You must get that.'

She waits for him and eventually he opens his eyes, but he doesn't look at her as he says, 'We had an argument.'

'OK.' She slides down onto the bed beside him, her hand stilling on top of his head. She's too frightened to move it in case he stops talking, but she can feel it shaking now against his scalp, her fear of what he might tell her. So they had *another* fight, she thinks, trying to keep her breaths even. They argued again last night, only she never heard them. 'OK,' she repeats, her head nodding frantically. Her chest constricts and makes it a struggle to breathe at all.

She doesn't like the way all this new information keeps rearing its head. It makes her wonder what's coming next. 'What was the fight about?' she asks.

Theo shakes his head. He isn't going to tell her still. What does she need to do to get through to him?

'I'm your mum, Theo,' she says. 'If there is anyone you can tell, it's me. There's only you and me here now. We're on our own so you can tell me anything. You must know that.'

'What about Rob?'

'He's gone out.' She shrugs. 'He had to do something. It doesn't matter where Rob is, just that it's only us.'

'I can't tell you, Mum,' he says, his words coming out in a choke. 'Please, can you stop asking me what it was about. Besides, it doesn't matter. It isn't important.'

'Everything is important, Theo,' she cries. 'How do you not understand that?'

'Mum! Stop!' He pulls away, catching her hand in his hair.

'OK!' she says, prising it out. 'Tell me what happened next then, after you argued.'

Theo fidgets, shuffling nervously. 'Isaac said he was going out.'

Her breath is ragged as she inhales deeply. 'He told you he was going out?' she repeats, trying to remain calm, but it's becoming increasingly difficult when Theo keeps adding layers to his story.

So he did know his brother had left the room again last night. She had been right about that. But if Theo lied to her on that occasion, what else has he lied about?

'So he went,' Theo goes on.

'What time was this?'

'I don't know. Midnight. Just after.'

Em thinks back. It was hardly any time after she and Rob had gone to bed. The boys were shuffling around in the bedroom for a bit, but she must have crashed out quickly. 'So, you were only in the room for about half an hour before he went out?' She is trying to fathom how she could have slept through her boys' argument. How she didn't hear Isaac opening the door, and how Rob hadn't either.

Theo shrugs. 'I suppose.'

'How could you have argued without me hearing?' she says. 'I don't get it.'

'We were outside.'

'Outside? So you went out too?'

'I followed him out.'

'So you were out on the decking?'

'Yes.'

'Why? Why did you both go outside?'

'Because he wasn't listening to me,' Theo says.

'About what?'

'It doesn't matter.'

'Oh my God, it does matter,' she says. It mattered enough that Theo followed his brother outside to continue the argument.

Now that woman's words come into her head. She had said they'd been arguing about something Theo had done, and if he doesn't want to tell her then she has no idea how she is going to get it out of him. He must have been convinced Isaac would tell her, scared enough to follow his brother outside at midnight.

Theo is tensing beneath her touch again and so, for now, she slightly changes tack and asks, as calmly as she can, 'What happened next?'

'He went off. I asked him where he was going but he wouldn't tell me—' Theo breaks off sharply.

Em balls her hands together in her lap. 'What did you do?' she asks. This is when Theo needs to tell her that he came back into the room and he didn't see Isaac again. Only she can tell from the look in her son's eyes that this isn't what she's about to hear.

'I waited around for a bit, then I followed him.'

'Oh my God, Theo. No, you didn't, please. Why did you tell the police you didn't leave the room? You lied to them,' she tells him, while all the time she is thinking, *Where did you go? What did you see?*

'So what happened?' she says.

'Nothing. Nothing happened. I just found him, wandering around the pool.'

Em closes her eyes. She feels the walls closing in on her. Theo was there last night, at the pool, only he has lied to them all. But sooner or later the police will know. Piece by piece they will break apart Theo's lies, like she has been able to so easily.

Theo is shuffling beside her, pushing himself to sit up, scooping his knees into his chest as he cradles them. When she opens her eyes and looks at him she feels like she doesn't know the child sitting next to her. 'Tell me what happened,' she says.

'I don't know what happened. We carried on arguing. I don't know. Isaac was really angry and it got out of hand.'

'In what way, Theo? In what way did it get out of hand?'

'I hit him. I just hit him. But I didn't kill him. Mum,' he says, reaching out and holding onto her arm. 'I didn't. I didn't do that, so you have to believe me.'

She cannot take in what her son is telling her. All these extra strands to his story that had been so vague and brief only earlier. Theo has gone from telling her he knew nothing to admitting he not only followed Isaac to the pool and stood in the place where his body was found, but also that they'd had another argument that he won't tell her about. That he hit him.

Was that the wound that the police had found? On the back of his head?

'How do you mean you hit him, Theo? What exactly happened?'

'He was shoving me and I shoved him back, that was all. It wasn't even hard, Mum.'

Her hands are shaking against her leg. She is fighting the urge not to vomit. They will know. It will not be long before Lieutenant Kallis and his team are able to place Theo there, surely. The forensics will find something and they will know he is lying.

As far as Em knows, Theo was the last person to see Isaac alive, and now he is admitting that not only was he at the pool, but that he was angry enough to have hit his brother. She cannot contemplate the gravity of what he's done or what more he might have done that he's not told her yet.

'Was it an accident?' she asks him. The words are out of her mouth before she can stop them, but they both know what she is implying. Did he kill his brother by accident?

Theo looks at her in horror. 'What?'

'I . . .' She shakes her head. She doesn't want to repeat the question. Asking him once was bad enough.

'If *you* don't believe me then no one's going to,' Theo shouts, uncurling himself, getting up, leaping off the bed. 'You said I could tell you anything.'

'I know I did.'

'But you think I killed him?'

'No, I don't think that,' she says.

'Yes you do. You asked if it was an accident, like you think I killed him.'

Well did you? The question is still there at the forefront of her mind.

'I just want to know what happened to my boy,' she pleads.

'I didn't do anything,' he yells. 'I didn't kill him. I've told you that and it's the truth. I promise you. I hit him but I didn't kill him.' He storms out of his bedroom and into hers. She hears the sound of the glass doors opening and slamming shut behind him.

Em clutches a hand against her chest. She tries to steady it and stay calm. She has to believe Theo. She has to believe he would not have done anything to hurt his brother. She knows that. She does.

Also, she reasons, why is he telling her all this if he has something to hide? If – God forbid, because she cannot even go there – if Theo was the one responsible for killing Isaac, then why is he telling her that he was there with him?

No, he would not have done that. He would have kept up his story that he didn't know anything, that he didn't even know when Isaac left the room. But he has told her this because she said he could talk to her, and now she has lost him again.

Only, once they know this, the police will have more evidence against her boy. There will be more reasons to suspect that Theo was responsible, and they don't know him like she does. All they want is to find Isaac's killer.

Em wants that too, of course. She wants that more than anything. But what if . . . ?

No, she will not go there. She will not allow herself to even question that Theo could have killed him. She saw the way he was just now. He was telling her the truth.

She gets up herself and walks through to her room. Theo is sitting on the lounger outside, punching his fist into the fabric of its cushion.

'I do believe you,' she says as she opens the door and joins him. She won't contemplate whether or not they are simply words. Right now he needs to hear her say them. 'I believe that's what happened.'

'No one else is going to,' he says as he stops punching. When he turns back to her his eyes are wide and wet with tears. 'I'm scared.'

'Oh, baby,' she says and rushes over to him, wrapping her arms around him.

'I'm scared, Mum,' he sobs into her.

'I know,' she whispers. 'I am too. But nothing is going to happen to you. I promise.'

Chapter Twenty-One

Every time siblings fight it is hard to know whose side to take. Em has seen it with her friends all the time. Often the older one will get the blame by virtue of the fact they should know better. She's always felt guilty when that happened, but then she feels guilty about most things when it comes to her boys. That pervasive feeling of never doing enough, or doing the right thing.

When they were little, Isaac would tell her she was always siding with Theo, especially when she would tell Isaac he needed to share the toy he had been happily playing with because his younger brother wanted to join in. 'It's not fair, Mum, Theo will ruin my game.'

Maybe she should have taken a step back and told Theo to find something else to do but he had always wanted to play with Isaac when they were young and she never had the heart to tell him his older brother didn't want the same.

And so she would insist that Isaac share his precious toys and more so his time, and Isaac, being the boy he was, reluctantly did what was asked of him, even if he wasn't happy about it. He told her it wasn't fair while all she was ever doing was striving to be fair.

Sometimes parents sided with their quieter child or the one who's less likely to stand up for themselves. Theo fell into both of those camps too. She relied on the fact Isaac spoke out if he wasn't happy. If her oldest felt wronged he would say and then they would talk about it.

This would happen when she heard screaming coming from upstairs and she would call out, 'What's happened now?' It was only ever a bump or a bruise between the boys or something might have got broken, but Isaac would readily tell her his side of the story while Theo rarely did. It annoyed her. She admits that. It frustrated her she couldn't ever get both sides out of her boys and she had to prise a few words out of Theo.

Now she realises how petty those squabbles are. Now, when she is tearing herself apart, not knowing what to do, because standing by Theo like she so desperately wants to means she isn't getting the truth for Isaac.

She had pressed Theo further about what happened last night, but he remained resolute that their argument was nothing more than that. He told her Isaac was OK when he left him to come back to the room. He was still alive. Theo has promised her this, assured her it is the truth. She could see the fear in his eyes, but of course he was afraid, his brother was dead and everyone was pointing the finger at him.

But what if Theo is still the key to knowing what happened? He has already lied to her once, does this mean he might start drip-feeding her more and more details when he feels like it?

Her phone rings out sharply at the same time as Rob appears. She glances at her husband and then at the phone screen: Charlie.

'All OK?' Rob says.

The phone rings out and eventually stops. 'Theo wants to pack up Isaac's things,' Em tells him. 'He'd tossed them in a pile on the floor. He wants me to put them in a suitcase.'

'Oh God.'

'I can't do that.'

'No well … I can, if you want. I can do anything you don't want to do.'

'I told him he could sleep in our room,' she says.

'Of course. That's fine. Of course he doesn't want to sleep in there.' Rob wanders over to the open door. 'I can sleep in their room tonight. What do you want me to do with Isaac's clothes? Shall I put them back in a drawer for now?'

'I don't know.'

'OK, don't worry. I can sort it. Did he say anything?' Rob asks. 'Did Theo tell you any more?'

Em looks back at her son. *Yes,* she thinks, *he told me plenty.* She shakes her head. She doesn't know why but right now she cannot bring herself to tell her husband what Theo has said. Probably it is because Rob will say they must go straight to the police. Maybe she feels she could not protect her child if that happens, and she needs more time to process it. Either way, she does not confide in him, and now this secret will start to eat away at her if she doesn't share it with someone.

Em calls Charlie back and wanders out to the path, where she can see Rob and Theo on the decking, but where they won't be able to hear her.

'Theo's told me something else,' she says as her ex picks up the call. 'He knew Isaac left the room last night. He says he followed him. He went after him and found him by the pool.'

'Shit,' Charlie mutters.

'He says they were arguing and that he hit Isaac.'

'Oh God, no, he didn't.' She can hear the fear in his voice.

'He won't tell me any more than that, I still don't know what they argued about, but it has to be pretty major, doesn't it? Surely he would tell me otherwise.'

'Do you have any idea?' Charlie asks.

'Only that it's about something Theo has done that he doesn't want me knowing about. Some woman overheard them yesterday. I think him saying it was about you was some cover-up. I need to give him time to open up to me, don't I,' she says.

'I guess. If you think he will.'

'Well he's started to. But what I mean is, I can't tell anyone what he's said, can I?'

'I don't know. God. I don't know, Em.'

'But what if someone saw him?'

'Saw him?' he cries. 'Em, the more you say, the more guilty it makes him sound.'

'I know,' she hisses, trying to keep her voice down through the will to shout. 'And I want to protect him because he's so scared, Charlie. He's like a child. He's been begging me to believe him, but—'

'But what?' he says, when she stops abruptly.

'I don't know. If it was anyone else – I mean, I realise how awful this is going to sound – but if it was anyone else who had been found and we thought one of our boys had something to do with it, we'd stand by them, wouldn't we? We'd do whatever we could for Theo.' Em knows how hideous her suggestion is. That if they feared their son might have harmed someone else's child, then surely they would protect Theo? She would go to the ends of the earth for him. She doesn't, of course, know what she would actually do if that was the situation, but the fact is it isn't anyone else's child. It isn't a stranger, it is her other son they are talking about. 'But if he hurt Isaac . . .' Her words trail off before she gathers them together again: 'I don't think I could ever forgive him.'

'You're running away with yourself,' he says. 'He says he hit him. Nothing more.'

'Yes. And I don't know, he seemed really adamant there was nothing more to it, but then he would, wouldn't he? If he'd done anything ...'

'But he didn't even need to tell you that,' Charlie points out.

'No. I've thought that too. He wouldn't have told me anything, would he? There was no need for him to say anything about hitting him. That's what I thought.'

'I want to see him,' Charlie says. He is stronger now, his voice has a hardened tone to it. 'I want to be there so I can see him for myself.'

'I can't do this on my own,' Em cries. She isn't on her own, but at the same time it feels like she is because she can't trust Rob with what she knows.

If she does, he will undoubtedly want her to tell the police. She couldn't even ask him for some time first; she knows he will say they need to tell them what Theo has told her. He is so unbearably righteous at times. She can even hear his words, saying that they have to be open with Lieutenant Kallis because it would enable them to rule Theo out. Rob would undoubtedly make out he believed Theo, that he was doing the right thing to protect him too.

But Em knows that's not all he'd be thinking. Deep down he would have his suspicions. How could he not when she does? And right now she cannot bear for anyone else to think her son capable of murdering his brother. It is awful enough that she is even contemplating it.

'I'll be there tomorrow,' Charlie says. 'As soon as I can. Em, just hold on, yeah?'

'OK.'

'I love you, babe,' he adds casually, the way he always used to speak to her, and she crumples to the ground on the path and stays there until Rob notices her and walks over to pick her up and take her back to their room.

It is the kind of thing you read about in the cheap magazines her mum used to buy, the real-life stories of families torn apart by rival siblings. They seemed so estranged from her own life that she couldn't recognise them, and yet now it is happening to her. On top of that she cannot even confide in her husband. This tragedy has hit her family and is ripping them apart even further.

Em paces the room that is becoming smaller as the hours pass, the walls closing in until she fears they will box her in completely.

It is not Theo, she tells herself. Someone else is responsible for what happened to Isaac and all the while she is trying to get Theo to speak, they are getting away with it. One of the other guests or staff in this hotel has killed her baby and they are trying to frame her other one.

And with this thought a surge of rage rises through her. More than nine hours have passed since Isaac was found and a killer is still walking among them. Maybe even watching them.

Did they single Isaac out? Might they be capable of doing it again?

Em knows there is only one way to stop the finger being pointed at Theo and that is to find out who killed Isaac. Now, with a renewed sense of purpose, she will not stop until she has found out the truth.

LAILA

Chapter Twenty-Two

'There are no ferries to Crete until Saturday.' James looks frustrated as he paces the room, kicking his case out of the way until it is half tucked under the bed. 'So we're stuck here for another two nights.'

I no longer know how I feel about this. One minute I'm desperate to leave, the next it feels wrong to run away, but the prospect of being here until Saturday sends a shudder rippling through me. I can't even imagine what the next forty-eight hours has in store for James and me, our relationship having taken such a severe turn for the worst in the last two days. With guests unable to sit around the pool, does that mean another day enclosed in our rooms along with everyone else? 'There's nothing at all tomorrow?' I ask.

My stomach feels like a leaden weight as I watch James's irritation. 'No. Do you want a drink?' he asks as he opens the fridge door and bends down to check its contents. It has been restocked. They must have come while we were at lunch because there are miniature bottles of wine and spirits where they were none this morning.

It's a heavy prospect, the idea of being cooped up with my husband in this room together. There are questions I want to ask him, but I am not sure I want the answers. *Where were you so keen to get to on Wednesday, James? Do you honestly think I'm capable of more than I'm telling you? How many lies are there between us?*

Only six weeks ago our lives had been so different. We were burdened with disappointment and loss of the one thing we never had in the first place. I wasn't happy, I see that now, even if I had briefly come out of that time with a renewed hope for our future together. I hadn't thought for one minute that our marriage was based on layers of deceit and secrets. That along the way we had lost each other too. Now, not only do I have no idea if we have any chance of getting it back, I don't think I want to.

'I don't want a drink, thanks,' I say. I can't imagine drinking alcohol again after last night. I am surprised I don't feel worse than I do, but there is the faint constant niggle of a headache in my temples and the idea of more alcohol is nauseating.

I watch James pulling out a bottle of amber liquid that looks like whisky and studying the label. Then he takes a

Coke from the top shelf and pours them both into a glass. He tips it into his mouth, a large gulp. I can see the relief in his face as he swallows it. This, another issue we need to address, is James's drinking. It is hard to know where to start any longer.

'What shall we do?' he says as he bends down and picks out another miniature bottle from the fridge and tips it into his glass, pouring the rest of the can of Coke on top. I'm expecting him to pour this down his neck too, but instead he takes it to the bed with him, where he sits down and cradles the glass in his hands. 'I don't see what options we have but we could get reception to call us a cab and get out of the resort for the rest of the day. Maybe we could find a restaurant, somewhere away from here. What do you think?'

I nod in agreement. While I don't relish the idea of an evening out with James, it's clear we both need to get away from White Sands.

'OK, great.' He checks his watch as he puts the glass down on the bedside table. 'We might as well go now.'

'Give me five minutes to get changed,' I say, and take myself round to the bathroom, where I splay my hands against the basin. I know that if I don't say anything, James won't either. We could easily drive away from the hotel and spend an evening talking about everything else and nothing that is important. We could possibly get through the next two days without addressing a single issue that is threatening our marriage, brushing everything under the carpet like I imagine my husband would be happy to do.

Like I now see I have been doing over the last few years, pretending our problems don't exist.

Only they do exist, and I can no longer pretend otherwise. We can leave White Sands behind us, just for a few hours, but we need to face up to everything this place somehow brought to the surface.

We wait in reception for fifteen minutes for a taxi to be called and to arrive outside. Walking through the revolving doors is like a step into freedom, and now I wish we were doing it for good. We sit in the back and James asks the driver to take us to a small cove ten miles away, where there is apparently a restaurant by the beach that the locals enjoy. He chats to the driver, who spends longer looking at us in his rear-view mirror than the road ahead of him. They talk about football teams and where we come from in England and James gives him the usual patter, 'a small town on the south coast. Yes, it's by the sea, but we don't have the weather they have in Greece. It's probably raining back at home right now.'

While he chats, I look out of my window and watch the scenery speeding past. The sense of freedom that comes from being away from the resort is only fleeting, and the idea of our conversation ahead sits heavily.

James surprises me by reaching for my hand and while I allow him to take hold of it, I want to withdraw it. I don't feel any closeness to my husband right now, I don't want him to have some misconception that everything is all right between us. He must surely know it isn't, but it's like he's willing to forget and move on.

It's such an odd gesture that I wonder what is going through his head. Is he merely buoyed up by his double whisky, or has he decided he's got nothing more to say? He's made it clear we will not be going to New York or anywhere else for treatment, an announcement that felt like punishment for going behind his back. He's delivered his accusation that I obsess over other women, and all the while he's kept quiet about whatever jaunt he had planned for the fishing trip, thinking he's got away with it.

Does he think we have no choice but to stay in White Sands and so we might as well make the most of it? *Is that it, James?*

The taxi driver turns off the main road, down a windy lane until he reaches the end and drops us outside a restaurant with whitewashed walls, stuck on the corner of a road that attaches itself to a beach. There are few people around, even on the sand, and only one couple sitting in the restaurant. 'This will do, yes?' he says as I retrieve my hand and James shuffles in his pocket for euros that he gives to the driver, telling him to keep the change. He passes us a business card and says that when we want to go back we can call him and he will pick us up.

'This place is a bit odd,' James says as we step out. 'It's practically deserted.'

I murmur an agreement as I look around me. It is completely off the beaten track, but this also makes it quite beautiful. The restaurant is circular and open almost all the way around, its tables and chairs stuck haphazardly and seemingly wherever the last customer wanted them. Each table is covered with a blue-and-white-checked tablecloth and its wooden chairs don't look at all comfortable, but it's by far the most authentic place I have seen since we have been here.

'What shall we do, is it too early to eat?' James asks.

It is not yet 5 p.m. but I am unsurprisingly hungry, having skipped breakfast and barely picked at my salad at lunchtime. A couple of chalk boards are positioned outside and while one is in Greek they have attempted to write some dishes in English.

'Maybe we could grab some mezze?' I suggest. No one is rushing over to pull us in, they seem completely laid-back about our presence. So we wander in and are told we can choose a table wherever we like. Opting for one with the best view of the sea, James orders a bottle of wine and I ask for some water. When the wine arrives I let him pour me a glass but I hardly touch it.

He relaxes back into his wooden chair and starts to talk about some guy he vaguely knows who has bought a house in Cyprus, and after a while I cut him short and say, 'James, we clearly need to talk.'

He parts his lips and it looks as if he is going to ask what about, but in the end he evidently thinks better of keeping up the pretence.

'I don't know what you think I might have done,' I say. 'But you were insinuating something when you suggested we needed to leave.'

James shakes his head and leans across the table, dropping his voice as he says, 'I wasn't insinuating anything. But you did let yourself into their villa, Laila. And you have been following them around.'

'I haven't been following them!' I cry. 'You make it sound sordid. I was people-watching, that's all. It's what you do on holiday.'

'It got out of hand.'

I turn away, tears pricking my eyes. 'I made a wrong decision, but it didn't get out of hand.'

'Laila, don't cry.' He glances quickly around him and then reaches for my hand again, but this time I pull away.

'What about you though, James?' I say. 'What have you not been telling me?'

He pulls back, frowning.

'I spoke to someone on the beach earlier. She told me you went fishing with her husband yesterday.'

He still doesn't say anything.

'I thought you went on your own?'

He shrugs. 'I thought I was going alone but then he booked on too.' He has that look as if he is trying to make out it is no big deal but at the same time is wondering what else I know.

'She told me you wanted to go to some island in particular, but the guy taking you didn't want to go.'

I wait for an answer but he sits staring at his glass in silence. 'James?' I say.

'It was nothing.'

'It doesn't sound like nothing. Not when her husband asked to be brought back because of it. He says you were pretty insistent. Where was it?'

'Just some place I'd heard of, that's all.'

'Don't lie to me, James. I know when you're lying.'

'I'm not, I ...' He hesitates and waves the hand that's gripping onto his wine glass in the air before taking a huge gulp. 'It was somewhere I had been before,' he admits. 'But I didn't say anything to you because I didn't want you getting the wrong idea.'

'What kind of idea could I get?' I ask. 'You beg some guy to take you to an island that I'm assuming you've been to with your ex-girlfriend, and even though you're told there's a chance you could get stranded there, you still insist he takes you? You were in a foul mood with me when you came back. I want to know why.'

'You know why. It was because of the clinic.'

'No, I don't believe it was. You were acting odd even before you answered that call.'

James sighs. 'Going there brought back memories. I should never have gone.'

'Then why did you?'

He places his glass down on the table, a little too heavily, and pushes it away. His jaw is set hard and he can't look at me as he works through whatever he's about to say.

'The truth, James,' I prompt.

'It was a place Stephanie and I went to,' he says eventually. 'That's all. The last place we went before I came back to England. It was so near to Ixos, and when I was out on the fishing boat I just . . .' He hesitates. 'I got it into my head that I wanted to go and see it again. There's nothing more to it.'

Nothing more to it? I have known James over ten years. It's hard to reconcile those early happy days of love and eyes for only each other with the couple who are sitting in this restaurant tonight, keeping secrets that threaten to tear them apart.

Our past and present selves are such very different images. Maybe this is true for many marriages, even if not to the same degree. Couples who reach the point of divorce must look back and wonder where their journey went so wrong.

For us it's unclear whether there was a single defining moment or if we meandered slowly off course. Either way, we've reached a place where we don't recognise ourselves any longer.

Maybe for my part I have been blind to the changes along the way, the little cracks in the road that have led us down different paths. I have been so intent on one track forward that I have forgotten to pay attention to me and James. I never stopped to ask him how he has coped with what we have been through, not focused on him in the same way that he has me.

But he cannot tell me there is nothing more to it. Not when he must have been thinking of the past more lately, maybe with regret. Is it my fault? Have I driven him away? I am certainly not blameless in this.

Now our holiday is soiled by a fight we may never come back from and a death that is inviting us to point fingers and question the person we should trust more than anyone. I know that there is more to the story, it is not *all,* as he hastens to tell me it is.

If I am really honest, something wasn't right before James came home to tell me he couldn't go through any more rounds of IVF. Don't they always say that women have an intuition for these things? But I chose to ignore it because mostly they were only small signs, like the frown lines pressed into his forehead, the nights coming home a little later, the nervous start if I walked into a room when he wasn't expecting me, as if I'd caught him out, and of course his drinking.

Only now we are here, neither of us knowing what the other has the potential for and what we are holding back from each other, and I fear we have gone too far.

'Are you still in love with Stephanie?' I ask him outright. I want to add that it is OK if he tells me he is, because in some ways it would be. I just want the truth now.

'No.' He shakes his head adamantly. 'No, Laila. God, no. I'm not.'

'I don't believe you,' I say. 'I don't believe you could suddenly get the urge to visit some island that you went to with her if she means nothing to you. You brought me out here on a holiday that's supposed to be about us reconnecting, but then you spent a day away from me on a "fishing" trip, begging a guy to take you to an island you went to with Stephanie?' I laugh, incredulous that he could expect me to be satisfied with the explanation he's offered. I grab my bag from beside my feet. 'I'm going to the toilet, and when I come back I want the truth. All of it,' I say.

A kindly old man who is sitting in an armchair points me towards the toilets and I take myself into a cubicle, locking the door and reaching inside my bag for my phone. It is just to check my messages, I'm not looking for anything in particular, only my hand brushes against something else. I can feel it, lumpy, inside a small inner pocket of my bag that I don't even remember being there, and that I certainly don't remember using.

The last time I used this bag was on Sunday. The day my watch disappeared. Since then I'd been loath to take much to the pool, only now, as I hurriedly unzip the pocket, I know what I am going to find.

'Shit,' I mutter, tipping my head back to the ceiling, closing my eyes as my fingers curl around my watch. I had been wrong, so bloody wrong about Theo. And if I was wrong about him taking my watch, what else have I been mistaken about?

EM

Chapter Twenty-Three

Day Seven – Friday

By 11 o'clock the following morning Charlie has arrived at the resort. The hotel has arranged for him to have a private boat transfer from Crete. Em meets him in reception. Her breath catches with the anticipation of seeing him climbing out of the taxi, the dread that it will open up a whole new raft of grief. Rob is right behind her, a support, but still she isn't prepared for Charlie walking through the revolving doors in a jacket that doesn't reach the wrists of his long arms and cargo shorts that have seen better days. He looks out of place. So confident but so fragile.

He drops his bags and she runs over to him, falling into his arms as she sobs into his chest, feeling it heaving against her. He is built so differently from Rob. Whereas Rob is slim, her ex is broad and built like a tank. It feels strangely normal to be held in his arms again when she hasn't been in so many years.

Em is glad he is here and she doesn't want to let him go, because in that moment she feels better. She knows it's a feeling that won't last more than a matter of seconds, but for that short moment, with Charlie's thick arms holding her, Em lets everything drain out of her.

When Rob wanders over it is Charlie who finally pulls away and shakes hands with him. 'Where's Theo?' he asks.

'I don't know where he is,' Em admits. 'He'd left the villa before we came to meet you.'

'Didn't he know I was coming?'

'Yes of course. But—' She breaks off and shrugs. 'You know what he's like. Come on, let's go back to our room, he might be there by now.'

But Theo isn't in the villa when they reach it and so Rob suggests he'll go and look for him. 'I'll see where he's got to,' he offers. He is already slipping back into the flip-flops he'd only moments ago taken off.

'Thank you,' Em replies and watches as her husband leaves. The three of them haven't ever needed to occupy the same space for more than a minute or two in the past, Em has always found ways to avoid it whenever she can. There have been times when Charlie has come to their house to pick up the boys and Rob has answered and both men keep it polite. There is, in fact, a surprising lack of hostility between them. Aside from Charlie's jealousy of

Rob's money, he has taken to the new man coming into her life reasonably well.

Not that he has any grounds to be put out when he's had a string of girlfriends coming and going since Mel, but deep down she knows Charlie would take her back. He has told her this a few times over the years since they split up, the last being the week before she married Rob, when she had said to him, 'I can't ever come back to you, Charlie, not when I don't trust you.'

'You *can* trust me, Em,' he'd said, with as much conviction as he was capable of. She wasn't sure how much Charlie believed his own words, whether he actually thought he was wholly able to remain faithful or if he likely knew it would happen again.

What neither of them had addressed was that, although Em had said she *couldn't* go back to him, she'd omitted to add whether or not she wanted to. It isn't that she doesn't love Rob, because she does, very much so. She has found a good man, one of the best, but Charlie ... well, there is something about their connection she will never find with anyone else. Em has simply had to learn she needs to let it go.

Charlie looks around the room with raised eyebrows. 'You've got your own pool,' he points out.

'I know,' she says bluntly. 'We can sit out there, if you like.'

He follows her through to the back and she removes a towel so that he can sit down. 'Very nice,' he comments, running a finger along the chair that sits on the decking.

Em knows what he's thinking, that it must have set Rob back a bit, but she ignores him.

'I want to see the place where they found him,' he says.

'OK.'

'Will you come?'

'I don't think I can,' she admits. 'I haven't been able to look at it— I can't bear the thought of seeing it.' She had avoided that route the two times she'd left the room. 'They've drained the pool,' she adds. 'They told me they were doing it yesterday but that they didn't expect it to help them. They said the water washes away any evidence, and anyway they don't think that was where Isaac was ... Where he ...'

She starts crying again and Charlie gets up and joins her on the two-seater that's already edging into the shade. He wraps his arm around her again and pulls her into him as she sobs against his chest once more.

'I can't believe it,' Charlie says. His words are full of his own tears and they come out shaking as his body convulses against hers. 'Not my boy.'

Suddenly he is hauling himself off the seat, pacing over to the pool. 'I want to see him. Can I see his body?'

Em goes to nod as Charlie suddenly falls to his knees. 'OK.'

'Oh God, Isaac,' he howls. He is balancing precariously by the water.

She has never seen Charlie cry. Even when his own mother died, who Charlie has always been close to, the tears never came. But to see this man a physical wreck as he rocks back and forth on his heels, breaks her even harder.

She goes to him, sinking onto her own knees as she wraps herself around him. 'I don't want to never see my boy again,' he says.

The pain slices through her raw, open wounds. She doesn't know how they can get through this. Perhaps they never will. How can you?

Em doesn't know how much time passes but eventually the tears dry up. 'How's Theo doing?' Charlie asks gently.

'He slept in my bed last night. He hasn't said anything more since he told me he followed Isaac out. He won't tell me what they were arguing about. It doesn't make any sense,' she says.

'Do you think he's protecting Isaac?' Charlie suggests.

'From what?'

'I'm not sure. Could he be, though?'

She mulls over the idea. 'I can't imagine Isaac confiding in Theo.'

'Theo could have found out something?'

'The police have Isaac's phone,' she says. 'So they'd tell us if there was anything on there, wouldn't they? They came for Theo's yesterday too.'

They are silent for a moment until Charlie says, quietly, almost to no one, 'What's he done?'

'Why do you say that?' Em snaps, pulling away from him. 'You were the one who told me yesterday there was no way he could have anything to do with it. Don't start making out you think he could have.'

'I don't think he killed his brother,' Charlie says. 'It's impossible. He wouldn't have intentionally hurt him, but ...' He trails off.

Em doesn't respond, because she will not go there. She no longer wants to contemplate the thought that Theo could in any way be responsible. No. Someone else on this island is.

Last night she barely slept, even though she'd taken another one of the pills Rob gave her. Whenever she did, her dreams were filled with her boys and she'd haul herself out of the nightmares, drenched in sweat.

She can understand that other people might blame Theo, but not herself and not Charlie. They know their son well enough, and while everyone else might start pointing the finger at him, they know he couldn't have done it.

But it doesn't help that Lieutenant Kallis is drawing conclusions about her son, or the fact that, as far as they know, Theo was the last person to see Isaac alive. She can only imagine what conclusions Kallis will draw if he finds out what Theo has told her, and so she has to go on protecting the boy she has been protecting his whole life.

It's one of the reasons she still hasn't confided in Rob. She cannot expect him to stand by Theo stoically as she will, because he doesn't know him like she does. He wasn't there when Theo was six years old and would care for the school hamster like his life depended on it. Neither did he know the eleven-year-old would sit by her bed after Charlie had left her, wrapping his arms around her, whispering into her ear that she would be OK, because she still had him. No one else knows for certain her son is incapable of murder so it won't stop them accusing him.

Finally Em sees Rob appear over the hedge, on the path with Theo in tow. Charlie gets up and walks around the pool. 'Hello, son,' he says when they reach the villa.

When Theo doesn't answer, Em prompts him. 'Theo? Aren't you going to say hello to your dad?'

Her son's eyes flick between her and Charlie, and then he turns and walks back along the path and disappears.

'What the hell is that all about?' she says. She is looking to Rob, but he is as surprised as she is.

'I don't know. He was fine when I found him.'

Now she turns to Charlie, but he just shrugs, his face full of hurt as he stares at the space where Theo had stood. She runs around the pool and onto the path and is about to yell out to Theo in the distance when she spots Lieutenant Kallis already speaking to him. The detective looks over Theo's shoulder, nods in her direction and eventually walks over to her.

'Good morning, Mrs Cross. I am sorry to disturb you, but we need to take your son with us for some more questioning.'

'No!' she says. 'No. I don't want you doing that. Why do you want to speak to him now?' She looks at Theo, who is standing at the side of the path, his head hung low so that she cannot see his face, but she notices his hands tapping against his legs. Theo is scared.

'I don't want you asking any more questions. He's been through enough already. I won't have you doing it.' Charlie and Rob are already at her side.

'We want to know what happened to Isaac. That means we need to do this, Mrs Cross.'

'*I* want to know what happened to my son,' she cries, slapping a hand against her chest. 'But questioning my other one is not the answer.'

'I think it is, actually,' he says. 'I think Theo knows a lot more than he is telling us.' He throws a look at Theo, who in turn stiffens beneath her arm. 'We will not take him off the island for now,' he says. 'But we would like to question him some place other than here. We have set up rooms in the main hotel.'

'I'm coming with him,' Em says.

'No. We want to speak to Theo alone.'

Em shakes her head defiantly. 'You can't do that. He's a minor, he needs someone with him. You're not allowed to talk to him on his own.'

She feels a hand grip her arm from behind and is sure it is Charlie's from the feel of his hand.

Kallis looks past and he says, 'Who are you, please?'

'I'm Theo and Isaac's dad, Charlie Lawson.'

'Ah, Mr Lawson.' Kallis speaks in Greek to his colleague who has now appeared on the path too, and then turns back and says, 'I am very sorry for your son's death, Mr Lawson. I know this is a hard time for all your family, but I hope you appreciate we have a job to do. Your son, Isaac, is our priority.'

Em feels his words cut into her. As if he's suggesting that Isaac isn't her priority. He is. Above anything he is, she thinks, while at the same time wondering if it's truly above anything. Because if it was, she would be forcing Theo to answer their questions. She would be doing anything Kallis wants if it will help him find out what happened to Isaac.

But Theo is her priority too. It isn't the first time she has been torn between her boys, but it has never before been so consequential. Because if she puts Isaac first, as Kallis wants her to, then she needs to hand him Theo. But if she puts Theo first, the boy standing next to her, scared to his very bones, then she might have to live with the idea that she could be jeopardising justice for Isaac, and potentially the truth too. Whatever way she looks at it, she will let one of her boys down badly.

'We would like to speak to you too, Mr Lawson. Please can you come with us so my colleagues can talk with you.'

'That doesn't sort out who is going to be with Theo,' Em butts in. 'He has to have an adult present, that's the law.'

She isn't certain it is the law in Greece, but Kallis raises his eyes and doesn't argue with her. Instead he says, 'Maybe your husband can come then. Mr Cross?'

'That's fine,' Rob agrees. 'I can sit with him, Em.'

'OK, good. Thank you,' Kallis says. 'You follow us please, Theo.'

'Why won't they let me?' she says to Rob as Theo reluctantly starts following the officers, Charlie dragging behind, his son still not having spoken to him. 'I'm his mum.' She trails behind Rob down the path too.

'I don't know, Em. Probably *because* you're his mum.' He stops and kisses her on the forehead. 'I'll look after him, I promise.'

She eventually lets him go because there is nothing else she can do. Watching them all walk down the path and then disappear out of sight, Em has never felt so empty, so useless and so much like she is not doing the right thing by either of her sons.

A scream rises inside her, and she turns on her heel and races back into her villa, pulling the doors shut tight behind her so she can let it out. She screams and screams, and wails along with it as she falls onto the bed.

How desperately she needs to know what happened to Isaac, but her pain is so much more than that. She *needs* him back, and now Theo has been taken away from her too, with Rob who knows nothing, and Theo who knows so much more than anyone else realises.

She is filled with a panic that she cannot suppress, yet she's being told that all she can do is wait. How the hell do they assume that is possible?

LAILA

Chapter Twenty-Four

Last night I purposely didn't put my watch back on. As soon as we got back to the room I zipped it into the lining of my suitcase where James wouldn't come across it. I cannot bear the thought of what he would say to me if he knew it was in my bag all the time. How he might satisfy himself that his accusations were right, I was out of my mind to accuse Theo in my head and steal into their room to look for it, when I had it all along.

When I went back to the table my thoughts were full of Theo and how quick I had been to assume the worst of him. He reminded me so much of Sam that I took a dislike to him. But now it turns out he hadn't taken my watch, he was innocent of the 'crime' that had made me suspicious of him. By then I was replaying in my head the fight between the brothers that I'd overheard, taunting myself with the idea I could have got it wrong.

James was shuffling uneasily on his chair when I sat down again, twirling his glass between his fingers. 'Laila, I'm sorry,' he said. 'I've been acting like an arsehole to you. You're right, I was in a mood when I came home last night. When I took that call for you, I blamed it all on you, and I shouldn't have.'

'OK,' I said.

'No, it's not OK. I didn't go out looking for anything in particular yesterday, I just remembered the place and took the opportunity, and then I guess I got a bit overexcited about finding it. Then when I did, I wished I'd never gone back because it reminded me of the past and Stephanie and ... well, that's why I wasn't in a good mood. I shouldn't have done it.'

I accepted his apology with as much enthusiasm as I could muster. I didn't know if I believed it, but I suppose it made some sense, and for the time being I was prepared to let it go. All I wanted was to get back to the hotel and for the day to be over.

This morning, in an attempt to restore some normality, the hotel moved the breakfast buffet to the Greek restaurant. And so at 9 a.m. we are walking there to eat – not hand in hand, though I feel a sense of relief in the air.

Guests are still being kept away from the pool and the crime scene; the area is cordoned off by tape while police officers continue to trawl through the shrubbery. Apparently there is little interest in the pool itself; it was drained and every inch examined, but the water had destroyed any evidence. Kallis and his team are therefore focusing on the surrounding area. There is talk of them refilling the pool later today, though I don't know who in their right mind would want to sit around it after what happened.

Today as I saunter aimlessly around the buffet, I can hear the way the other guests are openly talking among themselves and sharing their opinions and theories on what has happened, discussing Em's family and the fact they have remained holed up in their villa.

'No one has seen any sign of the mother,' one lady comments, ladling three fried eggs onto her plate. As if this comes as any surprise.

I don't get embroiled in their conversations, but I listen to snippets of them: the couple who speculate, 'Well, it's usually the family isn't it?' and the woman who tosses a comment to me that she always thought there was something funny about one of the waiters because he has been looking at her strangely since the day she arrived.

I ignore her, and all the assumptions in between, and back at the table I slam my plate down with such force that James looks up at me. 'OK?' he asks.

'Not really,' I admit. I don't like the way they're discussing Isaac as if he were a stranger in the news rather than a boy we have seen every day of our holidays. And neither do

I like the thought of what the police could be accusing Theo of. It's an idea that no longer rests easily with me.

After breakfast James goes for a walk on the beach. I tell him I don't want to go with him, I need the space because we have been dancing around each other since last night.

He has found us another hotel, in Crete. We'll check in tomorrow and stay for three nights until we fly home on Tuesday morning. The possibility of taking an earlier flight home has been dropped. James seems satisfied that we have tickets for the ferry on Saturday morning and somewhere else to stay. As if getting away from White Sands will enable us to make the most of the rest of our holiday, when surely he knows it is unsalvageable.

With him gone, there is something I have to do. I need to speak to Rosie again. Since last night I haven't been able to shake off the uneasy sense that there's more to the story than the version James has told me. I want to know everything her husband told her about his and James's trip. I need to decide for myself if what James said last night stacks up; only then can I think about what comes next.

Rosie's room is en route to the pool, I have seen them both coming and going from it on numerous occasions. When I get to their room I rap on the door, and when there's no answer I pound on it loudly. Eventually the door opens and thankfully it is Rosie who is standing the other side of it, but she holds it ajar, her eyes silently warning me not to say anything about the baby.

'I wanted to know something about your husband's fishing trip,' I say.

'Oh, OK.' She is confused but she opens the door wider.

'Can you find out where James wanted to go? The place where you said the guy didn't want to take them? I wondered if Spencer knew the name of it.'

Rosie looks at me curiously.

'I know it sounds odd, but please, could you ask him?'

She looks over her shoulder. 'Spencer,' she says, and then, when he doesn't answer she snaps louder, 'Spencer?' Her brusqueness surprises me. It isn't the way you would expect honeymooners to speak to each other. Then again, I've already seen that there is nothing about them that suggests they are happy to be married.

When she turns and opens the door wider still, I see Spencer hovering in the background, shirtless in a pair of shorts. 'Where did you say that guy, James, wanted to go on the boat? The place the driver didn't want to take him?' she asks him.

'I don't know,' he shrugs. 'Why?'

Rosie looks back at me. 'His wife wants to know.'

Spencer strides over to the door, pulling a T-shirt over his head as he does so. 'I can't remember the name of the place,' he says.

'Would you recognise it?' I ask, and pull my phone out, opening it up to where I have already loaded a map of Ixos.

I expand it and pass it over and watch Spencer's thumb and forefinger scrolling the screen. He shakes his head and then says, 'Oh, wait, this might be it. Halkion,' he says. 'Yeah, that was it. That small island there.' He prods a dot on the screen and then passes the phone back.

'Halkion?' I repeat, expanding the map further.

'Yeah,' he says. 'Why do you want to know?'

'No reason,' I say. 'Thank you though, that's really helpful.'

I smile at them both and turn to go when Spencer says, 'Your husband has a bit of a temper on him, doesn't he?'

'James?' I say, when of course this is who he means.

'Yeah. Bloody adamant we go there, despite Demetrius telling him it wasn't possible. If it hadn't been for the money, he would have ignored him.'

'What money?'

'The money your husband gave him. That's when I said they could drop me off first. I wasn't going to risk getting stranded.' Spencer shrugs. 'Can't you ask *him* all this?'

'Yes,' I tell him. 'I will.'

I leave Rosie and Spencer standing in their doorway, no doubt staring after me. Halkion. The name doesn't mean anything to me, I have never heard of it before, but clearly it means something to James. Enough for him to risk going there on Wednesday, and paying the boat driver a bonus to take him.

I don't want to go back to our room, because I fear I won't get any answers from him, and neither do I want

James to see me on his way back from the beach, so I head off to reception and find a quiet spot, a hanging chair that sits in the corner overlooking the outside. I curl up inside it, open Google and tap Halkion into the search bar.

As I wait for the search results to load, I'm distracted by the sight of Lieutenant Kallis coming through the door, followed by another police officer who is walking alongside Theo. Behind them is Rob and a man dressed in cargo shorts and a T-shirt who I haven't seen before, though there is something vaguely familiar about him. He has the same face shape and thick-set build as Theo. As I nestle further back into the chair I wonder whether it is the boys' dad.

If he is, then he and Rob couldn't look more dissimilar. The man is slightly dishevelled in his appearance, his hair hasn't been brushed and he has stubble that would take James a week to grow. His clothes are crumpled, as if he's been wearing them all night, and yet he has such dark, piercing eyes that they make his whole appearance quite attractive. If he is Em's ex, then she has gone for his exact opposite, and I wonder if it's a decision she made on purpose.

Kallis looks in my direction as they pass but he makes no attempt to acknowledge me. All the others ignore me too. As Theo passes, his head is down but I can still make out his expression. His eyes are wide with fear as he stares at the ground, his lips parted.

They disappear behind me and I peer around the other side of the chair and watch them heading through a door near the reception desk. They are taking Theo for a reason. They must want to question him without Em.

I watch the way the man, who I assume is the dad, walks. His gait is so similar to Theo's, yet while the teenager came across as posh, his dad appears casual and scruffy. There are no airs and graces, no pretences.

I turn away from them, shaken because seeing the two of them reminds me of those distorted images that, when you turn them another way, reveal something else entirely.

If I hadn't said anything, there's a chance they might not be questioning Theo. I can't help wondering if I've pushed them in the wrong direction. I can't help thinking that I've got everything about him wrong.

The thought preys on my mind, digging its claws in, but I tell myself that Kallis must know what he's doing. He wouldn't be questioning the boy if there wasn't good reason to. It cannot simply be because of what I have said.

Eventually I return my attention to Google. A few results have come up and I click onto Wikipedia, which tells me Halkion is a small island in the Aegean Sea, famed for its wildlife but little else. I scroll past facts about its size, its highest and lowest elevation points, down to its history and general information, which shows me little more than I have already learnt: *Because of its tides and shallow waters, Halkion is difficult to get to. Rip tides are common – time it wrong and you could be stuck on the island for hours.*

I come out of the site and look for more, though what I am searching for, I'm not sure. I don't know what I hope to find that will tell me why my husband was so desperate to go there, but then I am on the second page of results when I come across a headline that stops me short.

Search for British woman near island of Halkion

I click on it and read the article that was written sixteen years ago. A woman was reported missing near the island. Twenty-four hours later, her body was found.

It's a short story with little substance, so I come out of the page and try to find more. But there is nothing. No name. No information on how she died. All I have managed to dig up are the bare bones of the story, but my hands are shaking when I close down my phone and put it away.

The question lingers on the tip of my tongue: did this woman's death have something to do with James wanting so badly to return to that place?

And if it did, as by now I am sure it must have, then what has my husband done?

Chapter Twenty-Five

James is in our room, washing his T-shirt in the basin, scrubbing at a patch of food that he spillt at breakfast this morning.

I stand by the dividing wall as I tell him, 'I think the police have taken Theo in for questioning.'

He looks up. His hands stop scrubbing as he straightens his back.

'I guess they must have found more information,' I go on.

'Oh, well that's—' He stops. 'Good? I don't know, it isn't good I suppose, is it?'

'Why are you so interested in Halkion?' I ask. I have caught him off guard with my sudden change of subject because just as he was about to start scrubbing again he immediately stops. 'Was it something to do with the woman they found there sixteen years ago?' I am clutching at straws, but I don't know what I have to lose, and besides, James was quick enough to blame me for obsessing over Em.

I know I have hit on something, I can see it in his expression and the twitch of his lip. He doesn't look away but the silence is long enough for it to look like he's trying to work out how to answer.

'Who was she?' I ask, as calmly as I can, because inside my body is on fire.

'You already know who she was,' he says. His voice is low and flat, it sounds defeated. 'So please don't pretend you don't.' James is assuming my futile research threw up more than it did.

'No I don't, I—' I stop suddenly. 'Stephanie?' I say. I had thought that they might have been involved somehow, given the timing, and though I had briefly contemplated that it was her, I hadn't dwelled on the idea.

James drops the flannel in the sink, and his T-shirt beside it, still smeared with an ugly brown streak. 'This holiday was supposed to be about us,' he tells me. 'But I found myself going back there.'

I have no idea what he is talking about but I need to sit down. I step over to the bed and slide onto it, not once taking my eyes off him for fear that any minute he might stop or lie his way out of whatever it is that has happened. I don't say anything, until eventually he continues.

'None of it was my fault.'

'Tell me what happened,' I say as calmly as I can.

James inhales deeply and sits on the bed next to me. 'Stephanie and I came travelling out here, you know that.'

'I know you travelled the Greek islands. I didn't know you'd come to Ixos before we got here,' I point out.

'Well we stayed on Ixos for one night. Above one of the tavernas in the village. God knows how we got a room,' he goes on, 'but it would have been down to Stephanie, it was the kind of thing she used to do. Somehow she managed to talk people round to doing whatever she wanted. Everyone loved Steph,' he says. It's a sentiment that makes me curl up inside, despite the fact the poor girl is dead.

'Anyway the next day we took a boat out. I'd driven one like it once or twice before but I didn't have much experience, and not around here. I didn't know the tides like I should have done, or the sand banks around Halkion, but we went anyway.'

'Go on,' I say, when he hesitates.

'I thought we could drive the boat about a bit, maybe even head back to Crete, but one of the locals had told Stephanie about this island called Halkion and she wanted to get to it. Apparently there was some folklore about it and she was intrigued. She used to buy into anything like that, I don't even remember what it was, I wasn't interested. But I gave in and we headed there.

'The tides were low when we arrived. I told her we needed to turn back right away or else we'd get stuck, but

Stephanie jumped off the boat and we ended up having a huge fight. She was being pig-headed, she wasn't budging. That was another of her more annoying traits. You could never get her to do something she didn't want to, and that day it really pissed me off. I told her if she didn't come I was going without her.'

'You didn't?' I shake my head in disbelief as James turns the other way. I couldn't imagine him doing something like that to me, it's not in his nature.

'I didn't intend to leave her for long. I only wanted to show her she couldn't keep calling all the shots. I don't think I …' He is looking up now, but not at me, his eyes glazing over as if he's trying to remember exactly what happened. 'I don't think I was planning to go far anyway, but yeah, I left her there. And then at some point I think I turned the boat round and tried to get back, but the tide was too low. I couldn't make it, so the only chance I had was to get back to Ixos and call for help.'

James is rubbing a hand over his eyes, shaking his head.

'What do you mean you *think* you turned back?' I say.

'Because I don't know, Laila,' he says. 'I don't know exactly because I can't actually remember.'

'Why can't you?' I persist.

'Because I'd been drinking,' he cries. 'I was out of it. I should never have driven the boat in the first place. Again, another of Stephanie's ideas, but I did it, so I can't blame her, can I? But I can't remember everything.' He buries his head deep into his hands. 'I blacked out half the day.'

'What *do* you remember?' I say coldly. 'Did you go back to Ixos and call for help?'

James nods. 'Someone took me back but there was no sign of her. I don't know, I thought it would be typical if she'd managed to board someone's yacht. I didn't think …' He stops and shakes his head. 'I didn't think that she'd – that she'd be found dead. The next day. She must have tried to swim or something, but there were apparently rip tides and – I don't know, I have no idea.'

'Why have you never told me any of this?' I say. 'You never said a word, you never even told me she was dead.'

'Because – it was my fault. It was my fault she died. How do I tell you something like that? I just couldn't. So I thought it would be better if I buried the story and started again.'

My husband is sobbing on the bed, curled in on himself. His hands are splayed either side of his head and I can't see his face but he's softly rocking back and forth. He needs comfort that I can't give him. I don't feel pity for his sorrow, only anger that he has never told me this story in the ten years we have been together, and that for some reason he has brought me out here on the pretence of this being a much-needed break for the two of us.

'I don't understand why you've come back here after all these years,' I say. I am standing on the opposite side of the room, my back against the desk.

'Because—' James shakes his head, his hands still attached to the sides of it. 'Because I can't get rid of it,' he says, tapping the tips of his fingers against his scalp. 'I can't ever get thoughts of what happened out of my head. It's always been there. The guilt has never left me.'

'But why now?'

'There's no reason.'

'It's just that your timing is a bit odd, James. I know you'd started drinking again and then you tell me you can't go through IVF any more, and now here we are. You brought me on holiday to the place where your ex-girlfriend died. You sold it to me that *we* needed this break. It was meant to be a start of a new chapter for us, but it turns out it had nothing to do with me. It's all to do with you.'

'No.' He shakes his head, but that single word is a lie. 'Laila, I'm sorry. I didn't mean to hurt you,' he cries. 'I promise you I didn't. I just needed to come back and I thought I could do both and that I could make it something good for you too.'

'How could it ever be good for me? How could you secretly addressing your past demons be good for me? You've been pretending all this time. Our whole life together has been a lie.'

'No. It hasn't. Please don't think that, it's not like that at all.'

'Of course it is. If you can't get Stephanie out of your head then how can you have ever been committed to me and our marriage, and everything we wanted? I mean, *was* it what you wanted?' I shout. 'Did you even *want* children?'

'I wanted what *you* wanted, Laila,' he says. 'When I met you, I wanted to start again, I wanted to put the past behind me and forget all about it. That's why I never told you. I'd been sober for two years by then and I wanted to have this perfect marriage and family and everything—'

'But it didn't quite turn out like that,' I finish.

'No. No it hasn't turned out like that.'

'Because I couldn't give you the family.'

'No. That's not it. Don't say it like it's your fault because it's not. I found it hard, that's all. I found everything about my life hard – the endless rounds of IVF, how desperately sad you've been, me stuck working for my dad …' James trails off. 'None of that was what I wanted.'

'I take it he knows?' I say. 'Your dad? I presume he and your brother know what happened back then, to Stephanie.'

'Yes, of course.'

I nod. 'Is that why you kept me away from them? In case they ever told me?'

'No, it isn't like that, Laila.'

I let out a laugh. 'I don't believe you. I think that's exactly why you didn't want us getting together.'

'My relationship with my dad has never been good, you know that.'

'After Stephanie?' I say. 'Because of what happened?'

'I don't know. Yes. Maybe.'

'Tell me the truth, James: did you ever want us to have children?'

I watch in slow motion as he closes his eyes, wonders whether to lie to keep me happy or tell me the truth, and so I know without him having to tell me. 'Oh my God, James,' I cry, sinking to my haunches.

'I did want them,' he says. 'Because I knew that was what you wanted.'

'But you never wanted them for yourself?'

'I don't know,' he admits. 'If it happened I'm sure I would have loved it, but if it didn't—' He breaks off. 'I'm sorry.'

I crouch on the floor, hugging my knees to my chest. James is getting off the bed, coming over to me. 'Don't,' I tell him. 'Don't come near me.'

He stops where he is and sinks onto the floor too, a metre of space between us.

'You made out our fight at the gala evening was all about me,' I say. 'But now we both know it wasn't. It was all about her. The whole day had been about her. Are you sure you're not still in love with her, James?'

'No. I told you that,' he says. 'Whatever Stephanie and I had, it wasn't love, or at least it was nothing like the way I've always felt about you. If I didn't already know that I would have realised when I met you. Laila, it's you I'm in love with you, I always have been. You have to believe that.'

I laugh coldly. 'You have a very funny way of showing me that – if it's true.'

'I've always shown you that,' he says. 'Everything I have ever done is for you. Yes, maybe recently I haven't done so as much, but I never intended to hurt you, it's just that everything got too much for me. That's why I started drinking again, and that's why I had to stop us going through any more IVF.'

'And that's why we came here,' I finish.

'Yes,' he admits. 'Because I needed to face what happened, I had to try and remember it all, I guess. You're right, I should have done that a long time ago and told you the truth, because instead it's eaten me up and made everything worse.'

'And did you remember?' I ask.

James shakes his head.

'So you'd been drinking too much when you left Stephanie that day,' I mutter.

'Yes, and I shouldn't have done.'

'But then you came back on Wednesday and you drank through the evening with me,' I say, looking up at him, goading him to admit how wrong that was. 'The police wanted to know what time you got back,' I say. 'When they questioned me the first time, they asked me if I was on my own when I came back to the room.' It is something that has been playing on my mind, how I only have James's word for it that he came home half an hour after I did. He didn't wake me when he returned. I'm sure I would have only been in a light sleep by then.

I expect him to shout me down, ask me what I'm insinuating, but he remains silent.

'I told them you got back half an hour after me because that's what you told me,' I say.

'Yes—'

'Before you go on,' I interrupt, 'you need to tell me the truth from now on. I think you owe me that much.'

James blinks. Once, twice. His lips twitch, before he says, 'I don't know what time I got back.'

'Did you carry on drinking?'

'I don't know, I think so. I must have had another.'

'I'm sure,' I say snidely. 'So you lied to me and to the police.'

'I know.'

'Why? Why didn't you tell them the truth?'

When he doesn't answer, I go on, 'What happened? What happened on Wednesday night when you left me? Because if there is anything at all, then I need you to tell me.'

His breaths are shallow and tight. 'I don't know, Laila.' He looks up at me, eyes wide. 'I don't know. I'm trying to remember that too.'

EM

Chapter Twenty-Six

It has been over an hour. Em has been pacing the villa, her mind reeling with what is happening to her son. She hates that she isn't allowed to be with him and that she has no idea what's going on. When Rob finally lets himself in, he looks stricken.

'What is it?' she gasps. 'What's happened?'

'Kallis says they'll be arresting Theo.'

'No! They can't be. God, no. This isn't happening.' She feels all the air leaving her. For the second time in the last two days her world has fallen apart into irretrievably broken pieces. 'Why are they?' she begs. 'What have they found?'

'They don't trust his story. They know he argued with Isaac before he died and they know he was the last person to see him before he left the room.' He stops. 'Em, I don't trust his story either. There's something he isn't telling them. He's lying about something. I'm sorry, but it's obvious to me and it will definitely be obvious to them too. You know Theo, he isn't a good liar at the best of times.'

Em turns and strides across the room away from him, looking out at their pool so Rob can't see her face that she fears would give her away. Theo hasn't told them he left the villa on Wednesday night. Which means her son hasn't admitted he followed Isaac to the pool or that he hit his brother. So yes, he is lying to them, and as Rob says, he isn't good at hiding it. It's no surprise they don't believe him.

Maybe she should have told him to tell them the truth, because if it comes out now it will only be worse.

'Em, love.' Rob appears behind her and places a hand on her arm. 'I think we have to prepare ourselves.'

'For what?' she snaps.

'For whatever Theo tells us. Because he will,' he says. 'It will come out, you know that. As soon as he knows he's going to be arrested, he will speak.'

She feels as if she is doubling over as she sucks in air. A punch to the stomach, yet in reality she has somehow managed to stay upright.

'We have to be prepared he might somehow be involved.'

'No,' she says sharply, shaking her head. 'No. I can't believe that.'

'You can't believe it, or you won't?' His words are spoken softly but the sentiment is harsh.

'Where's Theo now?' Em spins around, ignoring his question.

'They're taking a short break,' Rob tells her. 'He's still in the room where they're interviewing him. They said I could come out and speak to you. I knew you'd be worrying.'

'And Charlie?'

'He's still in there too, as far as I know. I think they'll want to speak to you again. They want to find out if you know more than you're saying.' He pauses, watching her intently.

She knows what is coming.

'Do you?' he asks.

'I want to see Theo.' Em brushes past him. She can feel him turning, watching her, still waiting. Her husband would know she was lying if she told him she didn't know more. She and Theo are alike in the way the skin on their neck and chest always flushes if they are embarrassed. It is happening now. Burning a hole right through her. She is sure he knows anyway.

'Em,' he calls after her as she is at the door, already opening it to leave. 'Think carefully,' he says. 'I understand why you want to stand by Theo, but this is serious. This is a matter of them finding out what happened to Isaac. That's the most important thing, you know that. Whatever Theo may or may not have done, we need to help the police find out what happened.'

Once again she ignores him. She wishes he would shut up and leave her alone and stop telling her what she needs to do.

Rob follows her back to reception but with Em charging ahead, they don't speak until they get there. Though she refuses to believe her son will be arrested, deep down she knows this is a real possibility.

When they push through the glass doors to the lobby Rob tells her he'll ask at the desk for them to call through and say she is here. Reluctantly she drops onto a seat and waits.

Ten minutes pass before one of the officers appears through the door beside the reception desk. 'Where's my son?' she asks, flying out of the seat and propelling herself towards him.

'He is in a room,' the officer tells her kindly as he points at the door he has just come through.

'Is he OK?'

'Yes, yes, he is OK,' he says, though she doubts this is the truth. He likely doesn't even know.

'You're wasting precious time with him,' she says. 'You should be looking for the person who did it. There's a killer out there and you're too busy focusing on Theo. What about that woman? Laila?' she cries. 'I told you how she was watching my family for five days. It's her you need to be questioning, not my boy.'

Over the officer's shoulder she suddenly sees Kallis in the doorway beside the desk. He looks intrigued by her outburst as he wanders over to her. 'I'm glad you're here, Mrs Cross,' he says. 'I would like to speak to you too, please, if you don't mind coming with me?'

'Right,' she says. 'Right, yes,' she fumbles. 'OK.'

They know something by now, of this she is sure. She follows the detective through the door and down a short hallway to a room that must be used as a storeroom for the hotel but has been commandeered as a questioning suite. Theo has told them more.

LAILA

Chapter Twenty-Seven

'I don't understand,' I say to James. 'You mean you can't remember what you did after you walked away the other night? Not any of it?'

I have my own snatches of memory, the night itself has become hazy, but at least I remember getting back to the room and stumbling into bed.

'I remember some,' he says. 'It's like I have these missing periods of time between memories. Some are bigger than others.'

'A blackout?"

'A type of one,' he tells me. 'They call them greyouts. It's not total amnesia, it's like I'm missing pieces of a jigsaw.'

'And do they come back?'

'Not always. They haven't with Stephanie.'

'God, James,' I say. 'You actually have a proper drinking problem that I didn't even know about.'

'My grandfather was an alcoholic,' he tells me. 'In turn my dad was teetotal and hated me and Carl drinking. He was always on at us when we were teenagers, never allowing us to have a beer in the house even when we were eighteen. So we hid it from him, but I guess I went too far the other way and totally rebelled against him. Not that I knew it was an issue. Or at least not until much later.'

James pauses and takes a deep breath that he releases in a long sigh.

'I drank a lot with Stephanie because she did,' he went on. 'It was our lifestyle, we partied, we travelled, it was the way it was. But when I binged, I started getting these patches of memory loss. That was what happened when Stephanie and I took the boat out. I was drunk when we left Ixos, we carried on drinking on the way to Halkion.'

'But what about Wednesday night?' I ask.

'I guess the same thing happened because I drank too much too quickly. I knew I shouldn't have left you and carried on drinking. I should have finished when you went to bed, or probably much sooner than that, but I couldn't stop myself. I wanted to blot out all the old memories that had resurfaced that day. And I was angry with you too. Angry with myself more, of course, but I wasn't ready to go back to the room. So yeah I'm pretty sure I carried on drinking, but I don't know how much and I haven't any idea what time I got back.'

He reaches a finger to his mouth and starts biting his nail. It's a habit he once told me he had as a child, but it seems odd to see him chewing his way down it and only now do I see how the skin around the nail is raw and has started to bleed.

'Is there anything else?' I ask cautiously. 'Because now's the time to tell me.'

'I know I saw the kid. Isaac, the boy who died,' he clarifies in case I hadn't already guessed. 'Or at least I'm pretty sure it was him.'

'Why haven't you mentioned this before?' I gasp.

'Because ...' James cries, flapping a hand in the air. 'How can I? I can't possibly tell the police I saw the boy who died, and that it was most likely right before he died, when I can only give them half a story.'

'But you've always known it? Even yesterday morning when I told you what happened, did you remember then that you'd seen him?'

'Vaguely.' The fear in his eyes is palpable. 'Yes,' he goes on. 'Yeah, I think I knew then.'

'And you've been hiding it all this time?'

'I didn't know what to say,' he pleads. 'There's these small islands of memory floating around in my head and I can't connect them and I want to, Laila. I'm trying,' he says.

I listen to what he says and try to take it in. I am almost certain he is telling me the truth. Almost. But at this point I don't know if that is enough.

EM

Chapter Twenty-Eight

In the interview room Kallis does not give away what Theo has said and so Em has to follow the detective's lead as he questions her.

'Has Theo spoken to you about Wednesday night?' he asks her, his tone suggesting that he believes he has.

'Of course we have spoken,' she says carefully. They are playing a game that she doesn't want to be a part of. It is too one-sided and the stakes are too high. 'It is all that's on my mind.'

'Only, I believe your son isn't telling me something important,' he says. 'I believe he is lying when he tells me that he did not leave his bed all night.'

Em doesn't reply. So Theo hasn't said that he left the villa yet. She presses her lips tightly together, keeping her hands under the table where he can't see the sweat that films her palms.

She will never forgive herself if she doesn't do everything she can to find out what happened to Isaac. But she has two sons, and one of them is still alive. And so as much as Rob is right, deep down she would forgive herself even less if she did not stand by Theo.

She only has one son left and Em will not allow him to be taken from her too. And so she tells the officer that her son isn't lying. And that even though he admits he argued with his brother on the day Isaac was killed, as far as she knows, he did not leave their villa that night.

They let Em go after half an hour, either satisfied she is telling them the truth, or convinced she too is lying to them. She isn't sure which.

Charlie is waiting for her when she walks out into the bright and airy reception area. It's a stark contrast to the dimly lit square room with no windows that she has just come from and she has to blink back the glare of the light.

'And?' he says, taking her by the arm and steering her towards the sliding glass doors that lead outside. There is no one near, though he keeps glancing around to check they aren't being overheard. 'What's happening?'

'How do I know? I haven't seen Theo.'

'I thought that was where you've been?'

'No, they wanted to speak to me privately. They wanted to know if I'm hiding anything,' she tells him.

He sucks in a breath. If it is possible, his shirt is even more crumpled. She resists the urge to press her hand against his chest and flatten it out.

Charlie looks as exhausted as she feels. She barely slept last night with Theo beside her tossing and turning. He has always been an agitated sleeper, but she hasn't shared a bed with him in years.

Not that she would have slept anyway, of course, but it looks like Charlie has had the same fretful night. His flight didn't land in Crete until past midnight and he would have been up early again this morning to get the boat to Ixos. Never mind the thoughts that would have been rolling through his head, the fear that if you fall asleep you might wake up and not remember. Because right after that blissful second, the memory always comes searing back into your head, scorching your brain, making you relive the nightmare.

Em had thought it better not to try and sleep last night. And maybe she got a few snatches here and there, but she didn't want to risk any more.

'What did you say?' he asks her.

'I didn't,' she replies.

'Nothing?'

'No.'

'OK.' She wonders if it is a flash of relief she sees in his eyes but she cannot tell for sure. Whatever it is, Charlie doesn't persist, unlike Rob, but then that is understandable.

'We need to find out who killed Isaac,' Em says. 'It's the only way we can make any of this stop.'

They sit on the curved leather sofa in the corner of the lobby in silence. As soon as the door to the room at the far end opens, Charlie reaches over and takes hold of her hand. They stand together when they see Theo at the door. She expected him to be in handcuffs. That he would be led outside and into a police car and she wouldn't be able to speak to him. And so she is flooded with relief when he steps out and sees her, and comes straight for her with no one stopping him.

His eyes are bloodshot and rimmed with a red even more vibrant than before. As soon as he is close enough, she wraps her arms around him and pulls him into her. They are both shaking.

Rob is not far behind, and following him, though a little way back, is Kallis. 'What's happening?' Em asks. 'You said they were arresting him?'

'They're not going to for now,' he says, his voice low so no one else can hear. 'Honestly? I don't think they have enough evidence.' He stops when Kallis is near enough to hear him. 'But we're not allowed to go anywhere. Not just Theo – none of us. We aren't allowed to leave the hotel.'

'Where would we go anyway?' she replies. As Kallis draws up beside Rob, she turns to him and says, 'Can I take my son with me?'

'You can, Mrs Cross, but we would like you not to leave the hotel,' he says, repeating what Rob has told her.

'Please can you start looking for the person who killed Isaac now,' she snaps, and turns on her heel, walking Theo out through the glass doors, Rob and Charlie following behind.

'I don't want to go back to the villa,' Theo tells her.

'We don't have a choice.'

'No, I mean I want to go somewhere else. You and me.'

'OK. We can do that. Do you want to go to the beach?'

Theo nods and she turns to the others. 'We'll see you back there.'

They follow the path towards the steps as the two men continue walking back to the villa. It is an odd sight and an even stranger thought that they'll be alone in Em's hotel room, but she doesn't care. They are grown men, they can work it out between them.

On the sand she leads Theo to a spot by the rocks and they sit down. 'Are you OK?' she asks him.

'I didn't tell them everything, Mum. I didn't tell them I followed Isaac out.'

She nods. 'Why didn't you?'

'Because I'm scared they'll think I did it.'

'The problem is they think you're lying anyway, you know that, right?'

'I know.' He won't look at her. His knees are scrunched up tight against his body as he looks out to sea.

'Theo, you need to tell me what you and your brother argued about. I want to help you and I will, but I need to know what happened.'

Theo bites the corner of his lip and she gives his hands, which are wrapped around his legs, a squeeze.

'I found out in the afternoon that Isaac had been seeing someone.'

'Someone at home?'

'No. Here in the hotel.'

'Oh?' Em shuffles on the rock, trying to work out who Isaac could have been seeing, when she hadn't seen him with anyone at all. She can't even fathom a time when he might have met up with them. 'Who?'

'I don't know her name. But she's married.'

'OK.' She screws her eyes up at him. 'So does she work here?'

'No. She's staying here. With her husband.'

'Oh God. Theo, you need to tell me who it is.' Her skin is pricking like there are a thousand needles jabbing at her. This might be important. She can't believe he has kept this from them. A woman whose husband might have found out ...

'I don't know her name,' he repeats.

'Then describe her to me. Point her out. Theo, this is what could stop the police from looking at you, I can't believe you've kept quiet about it. Why haven't you said anything sooner?' Her voice reaches a high pitch.

Theo shrugs.

'Theo? Why haven't you told anyone this?' she urges. 'This is important.'

'Because of you,' he says eventually. 'Because of you, Mum. I couldn't say anything because of you.' His legs are shaking. Em gets up and shuffles around to face him, pressing her hands into his arms to try and calm him down.

'What do you mean, because of me?'

'Because of everything that happened before. To you.'

His eyes fill with tears and he wipes a hand roughly across them, but the tears keep coming.

'What happened before?' she repeats. 'You mean with your dad?'

'Yeah. Isaac is the same as him. They're exactly the same.'

'Oh, Theo,' she says, stroking a hand through his hair. She wants to tell him they are nothing like one another. Though there are many similarities between Isaac and his father, this isn't the same, however much Theo has twisted it to be in his head. 'You mean how I was after your dad left?' she asks.

Theo nods.

Em closes her eyes and hangs her head back. She can feel tears coming. 'Oh, baby,' she whispers. 'That was different. That was so so different. I wouldn't ever let myself get like that again, did you really think I would?'

'I don't know.'

'I wouldn't,' she tells him.

'Yeah, well, I didn't want to risk it.'

'But you thought I would if I found out Isaac was seeing a married woman?' Em shakes her head vehemently. 'Is that why you threatened him,' she asks, 'like you were overheard doing in the room?'

'I never threatened him,' Theo says bluntly, looking up at her confused.

'But that woman heard you.'

'I don't know how because the doors were closed. Anyway, it was Isaac threatening me. He told me if I ever said anything to you, I'd never breathe another word to anyone again.'

Em lets her hands slide off Theo's arms. That woman had got it the wrong way round. She'd overheard the conversation and thought it was Theo when it was actually Isaac talking. That stupid woman, Laila, has thrown Theo to the wolves because she couldn't get her facts straight.

'You're really all right with what he did?' Theo is saying.

'No. I'm not all right with it,' she says. 'I can't be all right with any of this, but I promise you I will always be here for you. In every way. I will never let myself get to that point again, so from now on you need to be truthful with me.'

She cannot believe Theo could have drawn comparisons between what Charlie and Isaac have both done. His actions have been driven by a deep-seated fear that mean he must have been much more deeply affected than she could ever have realised.

But right now she needs to focus on what he's told her. Em has no idea what Isaac thought he was doing, but whatever it was, it's meant he has ended up dead.

'Tell me more about this woman,' she demands.

'She's got blond hair, she's really young.'

'Wears white dresses?'

Theo nods.

'Oh, Isaac,' Em sighs, looking up to the sky. 'That woman's on her honeymoon. Come on.' She pulls herself up and holds out her hand to Theo.

'Where are we going?'

'To tell Lieutenant Kallis what you've just told me.'

LAILA

Chapter Twenty-Nine

'You have to tell the police what you've just told me,' I say.

'How can I?' James is pulling himself off the floor now, opening the fridge door. I wait to see what he gets out of it and am relieved when he pulls out nothing more than a can of Coke. 'They'll want to know more. They'll start questioning me about everything – what time it was, what state the boy was in, what he was doing. I've been through it all in my head.' His voice rises in panic. 'The fact is that if all I can say to them is that I don't remember because I was too drunk, how will that look? You can imagine it, Laila. I'll be hauled in for something I didn't do. And the worst thing is, I won't even be able to stand up for myself.'

James is manically opening the can, trying to get his fingers under the ring pull, swearing when he hurts them.

When he finally does it, he pours the drink into his mouth and marches across the room. Any worry seems to have fused into frustration and I'm concerned it is aimed at me for not sharing his point of view.

But I don't. There is not one part of me that thinks James is right to keep this to himself. 'You're withholding evidence,' I say. I stand my ground because I believe James has to tell the truth. However little of the story he can piece together, it is the right thing to do. My husband is not a murderer, I don't believe for one minute he could have harmed Isaac, not least because he had no reason to. But he has to tell the police what he knows.

'I'm not doing this,' he says. 'And I'm begging you to stand by me.'

'Did you stand by *me*?' I ask him in return.

'What do you mean?'

'You accused me of obsessing over that family, James. You told me I went too far and insinuated I might have been capable of worse, and the whole time you were saying that, you knew I was in bed in our room and you weren't.'

'I never thought you'd done anything to the boy,' he says, putting his can down on the bedside table and coming over, crouching in front of me. 'Never anything like that. I'm sorry if you thought that, Laila.' He presses his hands into my legs, his eyes imploring me to believe him. 'I should never have said you were obsessed with her, I was just worried after you told me you were in their room!' he cries.

'But I never thought it was more than that. I'm sorry. Laila, I'm sorry,' he begs.

'I don't know you any more, James.'

'Yes you do. You do still know me. I love you. I have always loved you.'

I shake my head, tears pierce my eyes sharply as they roll down my cheeks.

'Listen to me,' he says. 'I know this holiday hasn't gone as planned and I know how much of that is my fault. I wasn't honest with you about Stephanie, and I should have been. But when we met you were everything I wanted. A fresh start – my future. You know how we were, Laila, we only wanted each other.'

James is right. There was a time in the beginning that we lost contact with our friends because we didn't want anyone but each other. Claire and Melissa accused me of failing to make plans to see them, or making excuses if we had an arrangement, because I wanted to do something with James instead. It didn't last long, maybe only a couple of months before I realised how much I missed and needed my friends too, and after that they swept James up into our friendship group. They adored him as much as I did. But before then it had been a blissful few months of getting to know each other, of not needing anything or anyone else other than each other.

But it was the beginning of a relationship and a time when I thought I was getting to know my future husband, and yet I didn't know the real James as I thought I had.

There was a huge omission of truth lying beneath the surface that my husband was hoping I would never find out.

'I need some space,' I tell him, pulling my legs back out of his reach and pushing myself up.

'No, don't go,' he begs me. 'We need to talk about what's happening.' His eyes are wide with fear, though I'm not sure if it is the fear of losing me or what I might tell the police.

'Laila, please, we have to sort this out. We can't let this destroy us.' His voice is panicked. 'I can't lose you,' he says.

I close my eyes, trying to blot out the sight of him. Seven days ago when we stepped onto Ixos I wanted so desperately for us to discover some semblance of normality, and wasn't contemplating the thought of losing my husband. But now I don't know how I can ever trust him again. I don't even know that he is telling me everything about Wednesday after the gala dinner, because how can someone lose so many patches of the night?

'I love you,' James is saying. 'More than anything else in the world. I haven't handled things well recently. I turned back to drinking and I wish to God I hadn't.'

'You should have talked to me,' I say. 'You should have told me how you were feeling.'

'I couldn't talk to you, Laila. I couldn't because you were drowning. You must know that. For years, every decision we've made has centred around us having a baby – the next round of IVF, where the money would come from. All our savings have been ploughed into this one thing that I knew wasn't working and I couldn't see a way out of. So the last thing I could do was talk to you.

'I wanted to,' he continues. 'I wanted to tell you everything, but I didn't know how to start. All I could do was try to be there for you. That was all I was doing: trying to be there for *you*.'

James is crying now too. Tears streak his face, running into his two-day growth of stubble. Despite everything that's happened, there is a part of me that wants to hold him and wipe them away. Even knowing what I now know doesn't change the fact that this is the man I once loved with all my being. Who I have never been able to imagine my life without. He is right when he says that everything he does has been for me.

Up to a point, of course. 'But you weren't there for me in the end,' I sob. 'When you told me you couldn't go through with any more IVF.'

'I couldn't handle it. You knew I was feeling down, you'd attempted to ask me a few times but you never listened to my answer and I got to a point when I couldn't handle it. I love you, Laila. This was tearing us apart and I just wanted us to find a way to move forward.'

'And this holiday?' I ask.

'I knew we needed a break, and I did want us to spend time together and reconnect. I didn't want to lose you, but I was worried that after you knew I didn't want to go through IVF any more you might leave me, and so I thought that ten days away together might help us remember how it used to be in the beginning.'

'Yet you brought me *here*,' I cry.

'I know. And I'm sorry. I never had any intention of going to Halkion again,' he says. 'I didn't ever want to go back to that island. But once I was out here, all these thoughts kept coming back to me. I wanted to see if I could remember. I wanted to confront what I'd once run away from.

'And Wednesday night . . . I know I perhaps should have told the police at the time, but I haven't, and so I can't say anything now, because you know how it would look.

'Laila, I love you,' he says again, 'more than life itself. I would do anything for you. Anything.'

'What do you mean?' I ask, because he has a look in his eyes, which are sparkling now through his tears. His brows are pointed into a peak and he is grinning at me.

James nods as if in response and while I think I know what he means I don't want to go there. I cannot let myself go there. And so instead I say, 'Then you have to speak to the police.'

He shakes his head and takes a step back. 'I can't do that.'

'You said you would do anything,' I protest.

'I meant children. If you want to go to New York, I'll do that. We can go to the clinic and try again – you haven't cancelled, have you?' he says, and I shake my head, my mind trying to take in what he is promising me. There is still a chance? I don't have to give up?

But his sudden about-turn is too much to accept, his timing is dubious. When I give myself the space to appreciate that, I will understand what he is trying to do. James is throwing us a lifeline at the last minute, a lifeline for himself more than me though. One that he hopes means I will stoically stand by his side from now on. I won't make him talk to the police, or persist in my own interrogations. Because, as James knows well enough, I would still do anything to have a child.

EM

Chapter Thirty

Em waits in the lobby as the receptionist looks for Lieutenant Kallis. Theo is loitering outside the doors, reluctant to speak to the police officer again. She can understand why, but at the same time she's urging him to acknowledge this is the only way they can start investigating the right people and stop thinking he had something to do with his brother's death.

Eventually the lieutenant appears through a door and strides over. 'Mrs Cross, you want to speak to me?'

'Yes.' She beckons Theo in. 'My son has told me what his argument was about. There's a personal reason he didn't want to bring it up with you.' She pauses when Theo joins them. 'Theo, you need to tell the lieutenant what you've told me.'

'My brother had a girlfriend on the island. She's married,' Theo says.

'Oh?' Kallis raises his eyes. 'And why haven't you told me this before?'

'It's personal, like I said,' Em interjects.

'But it is also an important piece of information. Theo has withheld something that could help us find out what happened to his brother. So I'm interested in why he is suddenly telling me now.'

'Theo's father had an affair and left us,' she says bluntly. 'And off the back of that, Theo watched me go to a very dark place. He worried about how it might affect me. You might not understand any of this,' she says, 'but that's how it is.'

'OK.' He screws his lip up so it is skewed to one side as he seems to contemplate what she's telling him. Eventually he says, 'Who was Isaac seeing?'

'We don't know her name,' Em says. 'But she's here on her honeymoon.'

Em watches the way Kallis's eyes flick up to meet hers.

'She's got blond hair and she's about twenty,' she goes on.

'And how do you know this?' Kallis asks

'Isaac told me,' Theo replies.

'We don't have any other evidence of this,' Kallis replies. 'Just your word. Which has come at a rather convenient time, yes?'

'He's telling you the truth,' Em says. 'And so I'm begging you, will you please go and speak to her and her husband?

Because if the husband found out about them, who knows what he could have done?'

'Yes, of course we will speak to them,' Kallis answers, but he doesn't take his eyes off Theo.

'You say that finding out who killed Isaac is your priority,' Em says. 'Well then, this needs to be your priority now. You can joke about Theo's timing being supposedly convenient all you like, but the fact of the matter is one of my sons has been killed and while you're trying to blame my other one, someone out there is responsible and getting away with it.' Her finger shakes as she points it at him. 'And the likelihood is, right now they could be getting away from this place as quickly as they can – and then what?'

Em doesn't know whether Kallis believes Theo. She suspects he doesn't. The way his mouth pinched at the corners, as if he was trying to suppress his judgement, his accusation that Theo has likely made it up after an hour of being questioned.

She and Theo make their way back to the villa where Rob and Charlie are talking by the pool. 'Everything OK?' Rob asks when he sees them.

'Isaac was seeing someone on the island,' she says as they enter the back of the villa. 'A married woman. Well, I say woman – she's practically a girl. It's the one who's on her honeymoon,' she adds for Rob's benefit.

'How do you know?' Charlie asks.

'Because he told Theo.' She holds up her hands when she sees Charlie's quizzical look and knows he is about to ask why Theo hasn't said anything before now. 'The important thing is, hopefully the police are doing something about it.'

Now Charlie's expression is changing from one of curiosity to something that resembles anger as he processes what she is implying.

'What the hell was she doing?' Rob is saying. 'Isaac's a kid, he was probably swayed by the fact she's a pretty girl. But if she's here on her honeymoon . . . ?'

Em and Charlie's minds are in a completely different place. 'It has to be her husband,' she cries. 'I mean, it makes sense, doesn't it? Why would anyone else want to hurt Isaac? That was what I could never get my head around. Why anyone would have done it. But this makes sense,' she repeats.

Her heart is hammering. She knows that look in Charlie's eyes and she knows she can't – and doesn't want to – stop him from what he is about to do. Charlie is going to find this man, and she will go with him.

A moment later, as Charlie brushes past, Rob works it out too. 'You can't go and look for them,' he says, aghast at the idea of them taking matters into their own hands. This is Rob to a tee, always one to shy away from confrontation. Of course, he can afford to. Not like her and Charlie. It's not an option for them.

'You'll have to come with me, son, I don't know who I'm looking for,' Charlie tells Theo.

'No!' Rob shouts. 'You need to leave this to the police. There is no way Theo is going anywhere with you. What do you think you're going to do, beat him up? Charlie! You have to think about this clearly. Let the police question them first.'

'I can't leave it,' he says bluntly. 'Theo?'

But with Theo standing there, gaping at his father, Em says, 'No, he can stay here. I'm coming with you.'

'Em, don't be so ridiculous.' Rob grabs her arm, but she shakes him off.

'If he laid a hand on my baby then I want to hear it from him. And I swear to God, I'll kill him myself,' she adds as Charlie leaves the room and she follows him out.

Chapter Thirty-One

Em is too driven by fury to listen to Rob, though part of her knows he's probably right and they shouldn't go charging around the hotel trying to track down the man they think is responsible for killing their son. But it's easy for Rob to stand there and be sensible when it's not his flesh and blood who has been taken from him.

'Do you have any idea what villa they're in?' Charlie asks.

'No,' she says. She assumes the newlyweds are on the other side of the resort to the few villas on this side, as she hasn't seen either of them coming or going.

'So where do we start?'

'I don't know. The beach?' She doesn't remember seeing them when she went down with Theo only half an hour ago, but there were enough guests down there to suggest that most of them have nothing else to do.

'OK,' he says, and she is about to lead him towards the steps when she stops suddenly, seeing the husband veering off the path and towards a row of rooms ahead.

'That's him.' She grabs Charlie's arm and points.

Charlie charges forward, Em a few steps behind. Her pulse is racing and she can't think about what they are going to do; the mere sight of the man has triggered something deep inside her.

'Hey!' Charlie is shouting, his voice deep and growling as the man, who is turning towards one of the room doors, stops at his voice. His expression is one of surprise, though Em can see the sight of Charlie charging towards him has put the wind up him. The other man is not skinny but he is much slighter than her ex, who overpowers him as he approaches.

'What did you do to my boy?' Charlie is yelling. Already she can see he is losing control, and though she is on the verge of doing so too, she reaches out to take hold of him.

But Charlie pulls away. The man holds his hands up, pressing his lips together as his eyes flick about nervously. 'I honestly don't know what you're talking about.' She sees how he registers that she is Isaac's mum. His lips part as if he is going to say more but then thinks better of it.

'Your wife was having some kind of fling with my son, wasn't she?'

'What?' the man says. It comes out as a laugh.

'And you found out about it?'

'I don't know what you're talking about.'

Em's breaths are short and fast. Her hands are balled into tight fists that are clenched by her sides. The heat doesn't help. It has sapped the air from around her, making her struggle to take it in. She shares Charlie's rage and yet something doesn't feel right. The man's fear is solid but she isn't certain he knows what they're talking about. She is desperately trying to piece together what is happening, but it is too hard to do when your body is screaming out in grief.

'Did you want to get back at him?' Charlie is shouting. She can hear the pain in his voice, though she doubts the man is aware of anything beyond her ex's threats. 'Only what? You went too far?' Charlie is in the man's face. There are mere inches between them. His arm is outstretched over the man's shoulder and his hand is splayed on the wooden door behind.

'I don't have a clue what you're talking about,' the man is saying. 'I promise you. I don't.'

'I think you do,' Charlie says as the door suddenly opens and they both stumble into the room.

The young girl is standing the other side of it, watching them, her pretty face plastered in confusion. 'What's going on?' She's wearing one of the white dresses she always seems to be in.

'We know what happened between you and my son,' Em says. 'He told his brother the afternoon before he died.' She tries to remain calm but inside her anger is bubbling, merging with her grief, because this girl is to blame for what happened. She should never have approached Isaac.

'Rosie?' The man is screwing up his face, holding his hands out in a gesture that wants her to explain.

'Me and your son?' She shakes her head. 'There was nothing – nothing was going *on* between us.' She looks panicked and even more confused than she was when she opened the door.

Momentarily the girl's expression weakens Em, but she needs to keep going. 'Did your husband find out?' she asks. 'Is that how my son wound up dead?'

'No! Hold on. You've got this all wrong. There wasn't anything between us. I mean – I mean I know he liked me.' Her pretty, pale face flushes in bright red patches. 'He made that clear but – but no. Nothing happened. God, I wouldn't – we talked, that's all.'

The young girl, Rosie, looks frightened as she plays with the hem of her dress. Her eyes keep flicking over to her husband, who is trapped beside Charlie. 'I promise you, none of this is what you think it is.'

'Well you're going to have to explain that to the police,' Em says.

'I will. I mean, I've already told them everything that's happened, which really wasn't anything at all.'

'Maybe your husband didn't think that,' Em says, turning on the man.

'Spencer isn't . . .' She pauses. 'Spencer isn't my husband. He's my brother. So I promise you, whatever it is you think has gone on, you really have got it wrong. We didn't hurt your son. We have no reason to.'

'What do you mean, he's your brother?' Em spits.

'He is. He's …' She gestures towards Spencer, who looks crestfallen at the story that's unfurling. 'His fiancé left him a week before his wedding and he didn't want to lose the honeymoon, and he definitely didn't want her to have it so …' She gives a small shrug. 'We pretended so we could keep the upgrade and the wine, and I know it sounds pathetic but …' There are tears in her eyes that make the girl look so young. She is barely older than Isaac, barely an adult. Em takes a step back.

'I'm so sorry for what happened, I really am,' Rosie is saying. 'But it's not what you're thinking.'

Em feels all the air flooding out of her. She thought she was right. She wanted to be right, because now it leaves her back at the beginning. Not knowing what happened to Isaac, or, God forbid, to what extent Theo was involved.

LAILA

Chapter Thirty-Two

James finishes his Coke and tosses the can into the bin. He is smiling as he strides over to the coffee machine and presses it into action. 'Do you want one?' he asks, holding up a capsule.

I shake my head. 'No thanks.'

He is springy in his movements, and happy, like he can't believe he hadn't come to this conclusion earlier. As if going to the clinic in New York is actually what he wants after all.

This is the place whose website promises treatment that stands much better chances of success than any in the UK. The epitome of all my dreams, however much I've recently tried to pretend otherwise.

My body isn't clenched into the tight ball any more, I am getting up, shaking the pins and needles out of my right arm, listening to my husband tell me he wants to put me first.

'Where will we get the money?' I say. Now we have lost so much. Now we have spent £5,000 on a holiday. At the same time, I can't believe I am contemplating this. And yet I am.

'We can find it,' he says. 'We'll get it. I can – we can get a loan. Or,' he hesitates. 'Or there's always my dad.' James looks sheepish as he turns his head and I can see how hard it would be for him to ask his father for money. A father who would surely say no anyway, but as James is pointing out, there are ways if we want it badly enough.

My stomach feels fluttery; little butterflies are dancing inside me. After the way James has treated me over the last two days, and the way I have begun to feel, you would think that I wouldn't even consider the prospect of having a child with James right now, but then this is what I have been striving for for the last five years. And it's clear to me how any discussions we've had about adjusting our plans have been meaningless, when the chance of trying one more time is on the table.

I don't know if the butterflies dancing are down to excitement or nerves, but already I have a glimpse of a different slice of our future to the one that he has cast over us for the last few weeks. Can I put aside what I have learnt about my husband? Can I accept his stories and explanation for why he never told me what happened? Can I believe that there was nothing more to Wednesday night, when there's a potential for a child again in my life?

Or children. There could always be more. As an only child, I'd always hoped for siblings for my child, ready-made friends for them to play with, not the imaginary ones I made do with. Yes, two children running around my feet. And in this vision of my future I am so happy – why wouldn't I be? I have everything now. I have the children I have wanted forever. The pictures flick through my head on a showreel. James and I can start again. If we have this, we can go back to the way we once were.

'Anyway, think about it,' he says. He turns back to me again. He is beaming as he adds, 'As if you're going to say no!' And he carries on making his coffee and when he is finished he takes it outside and asks me to join him in the sun.

I follow James out to the small patch of garden outside our room, but I don't sit down with him. Though my stomach continues to perform its merry dance, as the minutes pass the sensation is drowned out by the shrill alarm bells inside my head.

I know what I should do and that is point out to James that this sudden change of heart cannot really be true, this can't be what he genuinely wants, not when he's been persuading me it isn't good for 'us' to go through IVF again. I even open my mouth to ask him how I will know that he won't change his mind again, but at the last second I clamp it shut. I have never wanted to take any chances and now, more than ever, I daren't.

But the bells refuse to stop ringing and there is a heaviness inside me where the fluttering once was and I am trying to shake it off, because I don't want it there. I deserve to feel hope and some kind of euphoria. Instead, the heaviness comes loaded with an apprehension that makes me hold a hand over my stomach to settle the nerves inside me.

I'm uneasy because of the way our conversation changed focus so quickly, from the lies and secrets of our marriage and the worry of where James was on the night Isaac died, to the prospect of a happy future and starting a family.

I think James is trying to blindside me. No, I know he is, of course I do, because I am not stupid. The real question is, will I allow myself to be blindsided?

He pats the chair beside him, and I say, 'Actually, I want to get out for a bit. Get some headspace, if that's OK.'

'Of course,' he says, but his frown tells me that he doesn't want me going and that he doesn't understand why I need space. Realising that he can't stop me, he doesn't try. All he says is, 'We need to leave at seven in the morning, by the way. I had an email from reception confirming the ferry to Crete, so we have to be packed and ready. We can get an early night.'

*

I leave James in the room to finish packing. The thought of escaping the island tomorrow plays in my head, I should be happy to get away from Ixos and everything that has happened in the last week, and in many ways I am, because as soon as James and I leave we could put these seven days behind us and focus on the future.

Thoughts oscillate in my head as I stride down the path, climb the steps down to the beach and slip off my flip-flops so I can feel the sand on my bare soles. I tell myself that what happened to Stephanie was tragic, James was wrong not to tell me, but it was an accident that happened years before I even met him. And so maybe he is right. Many couples enter new relationships with a secret or two, and those secrets become harder to reveal with each year that passes. I know I have withheld things in the past, though never to this extent.

Now my mind shifts to the gala evening. If James is saying he can't remember that night, maybe he is right to question what good it will do if he talks to the police. Surely they won't relent until he breaks?

Try as I might, I cannot shake off the many unanswered questions. My husband isn't the person I thought I knew, and if this is the case, then how can I ever trust him?

It is James's father who keeps popping into my head, breaking through the noise. A man I haven't spoken to in over a year, but the only person aside from my brother-in-law who truly knows the man I'm married to.

I imagine what he would say to me if I were to speak to him. The picture James has painted of his dad is of a man who wasn't there for his son. Who did nothing to help James when he needed him, save to offer him a job in the family business James wanted no part of.

But right now I am willing to take the chance. I don't know who my husband is and I need help.

The last time I saw either my father-in-law or Carl was at James's uncle's funeral, an occasion that James wasn't keen to attend, especially as his dad and uncle didn't get on. But still, he thought he should go and so I offered to go with him for moral support, even though I had never met the uncle.

We sat at the back of a half-filled church and on one occasion his father turned to look at the guests and caught my eye. He barely acknowledged me, a slight nod of the head and nothing more. After the service James lingered to talk to a cousin I had never met, and didn't bother introducing me to her before scooping up my hand and leading me away from the small family gathering. We bumped into his father at the car. 'Laila,' he said, another cursory nod of the head before turning to James. 'I'll see you in the office, James. I take it that's where you're heading.' The last sentence was pointed.

James shrugged and rolled his eyes. 'That's me told then,' he muttered. 'He clearly doesn't want me lingering around here.'

I felt for James, brushed off and pushed back to work, unwelcome at a family wake that I assumed Carl would be attending. But I didn't ask; I could sense James wouldn't want to discuss it, and anyway I was relieved to be returning to the office myself and not spending time with my husband's family who had no interest in us.

So now I don't relish the idea of speaking to the man who has never given me the time of day, but if he can at least give me one answer, I will try. I scroll through my contacts until I get to the never-used number and press my finger down, waiting for the international dial tone to kick in.

He answers on the second ring with a brusque, 'Hello?'

'It's Laila,' I tell him, wondering whether there's a need to explain who I am when he says, 'Laila, yes, is everything OK?' I realise he must have recognised my number and is panicked by my unexpected call.

I tell him, 'We're both fine.' Though we are not. We are far from fine and he must know this is why I am calling him, so I say, 'Something has happened and I don't know what to do about it.'

'Tell me.' His voice is different to how I remember it. Quieter, a little nervous; it doesn't have the harshness I expected and had thought I had heard on him answering. I let myself breathe out a long slow breath.

'We're in Ixos,' I say, wondering if the name will ring any bells for him.

'Yes,' he says. 'I knew, I— James didn't tell me where you were going but I'd told him to use the company credit card for the deposit and so I found out what he'd booked when the statement came in.' He doesn't sound pleased that we are here. 'I hoped he would take you somewhere ... I don't know,' he says. 'I told him to take the money and give yourselves a break, but I didn't expect him to take you there.'

'So it *was* a bonus,' I say.

'No.' There's a short laugh and then, 'Not so much a bonus, I don't think anyone could argue the case for James getting a bonus in these last six months, but I paid for it, so I suppose he could have made out it was.'

'Why would you do that?'

'Because I thought the two of you needed to get away,' he says simply.

I am completely thrown by this. Particularly the fact that his dad knows enough about us to think that, but even more so that he is caring enough to buy something as thoughtful as an expensive holiday. Especially when, by the sounds of it, James isn't pulling his weight at work.

'Only, like I say, I didn't buy the holiday you're on,' he says. 'I want you to know that, I would never have booked my son a holiday in Ixos.'

'Because of what happened?' I ask.

'Yes. Because of that.'

'I didn't know about it until today,' I tell him.

'I'm sorry to hear that, Laila. I always wondered whether James had said anything to you. I'm also sorry you had to find out on what was supposed to be a holiday.'

'Did you know about the IVF?' I ask. 'Was that why you booked it?'

'IVF?' He sounds confused.

'We're having treatment, to try and have a baby,' I explain.

'No.' There is a pause. 'No, I didn't know that. I booked the holiday because I knew there were problems, though I didn't know where they'd stemmed from.'

'How do you know – I mean, what problems did you think we had, if not that?'

His dad sighs. 'My son turned up at work one morning smelling of drink. That wasn't the only time though and he'd been supposedly sober for the last thirteen years, so I gave him an ultimatum: sort himself out once and for all, or lose his job. I bought this holiday for you both telling him it was a break to get away and think about it. I didn't want him going back to the same demons I had seen before. But then I found out he took you there.'

'I also didn't know James used to drink,' I say. 'He rarely had alcohol when we first met.'

'He did before you. When he was with Stephanie. Laila, you must know James and I don't have much of a relationship any more. I can only imagine what he has told you, but I promise you it isn't because I don't want one. Maybe it's because I didn't know what to do, but I did try. I gave him a job when no one else would, and the only reason I keep him on is because I'm trying to protect him. Protect you both,' he adds. 'James shut me out. Perhaps it's because

I know too much about his past and he doesn't like to be reminded of it, I don't know. But he doesn't want me to have anything to do with the two of you.'

I think about how James has never introduced me to any friends from his past, how there isn't anyone else in his life who knows about what happened to Stephanie. Right from the start he threw himself into my friendship groups.

'James went out to Halkion, the place Stephanie died, two days ago,' I say. 'He said he wanted to try and remember what happened.'

'Try and remember?' his dad says. 'What was he trying to remember?'

'He said he has blackouts and that he can't remember leaving her or what happened before he got back to the island.'

His dad is quiet.

'Is that true?'

'All I know is that he refused to seek help after the girl's death. I booked him into counselling and I paid for him to go into rehab, but he wouldn't do either. He told me he could sort himself out, although his way of sorting himself out was cutting out everything and everyone from his past life and starting again by trying to blot out the memory.

'I knew it wasn't healthy, but I couldn't force him to do what I wanted, and so all I could do was employ him at the company where I could keep an eye on him. He doesn't like that, of course. He sees it as me having control over him, and he made it clear that even though he works for me I wasn't to have any other part in his life.'

'Why *did* he carry on working for you then?' I ask.

'Because he knew he would never get a better offer anywhere else.'

'Do you think he does remember it all?' I ask.

'I think the only person who can answer that truthfully is James,' he says. 'I don't know.'

'I worry that my whole life with him has been a lie. I don't know my husband at all, and so I don't know whether he would answer me honestly. I no longer know what's lies and what isn't,' I say.

'James has never been a bad person. He simply has his own way of trying to deal with things, and clearly it's not working. He won't accept help and so he keeps screwing things up. But then I don't know my son any more because he won't let me in,' he adds, 'so I can't tell you if you know him. I'm afraid that's something you're going to have to work out for yourself.'

I hang up the phone and let the conversation play out in my head. I have no idea if James is telling me the truth about those gaps in his memory. But if he's lying, and he does remember what happened to Stephanie, then surely that means he also remembers exactly what happened on Wednesday night when he saw Isaac before he died?

It is a thought that strikes me, cold as a blade of ice. That James might know more, that he could even have somehow been involved ... But no. I cannot see how. What happened to Stephanie sounds feasible, but James had nothing to do with Isaac. There was no reason for him to have hurt him. His father is right: James is not a bad man. I can see with my own eyes how cut up he is about Stephanie. He wouldn't have done anything to Isaac.

Maybe the answer is to leave Ixos so we can put it behind us. Maybe I need to put my faith in my husband and believe he is right. What point is there in telling the police if he can't offer them more? We could salvage a future again. Everything I have ever wanted is within reach.

EM

Chapter Thirty-Three

Em doesn't want to go back to the villa. She knows Kallis will come to talk to the girl, Rosie, and Spencer, her brother. And that they will come to the conclusion that the two of them likely had nothing to do with Isaac's death. Because they didn't, Em is certain of that too.

'What are we going to do?' she says to Charlie, her voice shallow and hushed. They are on the edge of the cliff, looking out to the sea below. It looks aquamarine from here. A perfect green glass. When the boys were younger she used to take them to the beach in the summer holidays and they would stand on a clifftop and say what they could see below them as they ate their ice creams. Isaac was always the most excited, spotting ships in the distance, telling her what he was going to build in the sand.

She has grieved the loss of their childhood some days. When she feels particularly emotional, she looks back at photos of when they were young enough to hang off her hands and she could still pick them up. She would give anything to have those days back again. But it is only now that she can see their teenage years were just as precious.

'We can't let anything happen to Theo,' she says to Charlie. Her words sound stronger than she feels because Em is scared that all of it is out of her control. She had thought that someone else in the hotel must have had reason to hurt Isaac. It made sense if there was an outraged husband, however hard it was to bear, but now she knows that isn't the case then she cannot see who else the police will suspect. They will come for Theo.

And what if she has just made it worse for him? She pointed Lieutenant Kallis in the direction of a couple who will be able to convince them as easily as they have done her that they had nothing to do with Isaac's death. Surely Kallis will believe Theo is scratching at anything to get himself out of it.

As much as she loves her son, she would be thinking it too if she were them.

LAILA

Chapter Thirty-Four

The first time James proposed to me was a winter's evening only six months after we met. We had come out of our cocoon of the early days of our relationship but the intensity was still there.

That night we had been out with Claire and Greg and a handful of other friends to celebrate Claire's birthday, but I remember with clarity the way James looked so serious when he walked into our bedroom that night. I'd pushed myself upright and asked if everything was OK.

'I've never felt like this before, Laila.' He crouched down on the floor beside my side of the bed. A frown creased his forehead as he reached for my hands and took hold of them. 'I want you to be my wife.'

'What?' I had laughed at him, but he merely shook his head and said to me, 'I mean it. I honestly don't know what I would do if I didn't have you in my life. I want to grow old with you. I want you to have my children.'

I wanted that too. Just to hear those words took my breath away. James was the closest I had come to ever having a soul mate, but it was still so new and so fresh. In my mind's eye, I could see my mum, warning me not to rush into anything. She had only met James twice, how could I tell her we were getting married?

'Ask me again in a year,' I told him.

'That's a no?'

'It's definitely not a no,' I said. 'I want to make sure we both feel the same in a year's time.'

It was a year to the day that James took me out to dinner. Obviously his proposal had always been on my mind even though he hadn't once mentioned it again, and I worried he might have forgotten. By then I wanted nothing more than for us to get engaged; if it were possible, I had fallen even more deeply in love with this man.

The meal passed without event and James told me he wanted us to walk home. It was a cold January evening and there were a few fluttery flakes of snow but he was insistent and so we did, stopping at a bridge that overlooked the River Stour. He folded me into his arms and warmed me up.

'I still feel the same,' he murmured into my ear. I had closed my eyes, blinked back the tears. I knew in a heartbeat what he meant as he grinned and slid down onto one knee. 'One year on and I still feel exactly the same. I have never been surer.' He pulled a box out of his pocket. 'But now the question is, do you? Will you marry me, Laila?'

'Yes,' I cried. 'Yes of course I will marry you.'

'It's exactly a year,' he told me.

'Were you worried I might say no?' I asked him.

'If you did I would have asked you again another year from now,' he said. 'And I'd have gone on for the rest of my life. I mean it, Laila, I'm not going anywhere. I want to spend the rest of my life with you.'

James has packed by the time I get back to the room. His clothes are neatly folded into the suitcase that lies open on our bed, his Kindle and its charger on top, his washbag open in the corner.

'I thought we could get some dinner sent up to the room tonight,' he says. 'What do you think?' He looks up and chances a smile.

'Sounds good.'

'I haven't touched any of your clothes yet.'

'It's fine, I can do it.'

He closes his case and lifts it onto the floor, replacing it with my empty one that he pulls out from beneath the bed.

In half an hour I am packed. It never takes long to dismantle the room when you're going home. Though we still have another three nights in Crete before we fly to Gatwick and the holiday is over.

I don't want to spend tonight in the empty space. I want to go now, but we have no choice other than to wait for the ferry in the morning. At least we are leaving early and there is no hanging around, because I don't want to risk bumping into anyone, and especially not Em.

We order off the in-room menu. James chooses steak again. It has always been his go-to selection. Rare and red, piled with chunky chips and a mixed salad. I opt for a seafood pasta.

'You can share my chips,' he tells me, kissing my head as he calls through the order on the hotel phone by our bed. We don't get wine. Neither of us mention it, and I wonder how this non-drinking will pan out. To be honest, I could do with a glass of the Chablis that is staring back at me from the menu.

We sit at the two-seater bistro table outside as we wait for our food. The early evening sunshine has always been my favourite part of the day when I have been abroad. Ironically the image of our evening is a set of perfection. It could have been the most romantic night we have had since we arrived in Ixos if there weren't so many lies and secrets and dark pasts looming over us, whispering and taunting us to speak of them, knowing neither of us will.

'Will you talk to the police?' I ask him. I am only going to mention it once more and then I will leave it alone.

'Laila.' James shakes his head. 'I thought we had decided.'

'I just want to check you think you're doing the right thing,' I say.

'I am. We are,' he promises me. 'Don't you feel it? This is right.' He smiles and I smile back.

I don't sleep as badly as I had thought I might. I imagined a restless night, worrying my mind wouldn't settle, but I only woke once in the night, and even then I fell back to sleep with relative ease.

I wake at 6 a.m., as I have done most mornings of our holiday, and slip out of bed as quietly as I can. We have laid out our travelling clothes. For me it is a sundress and flip-flops and a wide-brimmed sun hat. The ferry over had proven hotter than I had expected and so I want to sit outside on the way to Crete.

I try not to wake James as I patter about the empty room, but he rolls over and opens his eyes as I am about to leave the villa. 'Where are you going?' he says. 'What time is it?' He shifts himself upright with the anxiety of someone who has overslept.

'Don't worry, we still have an hour,' I tell him. 'I just want to have one last early-morning walk.' I know I won't bump into any of the guests at this hour. No one else will be around and so I feel safe leaving the room.

'OK, I'll see you in a bit then.' He leans over to grab his phone, checking the time before he puts it back and rolls over, closing his eyes again.

I shut the door softly behind me and breathe in the Greek morning air. I hadn't wanted to leave three days ago but then everything changed within half an hour, throwing my world up into the air. I have been trying to catch the pieces ever since with no idea they could have scattered as far and wide as they did.

As I knew would be the case, I pass no one as I walk past the other few rooms on my way to the clifftop, along the path that leads towards the swimming pool and the steps to the beach. The pool has been refilled and the sunbeds are laid out in uniform lines, but I can't imagine any of the guests sitting around it today. Not with the police tape still flapping the other side of it, cordoning off the area of shrubbery that remains restricted while it's being searched for evidence.

I look straight ahead and carry on with purpose. I am not here to watch the sunrise, or meander across the sand this morning. I went to bed knowing what I must do, and I awoke with the same resolve. I take a deep breath as I reach reception.

Inside, the air conditioning hits me in a chilling blast and a shiver ripples through me as I cross the marble floor to the desk where a young Greek woman with dark shiny hair taps onto a keypad.

'Hello, can I help you?' She smiles as I approach.

'Is Lieutenant Kallis around please?'

'No, he hasn't arrived yet this morning.'

'It's important I speak to him now,' I tell her. 'Do you have a number you could call him on?'

'Yes. Yes, of course,' she answers, regarding me curiously as she turns to a cabinet and plucks out a card with ease. 'Who can I say wants to speak to him?' she asks as she taps out the number with long pink nails on her telephone.

'Laila Burrow.'

My stomach churns as I wait for her to make the call. This isn't a decision made lightly or quickly and even as I am going through with it I am haunted by doubt.

The woman hands the phone over to me and Kallis's voice fills the line. 'Mrs Burrow?'

'I need to speak to you,' I say. 'My husband and I are supposed to be leaving for the ferry at seven a.m. but I need you to come before that.'

Maybe he can sense the urgency in my voice, or the tremor that gives away my fear for he says, 'I can be there in ten minutes.' And then, 'Mrs Burrow?'

'Yes?'

'Don't go anywhere.'

'I won't,' I tell him, and hang up the phone. Then I sit on the leather sofa and wait for him to arrive.

PART THREE

LAILA

Chapter Thirty-Five

Day Nine – Sunday

I stand at the wall of the harbour in Crete, a takeaway cup of coffee in my hands. It is a hive of activity with fishermen trawling nets out of their boats and parents pulling their children along by their little hands pointing out the fish and the pretty brightly painted doors of the cafes that line the cobbled path behind me. They pave the street, all bustling with customers who spill out onto tables in the mid-morning sun. It is 11 a.m. and I have been awake for hours.

Yesterday morning I waited fifteen minutes for Kallis to arrive. His car pulled up outside the reception and he hurried through the revolving doors. I expected him to tell me he hoped I was going to make it worth his while, dragging him out of bed so early, but instead he walked over to me silently and sat down on the sofa beside me, steepling his hands in his lap.

'Is everything OK?' he said. Like there was any chance it could have been.

'My husband told me he saw Isaac the night he died.' My voice is low though there is no one else in the large lobby apart from the woman behind the desk, who is too far away to hear us. 'He says he doesn't remember anything else about it.'

'But you think he is lying?'

'Honestly? I don't know,' I replied. I didn't. I still don't.

But too much had unravelled the day before for me to hand on my heart believe my husband. Not only his admission about Stephanie's death and his involvement in it, but also the revelations about his drinking and the blackouts, or greyouts, whatever he wants to call them. Yes, he may be telling me the truth now, but what if he isn't? What if the gaps in his memory are simply convenient?

I couldn't leave White Sands with so many 'what if's hanging over us. Not when, in the worst-case scenario, my husband might know more about Isaac's death than he's revealing.

I gave him the chance to tell the police, but he chose not to take it, and in itself that told me all I needed to know. I suspect there is more to James's story than he makes out.

I told Kallis how James hadn't been happy with me when he'd returned from the fishing trip, how we'd drank too much and I didn't know what time he had got back to the room. What I didn't tell him was anything about Stephanie. I wanted him to treat Isaac's case and James's possible involvement as a separate incident and not be swayed by what may or may not have taken place sixteen years ago. I am sure it was nothing more than a dreadful accident, but while James pleads he doesn't remember, I don't know and doubt I will ever know whether that's true.

Kallis asked me what motive James might have had for killing Isaac and I admitted I could not think of any. 'There's no reason at all,' I said, emphasising the fact, and he nodded in response as if he were trying to fathom it too.

I hope he will not find James guilty. More than anything in the world, I don't want James to have been involved.

I wasn't sure what Claire would say when I called her yesterday. 'You think I've done the wrong thing, don't you?' I questioned her, when I had finished relaying the whole story and she was silent on the other end of the phone. 'You can't imagine how I could do it. Tell me the truth. Would you go behind Greg's back if he told you he had seen a boy who was later murdered, but refused to go to the police?'

I was desperate for my best friend to be honest with me, because that was all I craved right now: honesty from someone I loved.

'No,' she said eventually, 'I probably wouldn't. Because I have no reason not to trust Greg isn't telling me the truth, so I guess I would try and work it out with him first. But it's not the same as what you've been through, Laila,' she said. 'Not in any way. By the sound of it James has bit by bit broken any trust you have, so it's understandable that you suspect there's more he's not telling you. And you're angry with him too.'

'I didn't do it to get back at him.'

'I know you didn't.'

'I think a part of me hoped that if I couldn't get to the truth, the police might be able to.'

I did find out more snippets from Kallis when he called me to give me the news that they had arrested James. My husband had admitted he had seen Isaac on Wednesday night and had remembered more snatches of what happened. He and Isaac had spoken. A drunken (on James's part) conversation in the early hours of the morning when Isaac had woken him from where he'd fallen asleep at a table at the bar by the pool.

I still don't know if James has always had this memory or if, like he told Kallis, it had come back to him only yesterday. Either way, it puts him at the scene with the victim, though Kallis and his team are still scrabbling about for motive.

Meanwhile I have torn myself apart playing out images of James being woken from the sleep he likely drifted back into yesterday morning. Kallis and another colleague had gone to our room shortly after we spoke in the lobby. I picture my husband's surprise, shock and anger as he learnt of my betrayal.

I didn't see him taken in to be questioned. I couldn't bear to face him, all the time hoping he would tell Kallis what he knew and would then be released. That was my hope, but they held him longer than I expected, turning over question after question, updating me sporadically after I missed the ferry and spent most of the day waiting in our room for news.

At 3 p.m. I had a call from James. They had taken him to a small station in Ixos village.

'How could you, Laila?' He was close to tears.

'I'm so sorry,' I said. And I was, I was desperately sorry for everything that had happened. It was a horrible conversation. James asked me over and over why I had done what I had, and I kept telling him I'd had no choice. He would not have done the right thing himself and ultimately that meant I could never trust him. Only this last part I did not say aloud.

Not once did I ask James what happened that night, but neither did he tell me he had nothing to do with Isaac's death and that I had it all wrong. Since that conversation, I keep questioning whether this absence of denial means anything or not.

It was a short call that left me wrung out. When I hung up the phone I sobbed, flashes of regret and panic lurching through me, though ultimately I knew I wouldn't do anything different if I had the chance again.

Ironically I ended up getting a private transfer to Crete in the end. On Kallis's request, the receptionist at White Sands organised it when I refused to spend another night at the resort. I was picked up at 5 p.m. and taken to the harbour and they found me a hotel to stay in, a small guest house run by an elderly woman who doesn't speak much English. This is where I am now, or at least just up the road from it. I still don't know how long I will be here. I don't see how I can go anywhere until I know what is happening to my husband.

Yesterday afternoon I was waiting in my room, with only half an hour until my taxi was due, when there was a soft tap on the door. I peered out of the window and saw Em standing the other side of it. Her face was as ashen as it had been the day before, her expression blank. I opened the door to her and sensed her apprehension matched mine. For a moment we stared at each other, neither of us knowing what to say or what we were doing.

'They tell me your husband has been arrested,' she said eventually. Her words had no emotion in them. She was wrung out. I could see this in the black shadows that ringed her eyes and the hollowness of her stare.

I opened the door wider so she could come into the room. It was not a conversation I wanted to have outside. Em stepped in and I shut the door behind her.

'I'm sorry,' I told her. 'For what has happened to your family and for what I told the police about Theo. I want to make that clear: I never wanted to hurt you, but I got it very wrong.'

'You did.' I noticed the way her hands shook, her fingers tapping against her legs and I had to look away. Still no one knew that I had been in her room three days earlier, but now I worried whether it was a matter of time until James told them. I didn't know if he was capable of doing it, to get back at me.

I was pleased to be having this conversation with Em before he did. 'Did your husband kill my son?' she asked bluntly.

'I don't know what happened,' I admitted. 'But I hope to God he had nothing to do with it.'

'But you think he might have, or else you wouldn't have said anything.'

I mulled over how to answer her. 'My husband says he saw your son and that's what I told the police.'

'Only now they've arrested him. So they must think he did it. And I believe you do too.'

I shake my head. 'I don't,' I say.

'Can you imagine it?' she asked me.

I shake my head. 'No. Not the man I know.' I don't add that I have no clue whether I even know the real James or not.

'So why?' she says. 'Why would he have done it? What reason would he have had for killing Isaac?'

'There is no reason,' I told her. 'I know how hard this must be for you, and I'm sorry I can't give you more than that.

'I'm leaving in half an hour,' I said. 'There's a boat coming for me, I'm staying in Crete.'

'Why are you telling me that?'

'I don't know. I guess I don't want you to think I'm running away. I had nothing to do with any of this, I hope you understand that. I only found out yesterday that James ...' I looked away unable to finish the sentence.

Eventually Em turned away from me and walked back to my room door. She opened it and stood in the doorway for a moment before saying, 'You didn't need to do what you did.'

I nodded. I think it was her way of thanking me for doing it anyway.

As boats bob in the harbour I close my eyes and listen to the clinking of their sails in the light breeze. I am waiting for Lieutenant Kallis to call me with an update this morning; he has promised me he will, but it is already 11 a.m. and I haven't heard anything. I'm plagued with thoughts of what I must do, the calls I should make to James's dad and my parents, who I still haven't been able to speak to, as well as work and of course the clinic in New York, which I will have to cancel. I can't find it in myself to do any of it.

And then it rings. From deep inside my bag I pull out my phone and check the screen. It is a Greek number and I know it must be Kallis. 'Hello?' I answer.

'Laila?' It isn't the lieutenant but James's voice that fills the line. 'They've released me,' he says.

'They've ... ?' I step back, feeling for the railing behind me. 'That's great,' I say, 'that's great,' all the while thinking, *What now? What happens now?*

Chapter Thirty-Six

'I'm getting a boat to Crete, so I'll see you later today. I assume you'll still be there?' James says. I detect a hint of sarcasm.

'Yes. Of course I'll be here. What happened?' I ask. What did …' my words fade. *What did the police decide?*

'There isn't enough evidence to convict me,' he says, adding hurriedly, 'Which of course there isn't because I didn't do it. Anyway, we can talk later.' He hangs up the phone.

My stomach twists at the thought of seeing him again, of having to explain myself to him and of not knowing what my future holds any more.

It is almost 6 p.m. when James finally arrives in Crete. I am waiting at the harbour, my heart in my mouth as he steps off the boat and sees me. He goes to hold his hand up in a wave but then drops it back to his side, his other pulling his suitcase behind him.

His face is blank when he walks up to me, although there is a coldness in his eyes that resembles hurt. 'Hi, I ...' I fumble over my words. 'It's good to see you,' I try, finally.

'Where's the hotel?' he asks. 'I want to get rid of this.' He tugs at his case.

'It's over this way. It's not really a hotel,' I say, 'it's fine, but it's not much.'

James doesn't respond. I hadn't thought through the logistics of us sleeping together in the room until after I had spoken to him earlier. It is a small space, with a double bed, and the idea of James and me sharing it tonight seems implausible.

We don't speak as I lead him over the road and around the corner, up the steps of the small guest house. 'What are you doing here, Laila?' he says as he looks up at it. 'I had a hotel booked for us.'

'I know, I just ... it's what they found me, I went with it.'

He silently raises his eyes as he follows me up the stairs to the room.

'What do you want to do?' I ask. 'Have you eaten?'

'Barely.'

'Shall we go and get something?'

James nods, wandering over to the window and looking out on the harbour below. I tell him there are plenty of little tavernas we can grab something from and so he follows me back down again and onto the street, a narrow, cobbled alleyway with brightly painted buildings either side. We walk to the front where the canopy-lined road shelters restaurant upon restaurant, buzzing with customers and people stopping to read the menus, or take photos of the port.

'What do you fancy?' I ask.

'Anything.'

'Shall we try here then?' I point to a nearby cafe where there are plenty of free tables and we can sit on one at the edge away from other people. We order two Cokes and accept the menu. James is quiet and in return I have no idea how to act.

As soon as our drinks have arrived, he says to me, 'Why did you do it? You handed me over to the police. You must have thought I was capable of murdering that boy.'

'I didn't. It wasn't that,' I insist, reaching for his hand that he pulls just out of my reach.

'Of course it was. You left me sleeping in bed and you called the lieutenant. He came to the room and woke me and then dragged me out of there like some criminal.'

'I know. And I'm sorry,' I say. 'Only—'

'Only what?'

'I don't know,' I cry, 'I don't know what to say.'

James's eyes are filled with tears too as he looks away and towards the port. He bites down on his bottom lip, willing himself to be strong and for them not to flow. A drop hangs precariously close to the edge of his eyelid and he needs to wipe it away but I can see he is trying to ignore it until it's too late.

'I didn't kill him,' he says quietly. 'I didn't do it, Laila.' Now he turns to me, narrowing his eyes. He looks as if he is trying to think it through.

'You told me you couldn't remember what happened.'

'I know and I—' James stops abruptly. 'I didn't kill him.'

'Have you remembered more then?' I ask.

He hesitates for a moment. It's a moment too long I think, he has remembered. Something has come back to him, but he shakes his head and says, 'I remember talking to him. He was at the bar, though it was closed by then. But after that—' He waves his hand in the air and then leans across the table towards me. 'Laila, I didn't do it.'

I nod cautiously. I want to believe my husband, of course I do. He looks sincere as he tells me he didn't, and the police have questioned him and let him go. I have known this man for ten years and yes, there are secrets he's told me about recently, but his father was right when he said that James is a good man.

'You need to figure out if you believe it too,' he says to me.

I nod, but don't answer. I so desperately want to. If he is lying to me now, then it feels like our whole life together has been a lie too.

'The last twenty-four hours have been bloody hard,' he says. 'It wasn't even the questioning, it was trying to reconcile what you did. But then, I suppose I can't blame you. Of course you must have considered I could have killed him right after I told you what happened to Stephanie.'

'No, James, it's not that I thought you did it—'

'What I'm saying is, I get it. I don't like it but I get why you did what you did. But we're here now, Laila. Look at us, look at me,' he says. 'I love you. I always have, and I always will, and all I need to know is that we can move on? Together?'

I don't know what to say. My head is spinning. I never thought I would find myself contemplating whether or not I wanted to stay with my husband. It has only ever been James for me, but so much has happened that I'm not sure I can move on from.

'Laila?' He shuffles in his seat, sensing my hesitancy.

'The clinic—' I say. 'Is that still what you want too?'

'If it's what you want,' he tells me.

I take a deep breath. Is there still a chance we can get through this? Because if there's any possibility of me getting pregnant …

'So?' he says. 'Do you believe I had nothing to do with Isaac's death?'

I nod. 'I don't believe you did, James.'

My husband smiles at me. 'Thank you,' he says. 'Then let's do this!'

ISAAC

Chapter Thirty-Seven

Day Five – Wednesday

Isaac presses his phone and the screen flashes up. No new messages. He had hoped she might reply to him but deep down he knows she isn't interested. She's twenty-one and he's four years younger. She left school and he's taking his A levels next year. They are worlds apart but he had hoped, when they spoke earlier, that she might have wanted to see him again.

He couldn't believe it when she'd come over to him. They had been looking at each other for the past few days, he knows she had seen him too. He'd caught her eye a few times over the swimming pool. He couldn't help looking at her, because, come on, she was so hot and especially in that little white bikini she wore most days. She would see him looking but he wouldn't turn away. He didn't feel guilty or embarrassed and he wanted her to know that. That he could handle older girls like her.

Earlier today she'd come over and started chatting. The guy she was here with was out on some fishing trip. 'Isn't he your husband?' he'd said.

Eventually she admitted to him, 'No, actually he's my brother.'

Isaac had tried to hide his surprise. Their fingers were so close he could almost touch her. He had wondered if he should, let her know he was interested and see what she did, but in the end he thought it would be better to play it cool for now. She'd only just told him she was here with her brother, there was time for them to see where it went.

He had got her number though. Tapped the digits into his phone straight away. She didn't ask for his, but that was OK as he sent a text fifteen minutes later. *Do you want to meet up tonight?*

Theo had followed him back to their villa after that. His brother. Always there. He knew that Theo had been watching him and Rosie talking, and that Theo was spoiling for a fight. He'd been in a tossy mood all day and now he was worse.

'What the hell?' Isaac said when his brother followed him off the path and to their pool, kicking a pair of Isaac's shorts into the water as he passed. 'Get them out.'

'She's not interested in you,' Theo said. 'She's married.'

He had a knack of always getting Isaac's back up. Even when they were kids he did it, and their mum always took

Theo's side. *Be nice to your brother, Isaac. Let him play with you and your friends.* He used to wish Theo would get some friends of his own to play with.

It was an unkind thought, he knew. And Isaac wasn't cruel, because he did actually love his brother. But they were older now, and there were times when Theo really pissed him off and this was one of them.

Rosie had made him promise not to tell anyone they weren't actually married because they were pretending to be on a honeymoon. Something about her brother's ex-girlfriend jilting him and she'd stepped in for the free holiday. He said to Theo, 'Yeah? That's what you think 'cos she is interested. She gave me her number.' He held his phone up as if to prove it though he wouldn't show him. He wouldn't put it past his brother to toss that in the pool too.

'That doesn't mean anything.'

Isaac could see that he had caught him off guard. His brother who wasn't making any move to get his shorts, and nor would he. 'And we're meeting later,' he told him.

'She's married,' Theo repeated, narrowing his eyes. Isaac could almost feel the heat burning off him.

Isaac laughed. 'So what?'

'She's married,' he said again, striding towards Isaac and getting into his face. 'So you wouldn't do it.'

It was so easy to wind Theo up. It always had been. His mum was always giving Theo slack if he got angry, blaming Isaac for pushing him too far. She was overly protective of his baby brother and would always side with him but this holiday she had been spending more time with him and not Theo. She wanted to talk to him instead and maybe that was because she'd realised how irritating Theo could be.

'I would and I am,' Isaac told him. It was a version of the truth because he still held out hope it would happen.

Isaac pushed aside the sliding doors and slipped into their room. Theo was close on his heels, biting at him like a dog, telling him he was going to tell their mum. Now might have been the time to confess there was nothing happening, but there was no way Isaac was going to do that. He wanted to shut his brother up. What business was it of his anyway who he did and didn't see?

But anyway, it's irrelevant now because more than eight hours have passed. It's gone 11.30 p.m. and she hasn't replied to his message. He presses delete and erases it, along with her phone number. He isn't going to waste his time on some girl if she doesn't want to know him but he's certainly not going to give Theo the satisfaction of knowing the truth when he's still arsey with him. He really can't believe that anyone can hold a grudge for as long as his brother does. It's another of his annoying traits.

Isaac sighs as he sits on top of the covers and scrolls through his phone. Theo is standing by the en suite door, brushing his teeth and staring at him. 'Your brother's watching us,' Rosie had said to him earlier. 'He's right behind us.'

'Ignore him,' Isaac told her.

'What's he doing?'

It was a good question that half the time Isaac couldn't answer. There were a number of reasons why Theo did what he did. His mum once said that she thought Theo couldn't handle Isaac growing up and moving on from him, but Isaac thought it was nothing more than the fact that Theo was jealous of him. And most likely their mum spending more time with him has wound him up too.

'Where are you going?' Theo asks him now.

'Out,' Isaac replies. He checks his watch, it's gone midnight.

'Where?'

'Just out.'

He slides open the door and closes it quietly behind him so he doesn't wake his mum or Rob. He wishes he didn't have to share a bedroom with his brother, it's so hard to get away from him. But Isaac is barely out when Theo emerges too, starting on at him again. Isaac tell hims to piss off and walks away, picking up his pace as he dips into the trees and runs towards the pool.

There are still a few people out after the gala dinner. It's a hotel that usually seems to go to sleep quite early. There isn't much to do here and Isaac has been bored out of his mind in the evenings. He didn't mind coming away with his mum and Rob, but he doesn't want to do it again next year. When he's eighteen he wants to be out with his mates, holidaying in Mykonos like two of them are already doing this summer.

Isaac lies out on one of the loungers and watches the stragglers at the bar and the staff who are clearing up, probably hoping the guests will all hurry up and go to bed. No one looks in his direction. He is tucked under one of the trees the other side to the main restaurant. No one knows he is here and that's the way he likes it.

He might have taken Rosie's number out of his phone but now he is hoping he'll see her. He pats his jeans pocket and realises he'd left his phone in the room. He can't even see if it's still on his last-dialled-number list.

At some point Isaac falls asleep. He's cold when he wakes up. A slime of dribble runs out of his mouth and he quickly wipes it away before anyone sees but the place is deserted now. He looks at his watch again, he must have slept for over forty minutes.

He starts to get up when he sees the guy from earlier who had been arguing with his wife at dinner. The one he and his mum had been laughing about. The man has his head down on one of the tables, lying on his arms that are spreadeagled in front of him. Isaac wanders over and gives the guy a shove on the arm. 'Hey, mate,' Isaac says. 'Wake up.'

The man stirs and looks up, bleary-eyed and staring around him as if everything is out of focus and he is trying to work out where he is.

'Don't you think you'd better go home?' Isaac says.

He grunts and slumps back in his chair, reeking of alcohol. His poor wife probably doesn't want him back, Isaac thinks, maybe he's better off sleeping out here for the night. 'What was that?' the man slurs.

'Nothing, mate, just checking you were all right,' Isaac replies.

'All right?' the guy laughs. 'No. The one thing I'm not is all right.'

'Sorry to hear that.' Isaac rolls his eyes. This isn't a conversation he wants to get into but the guy has other plans.

He goes on, 'And besides, I don't want to be a father. I don't deserve to be one.'

'OK.' Isaac grimaces.

'I love her though, you know? I'd do anything for her. Anything. But I can't give her that, so?' He shrugs. 'I was responsible for ...' The man drifts off and then picks up again as he says, 'I was responsible for someone's death. Out here. Or near here.' He waves a shaky arm in the direction of the sea.

'What?' Isaac automatically takes a step away from the table.

'Not outright. I didn't mean to, it just happened. I went back there today. I couldn't ... I didn't want to ... I wanted to see the last place she was. I left her,' the guy goes on. 'I left her and she died.'

'OK, listen, mate, maybe you should get back to your wife now?' Isaac says. He is way out of his depth, he doesn't have the right words to tell this stranger. His mum would know what to do, she's always good with stuff like this, but seriously, what the hell?

'Laila doesn't know about it. I never told her.' He pushes back his chair with a screech as he stands up, stumbling into the table as he rights himself. 'I wish I could forget it all,' he says. 'Forget it ever happened.'

'OK. Are you going back now? Because I need to ...' Isaac waves in the direction of their villa, over the other side of the pool. He starts to walk towards it but when he glances back, the man is following him in wavy lines that slowly meander towards the water.

'Christ,' Isaac mutters. What's he going to do? Isaac can't leave him here, the guy is so drunk he could easily fall in the water and drown. He goes back to him and holds onto his arm but it's almost impossible to shove him in any direction other than onto one of the sunloungers, which is what he does.

He is walking back around the pool when a voice calls out, 'What are you doing here?' Theo is emerging from the bushes.

'Theo, go home,' Isaac hisses. He's glad the guy is still lying on the lounger and Theo doesn't seem to have spotted him. If the man starts muttering about killing people again and Theo overhears him then his brother would be straight to their mum, telling her, sensationalising it. The guy needs a break. The last thing he needs is for Theo to get involved.

But thankfully the lounger is practically completely in the dark and so Isaac shoves his hands against his brother's chest. 'Come on,' he says, trying to get him going in the right direction.

'Stop pushing me about.' Theo splays his hands against Isaac's chest, two flat imprints onto his white shirt as he pushes him back.

'Don't even go there.' Isaac isn't in the mood. All he wants now is to go to bed, only his brother is wound up and spoiling for a fight and he knows that if they go back to the room, Theo won't stop. He'll keep on and on at him.

All it would take is a handful of Theo's T-shirt, squeezed tight, telling his brother to stop acting like an idiot. He has always overpowered him, even though Theo's the one who's built like their dad.

Ironically in that moment Theo is telling *him*, 'You're just like Dad.'

'Like Dad? How?'

There are tears in Theo's eyes, he can see. Something's got to him, but Isaac doesn't have a clue what. 'Having affairs, you don't care about Mum. You didn't even care at the time when Dad left her. You always think you can do whatever you want.'

Isaac screws his eyes up as he pulls his head back. Probably he should tell Theo that Rosie isn't even married, but now Theo is yelling at him, 'Don't laugh at me,' when he wasn't even laughing at him.

He goes to tell him that he did care what happened when Dad left. He cared very much, and was worried sick that his mum was spiralling into a deep depression. But he was thirteen, and he was the man of the house then, and so instead of waiting outside her door for her to get up most days like Theo did, he got on with the things that needed doing. He pretended to his mum that he was happy and life was good so that she might think it was too, while meanwhile his brother was drowning alongside her.

He didn't realise that Theo hadn't moved on from that fear like he had, and while all those thoughts take seconds to float around his head he doesn't have the chance to speak any of them because he could never have predicted the speed of Theo's fist as it comes hurtling through the air, catching him smack in the jaw as it pummels him backwards.

Isaac hits the tree with a thud to the back of his head. He lays on his back, dazed, his eyes trying to focus as the drunk guy's had earlier. He can make out Theo's face looming over him and so Isaac manages to reach out and grab his brother's ankle and swing his arm to one side, tipping him off balance so that Theo falls to the floor, his leg flinging behind him, catching Isaac square in the ribs.

The air punches out of him, his eyes flicker as he tries to catch his breath. The pain is searingly intense. Not just in his stomach but his head too where he'd hit the ground. He can't move a muscle. His eyes won't stay open. Over the other side of the pool he can barely make out the guy who was facing him but who had passed out again on the lounger.

Isaac's eyes gradually shut. Then open again, only marginally in a narrow slit, before closing again.

Theo's hand is around his wrist. He can faintly feel it along with his brother's voice. 'Shit,' Theo is saying in his ear. 'Isaac, wake up.' His fingertips are pressing into his skin as if he is feeling for a pulse. 'Isaac?' Theo is panicked and even though his voice is fading Isaac can feel his breath on his cheek.

''Sfine,' Isaac mutters. 'Fine,' he says again, although he has to admit he feels anything but fine.

He feels Theo moving away from him now. 'I'm going back,' his brother is saying, though the words are fading fast, ebbing away. 'You better come …' Whatever he says next Isaac doesn't hear him.

He wants to call him back now, stop him going. It's just like Theo to run, pretend like nothing happened. He never wants to get in trouble. Isaac doesn't feel good. This isn't right. But his words trickle around his head like water and he can't catch them.

His hand falls limply until it hits something wet. How funny that that is his last thought.

LAILA

Chapter Thirty-Eight

One month later

It is a rainy Saturday morning, weather I've come to expect in August, yet it feels like the summer is already a long way off.

Still the river is busy with paddle-boarders and kayakers and hooded walkers with their dogs strolling alongside it, or queuing for a bacon sandwich from the restaurant on the quay. The sky is grey and the rain feels fresh, but there's an optimism that the day will improve.

Ever since my early morning walks in Ixos I have found the solitary time good for my soul. James is at the gym and so I have come out on my own to breathe in the fresh air and let my mind drift to whatever place it wants to take me. My boss once told me that sometimes we only make decisions when we don't think about them, when we let them come to us, and recently I have been trying to live by this motto, because ever since we left Greece I've been drowning in choices.

I had told James in Crete that I believed him, because I desperately want to, but I am still plagued by the conviction that he isn't being honest with me. That his memory has in fact always been intact, and that if this is the case there may be more he isn't telling me.

James and I have fallen into a pattern of talking at night over bottles of alcohol-free beer and dishes that I have spent time preparing. Sometimes we go out for dinner and pick at Thai curries and noodles and dissect our days and where we might find the money for the clinic in New York that I postponed to another two months' time.

He is working hard to prove he is the perfect husband, assuring me he is more focused on work, that he will get the promotion that his dad has spoken to him about, as we laze in bed on Sunday mornings. We even have my father-in-law coming over to lunch tomorrow.

On paper we are moving forward together, heading in the right direction. When I can manage to block out the questions in my mind, it's exactly like the old days.

JAMES

Chapter Thirty-Nine

Day Five – Wednesday

James opens his eyes. He doesn't have a clue where he is. Outside. Definitely out. Oh God. What's happened? He is sprawled out on one of the loungers by the pool. He thought he was sitting by the table.

Laila. They had a fight. A huge row. God even knows where she is. Probably still at the table having dinner. His head is banging. He reaches for his phone to see what the time is but it's completely dead.

Why did he ever go on that fishing trip? He didn't really want to see that place again. He was torturing himself. Making himself live through it again, and for what? A few more snatches of memory he doesn't need.

A part of him thought he owed it to Stephanie when he hadn't been able to get what happened out of his head.

Over the years most of the memories came back to him but he'd believed he could go and come out the other end and then be able to put it behind him. But it made everything worse.

He rolls his head over, searching for the bar. He'd order another drink if there was someone there. He wants to blot out the memories of Stephanie again.

Laila has been annoying him though he can't recall why. But it wasn't his fault, he was sure of that.

He needs a drink but there's no barman. The bar looks closed. The lights are off, a shutter down at one end of it. Now he thinks about it there's no longer any music playing. Christ. How long's he been here?

James closes his eyes again. He'll have to sleep here tonight. Or he would if it wasn't for the bugs. He's been bitten again and scratched his ankle raw. Why do they like him so much? He thumps his leg against the bed trying to rid it of anything that might be crawling over his flesh. Maybe he should go to the bar inside to get another drink.

He rolls himself up, sitting on the edge of the lounger, rubbing a hand over his eyes to focus as he lets out a deep sigh. What a night. How the hell he ended up on the sunlounger he has no idea.

There is someone else lying on the other side of the pool too, except they aren't on a sunbed, they are sprawled out on the ground, one arm hanging off the edge, the hand trailing into the water. James laughs at first. They're in a worse state than him.

But there is something about the body that looks too … wrong? He pushes himself up and stumbles towards the pool. He isn't that drunk, surely? He manages to stagger around it to the other side and nearly topples on top of the body when he leans over to crouch down. He puts a hand out to stop himself and it falls onto the body's chest.

James recoils. It's too still. He manages to lift up the wrist but there's no pulse. He falls onto his backside dropping the body's arm and looks around. There's no one else here, he has to get help.

A flash of a memory comes searing into his head. The boy in front of him, talking to him. James told him about Stephanie. He remembers that. He said he was responsible for her death and then … he can't remember a thing. His whole mind is blank. But then he woke to find himself lying one side of the pool and here is the boy lying the other side. Dead.

James brings his own hands in front of his face and stares at them. Did he do this? Could he have? No. He couldn't. There is no way. But then he told the boy the one thing he has never told anyone, not even Laila. Only his father knows the truth. And so maybe, maybe he did.

James pushes himself backwards, still on the ground, trying to get away from what he may or may not have done. He wants to be sick, but he knows he can't. Not here. His heart is racing but his memory is black. He can't leave the boy but he can't tell anyone because what if they find evidence that he has killed him?

He hits himself on the side of the head, trying to slap some memory back in there, to string together conscious thoughts of what to do, but all James can think is *I killed him.*

Slowly he eases himself up to standing, takes a step back until he is hidden within the trees. His heart isn't easing. He cannot walk away. He has to cover his tracks. The body is so near to the water, it wouldn't take much to push it gently in. Make it look like an accident.

EM

Chapter Forty

One month later

It is an unseasonably cold day for late August and Em is wrapped up in a large woollen cardigan on the bench in the park. She is a distance from the other parents who stand on the sidelines and cheer their children, she can barely see Theo, but it is the closest she can bring herself to be right now.

Rob sits down beside her and hands her a cup of coffee that he has bought from the van nearby. Wafts of bacon drift over, a smell she would usually love but today it makes her nauseous.

'He's playing well,' Rob says. 'He deserves a place in the team.'

She nods. She wants to be able to say she is pleased for him, that he needs something like this, but she can't bring herself to say anything. It is the first time in the month since they have been back at home that she has seen her son have the inclination to get out of the house and do anything. She has worried about getting him back to school in September, about how he is going to cope this year, his GCSEs coming up next summer.

Her gaze stretches to Charlie at the far side of the field, pressed as close to the spectator line as he is allowed to go. She doesn't recall a time when they have both been at the same match, and especially not for one as unimportant as this friendly. It is OK for Charlie because the other mothers won't harass him and give him their pity and their condolences as they would with her, as most of them don't know who he is. She is the parent who was always on the sidelines, or at the school open evenings. Since either of the boys left primary school, Charlie has not been involved in their activities.

That's why Em keeps her distance now. She doesn't want a well-meaning mother wandering over and offering her sympathy while either looking at her like a deer in headlights or trying to embrace her. She doesn't want to speak to any of them. There is nothing they can say to remove any of the pain that sears through her heart and so for now the best thing she can do is keep away. She would think that they might acknowledge it is hard enough to walk out of the house without having to confront people and relive her agony, but then many don't know how to deal with grief.

Out of the corner of her eye she can see someone making a beeline for her and so she nudges Rob, who in turn gets up ready to bat them away. Thankfully they have second thoughts as they steer around in an almost 180-degree turn and head towards the coffee van as if that is where they were going the whole time.

'I don't know how this will end,' she says to Rob.

'How what will end?' Rob says. She is pleased for his calm and constancy. After those early unthinkable days Rob fell into place beside her, judging her needs with a quiet sixth sense. She doesn't ever want to be without him. She couldn't envisage not having him in her life.

'All of it,' she says. 'I don't know. This. Us. It's all just a matter of trying to survive every day,' she says. 'I can't see a way it's ever going to end.'

'No,' he tells her. 'No, nor can I.'

'I'm sorry, Rob,' she says.

'Sorry? What for?'

'This isn't the life you bought into when you married me.'

'Em!'

'I mean it. I'm just saying . . .'

'I'm not going anywhere,' he says. 'You must know that. I am never going anywhere.'

She nods again. 'Thank you,' she murmurs.

Rob takes hold of her hand and squeezes it. 'I love you,' he tells her. 'Please don't forget that.'

She carries on watching Theo, her mind slowly filling with the things she hasn't ever told Rob, and never will.

She won't confide in her husband about how she lies awake at night and lets her mind wander back there, picking over the fragments of their holiday.

Em knows Theo too well. One night, not long after they arrived home, and she was trying to live with the news that James Burrow had been released and not charged, she said to her son, 'You have to talk to me or it will eat you apart. You have to trust me, Theo.' She knew he was holding out on her still.

Finally her son opened up and told her what had happened during the night of Isaac's death. How he had fought with his brother and it had gone too far. How he hurt Isaac and walked away when Isaac told him he was fine. He had thought he was, but he hadn't hung around. Theo had been too frightened and had come home, gone straight to bed. Only Isaac must have somehow slipped and fallen into the water.

It was an accident. He never intended to hurt his brother. He made a mistake in not checking he was OK, in leaving him there. A mistake that cost his brother his life. A mistake that will haunt them both forever.

Em remembers how Theo had turned to her at the gala dinner and said, 'You would never forgive Dad for what he did would you?' He has asked her the same about himself since. 'How could you ever forgive me, Mum?'

Forgiveness. It is too big a word for her to consider. Before, she would always have said she'd forgive her sons anything. But now …

In truth, Em cannot even consider the question because she isn't able to confront the answer. And so she pushes it down, deep into her soul, where she hopes it will not eat away at her. Besides, Em has had to put that aside, because she had a decision to make. As it turned out, it was not a hard one.

When Lieutenant Kallis called her again to remind her that he would not stop until he found out who had killed Isaac, she now prayed he never would.

Because Em had two beloved sons, but one of them was dead. She refuses to lose the other and she will have to live with that decision for the rest of her life.

For now it is all she can do to survive every day. And some days, like today, there are small glimmers of hope. Watching Theo playing in a team, seeing her son smile. She knows that if that is all she has to carry her through today then she will take it. And she will remind herself that she made the right choice, whatever it has cost her.

She knows the truth of what happened to Isaac and she also knows that justice has been brought because she and Theo will have to live with what happened every day of their lives. But Theo is also her son, and she understood the day her boys were born that she would do anything for them until the day she died. And she will not lose him too.

LAILA

Chapter Forty-One

I know it will never truly be like the old days ever again. How can it be when there is a black spot that sits in the corner of my mind, threatening to expand if I give it air to breathe. Its mere presence makes me feel like I could lose control at any moment, reminding me this life we are recreating is built on a pretence. Deep in my gut, in the place where my intuition resides, I don't know that I believe James is being honest with me.

There is no substance to my belief and this is what makes it harder. It means that I can shake the thoughts away and slip back into this imperfectly perfect life. And yet those doubts will always come back.

On our first night in Crete harbour, when James had left Ixos, he said to me that the only thing I needed to do was to work out if I believed him. It is an impossible task.

He is already back at the house when I get in from my walk. He reaches to touch my wet hair and grimaces. 'Let me get you a towel,' he says. 'What were you doing out in this anyway?'

'It's only drizzle,' I say. 'It was nice.'

'Was it?' he laughs. 'I bought some fresh bread for lunch, and cheese from the deli.' He calls back as he goes to the airing cupboard and pulls out a towel.

'Sounds lovely.'

'I've been thinking about how we can pay for the clinic,' he says as he returns. 'We can talk about it over lunch.'

I nod. And this is it, I think. My reason for arriving at my decision. There were many years when all I wanted was for James and me to bring children into the world. Now it is the one thing that makes me realise I can't let this carry on. How can I have children with a man I do not wholly trust? I would be tied to him for the rest of my life, and I cannot risk that. The years ahead of not knowing, of always questioning. I need to stop now.

And so I pull out a chair in the kitchen and begin to break it to James that *we* will not need the money for IVF any more. I will be moving in with my mum and dad.

His face falls and I listen to the inevitable protests that begin. The hardest part of all is that I might never know what happened the night Isaac died. I will never know the truth, because I don't believe my husband will ever tell me.

And so my future is not with him. It is on my own. But I have already signed up for an evening course in counselling, and I have spoken to the clinic about sperm donors and the potential to have children as a single mother. And if I am being perfectly honest, I am pretty bloody excited about all of it. Because, after all, I think it's no more than I deserve.

Acknowledgements

I wrote this book during 2021, a year when we were still in lockdowns and living under rules, but when we were also beginning to be allowed out for walks – and by the summer there was some semblance of normality. I actually found it a lot harder to write that year than I had the one before. My concentration and dedication to the hours I need to write was waning, and so *The Other Guest* came with more than the usual amount of challenges along the way.

But I got there in the end. Mainly thanks to the help of both my agent and editor, as always, but also because I work better under pressure, and I knew this book could be so much more. I am now thrilled with *The Other Guest* and I hope you enjoy it too.

In my story Laila has been through multiple rounds of IVF and I spoke to many wonderful women who graciously shared their own personal stories with me. They opened up with honest and personal accounts of what they have been through and I am grateful to them all. Thank you to Deborah Dorman, Vicky Fowler, Kathryn Tucker, Melissa Carr, Vik Brinson and Francesca Reina, and to all the others who spoke to me about their experiences.

As always to my agent, Nelle. You are amazing. I am so lucky to be working with you. Thank you for your insights, ideas and for asking the questions that challenge me to think about things in a different way. And to Emily, my wonderful editor. For always being there, listening to every worry I have and persuading me that it's all going to turn out well in the end. I couldn't do any of this without you.

My books would not be a success without the great teams behind them. Along with Nelle Andrew there's an amazing team at RML who help sell rights around the world, including Charlotte Bowerman, Alexandra Cliff and Rachel Mills.

Thank you to all the people at Century who promote, market, talk to the journalists, sell into stores, copy-edit, proofread and design the beautiful covers. A massive thanks, therefore, to Rachel Kennedy, Natalia Cacciatore, Claire Simmonds, Helen Wynn-Smith, Rose Waddilove, Anne O'Brien, Jane Howard and Emma Grey Gelder. I appreciate everything you do to make my books the biggest success they can be.

I am so pleased to have some wonderful writer friends around me who encourage and listen and help. To Lucy Clarke for all the book chats and lunches and to Alice

Clark-Platts, Alex Tyler, Dawn Goodwin, Elin Daniels and Julietta Henderson for the most amazingly fun 'writers' retreats' we have had over the last year, where we laughed until we cried, and did no writing whatsoever.

Thank you to *you*, my readers, because let's face it: you're really who I write the book for. I am always grateful for your support in buying the book and telling everyone you know about it. And to the many bloggers and journalists who continue to write such lovely things about me and my stories.

And finally, to my family who give me so much love and support. Mum, for your unwavering belief and pride in everything I do, and always being one of my very first readers. To my wonderful husband, John, who continues to encourage me and is always in my corner. You still make me laugh every day. And finally, Bethany and Joseph. I love you both so much and am so proud of you. Keep following your dreams and doing what makes you happy. When you want something enough, you can make it happen.